ELLE GRAY

THE
LIES IN THE
FALLS

The Lies in the Falls
Copyright © 2024 by Elle Gray

All rights reserved. Without limiting the rights under copyright reserved above, no part of this publication may be reproduced, stored in or intro-duced into retrieval system, or transmitted, in any form, or by any means (electronic, mechanical, photocopying, recording, or otherwise) without the prior written permission of both the copyright owner and the above publisher of this book.

This is a work of fiction. Names, characters, places, brands, media, and in-cidents are either the products of the author's imagination or are used fic-titiously. The author acknowledges the trademarked status and trademark owners of various products referenced in this work of fiction, which have been used without permission. The publication/use of these trademarks is not authorized, associated with, or sponsored by the trademark owners.

CHAPTER ONE

S PENSER FLINCHED AND GRITTED HER TEETH AS THE MAN fired his shot, unable to do anything but watch as it streaked toward her like a bolt of lightning. Her body grew taut as she waited for the impact. She heard it hit with a solid thump a moment before she heard the ring of the bell and then the world opened up beneath her. Spenser let out a sharp yelp as she plummeted and a moment later, she hit the frigid water and sank to the bottom of the tank.

Even submerged, Spenser could hear the roar of the crowd, though it was dull and muted. Pushing off the bottom, she launched herself upward and broke the surface of the water, sputtering and gasping for air as she spat out a mouthful of water.

"I tried to tell you to keep your mouth closed," Marley said as she howled with laughter.

"I hate you so much right now!"

Still giggling, Marley pulled the lever to reset the bench in the dunk tank. Spenser climbed the ladder and settled herself on the bench again, glaring balefully at Marley, who'd talked her into volunteering for the tank. Manipulated was probably the better word for it.

"I'm never going to forgive you for this, Mar," Spenser said.

"Yes, you will!"

The crowd on the other side of the barricades in front of the tank were laughing and patting the young man who'd thrown the ball on the back. He lifted a ball in the palm of his hand, a cocky grin on his face. David Copley is a star pitcher on the Taft High School baseball team and an aspiring deputy. Spenser had talked with him several times and rather than go to college, he wanted to join her department. It was a plan she had been trying to talk him out of, arguing for the importance of college, but he seemed set on his path.

"David Copley, if you throw that next ball, I swear to God that I will never approve your application to my department!" Spenser called.

The ball was such a blur, she didn't see it coming until it again hit the target. She yelped as the bell rang and she was, once again, dropped into the frigid water, the howling laughter of everybody at the tank the soundtrack ringing in her ears. Once more, she swam to the surface of the tank and spit out another mouthful of water.

"When are you going to learn to keep your mouth closed?" Marley squealed.

Still glaring at Marley, she seated herself on the bench again. "I will get you back for this, Mar! Payback is a bit—"

The bell rang and David Copley dropped her into the tank for the third time. As she breached the surface of the water, she looked at the line of people waiting to take their turn at her in the tank. Thankfully, she didn't see any of the other star pitchers in town. For the next two hours, though, Spenser endured the humiliation of being the clown sitting in the dunk tank on a chilly afternoon. She was wearing a bright pink and black, long-sleeved neoprene springsuit, but her dark hair was sopping wet, which made her head feel cold, which in turn, made the rest of her cold. She should have opted for the full winter wetsuit with the hood instead.

"Okay, I guess you've done your time," Marley said.

"That's so kind of you."

"Unless you want to spend a little more—"

"Nope. I'm done," Spenser cut her off.

Marley laughed as she unlocked the cage then stepped to the front of the tank and raised a bullhorn. "Okay, guys. The sheriff is done for the day—"

The line was still fairly long and everybody in it groaned in disappointment. Spenser climbed down the ladder and laughed to herself.

"I'll try to not take that personally, guys," she called to the crowd.

"If you've already bought tickets, don't despair. Next up for your dunking pleasure is City Councilman Harvey Pace," Marley announced through her bullhorn. "Come on now, give the sheriff a hand, everybody!"

The crowd applauded, laughing and cheering as Spenser gave them a wave. She turned and headed back to the tent behind the tank, slipped inside, and grabbed a towel from a stack sitting on a table to the right of the entrance. A pair of stand heaters stood in the corner of the large tent pumping out warmth. Wrapping the towel around her hair, Spenser made a beeline over to them. She groaned with pleasure as she soaked in the heat.

The tent flap opened, and she looked over to see Ryker step in. He stopped just inside the tent flaps and hooked his thumbs through his belt loops, looking at her with a wide smile on his face. As it always did whenever she saw him, Spenser's heart skipped a beat. Six-two with a strong, chiseled build, she thought he was a beautiful man. Even though they were rapidly approaching winter, Ryker's naturally tawny complexion made him look like he was still well-tanned.

He'd grown a beard, thick and dark—his winter coat as he called it. His Grizzly Adams look, she called it. It only made him look more rugged, which made him even more attractive. It came as a surprise to Spenser since she'd always favored the clean-cut, babyface type—like her late husband, Trevor. Ryker was the opposite of Trevor in just about every way. Spenser had sometimes wondered if that opposite nature was the reason she was so attracted to Ryker. Maybe she wanted to get as far away from Trevor's memory as possible. She didn't know. But she did know that her attraction to Ryker, whatever the underlying reason might be, was undeniable.

"Well, look who came down off his mountain to join the unwashed masses," she said.

"And miss watching you get dunked all day?"

"I'm surprised you didn't buy tickets."

"Nah. Watching you take that abuse was fun enough," he said.

"You say the sweetest things."

Spenser ran over and gave him a quick peck on the cheek before disappearing behind a privacy screen. She peeled off her wetsuit and hung it on a rack to dry.

"I didn't think you were coming," she said as she toweled off. "I thought you said Founders Day was lame."

Ryker laughed. "It is lame. But Kelli called and I had to drop some things off at the shop for her. I figured since I was already here that you might want to go grab a bite."

"Look at you, being all social," she said. "I think we're making progress, Ryker Makawi. Keep this up and people will have to stop calling you the hermit on the hill."

"Well, that's still better than them calling me the cave troll," he replied. "But yeah, I think we're making some progress. Both of us. I mean, look at you taking part in town festivities."

Spenser groaned. "Just doing my civic duty."

Founders Day in Sweetwater Falls was one of the biggest events of the year. It served to not only celebrate the founding of the town back in the late 1800s, it was also the official kickoff to the holiday season. And Marley already warned her that people in town went all out for the holidays. Carolers in Dickensian costumes strolling through town, awards for the biggest and gaudiest Christmas displays, and a host of other holiday-related activities—Sweetwater Falls had it all. And according to Marley, much, much more.

Spenser had never cared for the holidays very much. Christmas was not her thing. She would have been happy to grab some Chinese food, curl up on the couch with a horror movie marathon, and forget the day entirely. But that wasn't in the cards for her. One of her duties as the town sheriff would be to light the traditional Christmas tree in the town square. Where that tradition came from was a mystery. Why the town sheriff? Spenser would have thought the mayor or some other prominent figure would have been more appropriate. But that was required of her and so, she would have to suck it up and do it.

Spenser pulled on her jeans, then slid a black, long-sleeved t-shirt over her head and tucked it in. After getting into her boots, she stepped around the privacy screen and grabbed her coat from the rack standing near the heaters. She slipped into it, relishing the warmth the fabric had soaked up.

"Cozy?" Ryker asked.

"Very."

"Good," he said with a grin. "Are you hungry?"

"Famished."

"For anything in particular?"

Spenser shook her head. "Dealer's choice."

"I know just the spot then."

They stepped out of the tent and Ryker shocked her by grabbing her hand and lacing his fingers through hers. As they walked down the street, Spenser couldn't help but notice that people were looking at them, making her cheeks flush. They had never really acknowledged what was happening between them. And they certainly hadn't progressed to the public displays of affection stage of their—whatever it was. It wasn't like they'd put a label on it or anything. And yet, she couldn't deny that it felt natural. It felt... right. They really were making progress.

"Sheriff!" Young exclaimed as she walked over to them.

With Spenser on duty in the dunk tank, she'd left Young, her undersheriff, in charge. Young had handed out the assignments to the dozen deputies working the festival. Not that there was likely to be any trouble, but the presence of uniformed deputies was a deterrent against anybody who might be thinking about stirring the pot.

Young stopped in front of them with her usual smile on her face. She was one of the cheeriest people Spenser had ever met. Young seemed to be able to find the good in almost every person and situation. Her eyes widened when she glanced down and saw Spenser's fingers interlaced with Ryker's, but she covered it well and didn't mention it.

"How is it going out here?" Spenser asked.

"All quiet. No problems at all. Everybody seems to be having a great time," she said.

"That's good news," Spenser replied.

"It's what we expected. But yeah, good news all the same," Young said. "I'm just sorry I didn't get over to the dunk tank before your shift was done."

"I'm glad you didn't," Spenser replied. "I would have hated to fire you."

Young laughed. "Anyway, I'll let you two get going. Have a great time, doing… whatever you two are doing."

She tipped Spenser a wink and laughed to herself as she walked away. Ryker turned to her with a grin on his face.

"She's subtle," he said.

"Yeah, not the word I would have chosen."

Despite Young's antics, Ryker didn't let go of her hand as they continued their walk down the street. Spenser nodded and greeted the people they passed. Young was right. Everybody did seem to be in a good mood and having a good time.

"You seem to have settled in nicely," Ryker said.

"Still working on it," Spenser replied. "Maybe twenty years from now, they won't all look at me like I'm some outsider who's come to ravage their town."

"It might take longer than that before you're not considered an outsider," he said with a chuckle. "But it looks like you're making good inroads with the people in town."

"You mean all the potential voters in town."

"That, too."

"That's how Marley convinced me to do a shift in the dunk tank. She framed it as currying a little goodwill among the people and putting a human face on the sheriff's office," Spenser replied. "She reminded me that my position is an elected one and that eventually, I'm going to have to run to keep my job."

"She's a smart lady. She's not wrong."

"Yeah, I still hate the fact that my position is so... political."

"You're doing good work in town, Spense. People respect you. I've seen it on their faces just walking down the street here," he replied. "Old Howard Hinton never lost an election, and he didn't do a fraction of the good in his entire tenure that you've done in the time you've been here. People notice. And believe me, they'll remember that when it comes time to vote."

"I hope you're right. Truth be told, I kind of like this job. And if I'm being even more honest, I like this town and the people in it. Once upon a time, I never would have considered myself a small-town girl, but I've been proven wrong. Pleasantly so," she told him.

"Trust me, the people like you back. I see it and I hear the whispers around town," he replied. "That being said, sticking yourself in the dunk tank was not only amusing, it was a smart play. You should do that more."

"Yeah, I don't think so. Three hours getting nearly drowned was enough for me, thanks."

They laughed as they walked along, hand in hand. As she looked up at Ryker, Spenser's heart swelled to the point it felt like it might burst. She hadn't felt that rush of emotions since before Trevor was killed. Part of her didn't think she was even capable of feeling them anymore. But as Ryker's soulful eyes locked onto hers and she felt that flutter in her heart again, she was glad to know that she was indeed capable of still feeling those things.

She had no idea what she and Ryker had between them, but for now, just enjoying his company was enough. For now, enjoying the feeling of the emotions he stirred inside of her was enough. She was making progress. She was healing.

And that too, was enough. For now.

CHAPTER TWO

"Oh my God, I'm stuffed," Spenser said. "That was incredible. Thank you."

"You're very welcome."

"I don't even remember the last time I had Indian food, but I can tell you it couldn't have been as good as what we just ate."

"This place is still relatively new, but they do it up right."

"That they do."

As they walked down the sidewalk together, Ryker slipped his hand into hers again. She smiled to herself. This was apparently a thing now… not that she minded. In fact, it was quite the opposite. It filled her with a sense of warmth that had been so uncommon in her life for so long. Being near Ryker was thawing the frozen parts inside her.

"So, what do you want to do now?" Ryker asked.

Spenser patted her belly. "Let's walk this off."

"That's a good idea."

Hand in hand, they strolled through the town square. It was getting late in the day and the sun was slipping toward the horizon, casting the sky in vivid shades of red and orange. The square was lit up with strings of festive lights and lined with booths and pop-up tents put on by independent vendors as well as many of the local businesspeople. There was a cornucopia of food and sweet treats all around and the air was saturated with a hundred different delicious aromas.

"If I wasn't already all fat and happy, you better believe I'd be stuffing my face with all the sugary treats I could find," Spenser said.

"Well, I don't know about happy, but you're definitely not fat. And you work out so much, I highly doubt a sugary treat or two is going to make or break you," Ryker said with a grin.

"Why, Ryker Makawi, are you trying to talk me into getting some sweets?"

"I might be."

Spenser laughed. "Just say you want some sweets and I'll be happy to oblige."

"Oh, you'd do that for me? You'd be willing to make that sacrifice for little old me?" he teased. "That's so kind of you."

"I do what I can."

They shared a laugh as they wandered the square, trying to settle on which sugary snack to stuff their faces with. The problem was, everything looked so good, Spenser wanted it all.

"So? What do you think?" Ryker asked. "Funnel cakes? Gourmet donuts? Caramel apples?"

"Actually, I think I have a craving for those fresh waffle cones with some chocolate ice cream, hot fudge, and some sprinkles. You okay with that?" she asked.

"Well... as long as we get sprinkles, I guess that sounds okay."

Spenser laughed and playfully punched him in the arm. "I appreciate your sacrifice."

"Anything to keep you fat and happy."

"You said I wasn't fat."

Ryker didn't say anything but pointedly looked down at her stomach and grinned wolfishly. Spenser's mouth fell open and her eyes grew wide but she was unable to keep the smile from her lips as she elbowed him in the ribs, making Ryker cackle wildly.

"You're such a jerk," she said.

"I'm teasing you," he said.

"You're awful," she exclaimed.

"Sometimes," he replied. "But that's why you like me."

"Why does everybody seem to think I like them because they're terrible?"

"Because it's true."

Ryker pulled her into a hug and gently kissed the top of her head. It flooded her with warmth and put a wide smile on her face as she leaned into him. The fact that he seemed comfortable with showing his affection for her was new and seemed to take things between them to a different level. It was unexpected. But Spenser couldn't deny that it was nice. Really nice.

They walked over to the Sweet Dreams booth and ordered their waffle cone sundaes. It was the most popular sweet shop in town and in addition to the thousand other delectable delights on the menu, they had incredible homemade ice cream. Many of the kids in town hung out after school and on weekends there. It was almost like one of those old-fashioned shake and soda shops they had back in the day. It was just a nice, safe local hangout spot the kids flocked to.

"Evenin', Sheriff," said Lori Kavanaugh, the owner of Sweet Dreams. "How you doin', Ryker? Good to see you out and about."

"Good to see you, too, Lori," he replied.

She was a tall, thin woman—not what you might expect of somebody who spent their days around a plethora of sweet treats. Or perhaps Spenser thought that because she herself didn't have the willpower to not constantly indulge in the goodies. Lori had mousy brown hair, rosy cheeks, and hazel eyes that sparkled. And she always had a smile on her face.

"Hey, Lori. How's it going this evening?"

"Can't complain. The festival seems livelier than it has in past years," she said.

"We'll just call that the Song Effect," Ryker said with a smirk.

"Hardly," Spenser said.

"I don't know, Sheriff," Lori chimed in. "People really respect what you're doing with the department. They feel safer."

"It's not like Sweetwater Falls was a crime-ridden place to begin with," she replied.

"No, not exactly. But we had some troubles now and then," Lori said. "But what you've done with your department, what with the way you're modernizing it the way you have, and actually making it a formidable and functional police force has people feeling safer than before. So, yeah. I think we can call it the Song Effect."

Ryker grinned at her, and Spenser felt her cheeks flare with heat. She didn't think she deserved the praise or credit for doing what she thought were the obvious things to do and shoring up what she saw as chinks in her department's armor. But hey, if it helped people feel safer—and helped them to remember that feeling when it was time for her to run for office—then, so be it. Spenser would be happy to take the credit then.

"Well, I appreciate that vote of confidence," Spenser said.

"We appreciate good police work," she replied. "So, anyway, what can I get you two?"

Spenser placed an order for the peanut butter and chocolate ice cream in a waffle cup with hot fudge, nuts, and sprinkles. Ryker ordered the same. Lori chatted them up as she dished out their sundaes. Spenser and Ryker paid for their treats and said goodbye before turning and walking through the festival, eating and looking at some of the products—mostly holiday-themed—being sold by the army of vendors filling the town square.

"Okay, if I eat any more of this, I really am going to explode," Spenser said.

Ryker laughed and looked at her cup. "I'm impressed. There's not much left."

Spenser looked down into her cup and saw there was only about a quarter of the sweet treat left. She raised her gaze to Ryker and shrugged.

"Yeah, well, like you said, I work out a lot," she said.

"You're going to need to work out a little more."

Spenser squealed with laughter and slapped his upper arm playfully. They threw their cups in a nearby trash can and used their napkins to wipe their faces and hands. They stood in silence for a couple of moments, their eyes locked, the air between them crackling with electricity and a sense of anticipation. Given the way they'd been together that day, Spenser found herself wondering what the rest of the evening might hold for them. And whether she was ready for it.

Spenser smiled at Ryker. "I've had a really nice time today—the whole dunk tank thing aside anyway. Thank you."

"You're welcome. It has been a nice day," he replied. "And say what you want, but watching you in the dunk tank was a highlight for me."

Spenser shook her head. "I'm glad my discomfort amused you."

"It's not that," he said. "It was watching you interact with the people. The way you were barking at them, chatting them up, and most of all, the way you were smiling—it was nice to see. It was like people were finally getting to see the real Spenser Song."

Her cheeks warmed and she looked away as her lips curled upward. She wasn't sure what to say to that. It wasn't often that anybody left her too flustered to speak but Ryker seemed to be making a habit of it. She looked up and was still trying to think of something to say when, from the corner of her eye, she saw somebody approaching them, a timid look on her face. Ryker frowned, obviously annoyed that the girl walking up to them was ruining the moment.

Spenser couldn't say she didn't feel just as annoyed as Ryker looked. It seemed all too rare that she was off duty, so to have one of those few times when she wasn't on the clock interrupted—especially with the way things with Ryker were developing—was a bit irritating. But as the public face of the department, she had to stuff that all down.

"Sheriff Song? Can I talk to you?" the girl asked, her voice as timid as her expression.

No more than twenty-one or so, the girl was small with a wholesome, almost innocent look about her. She was no more than five-four and petite but with womanly curves, and a smooth, milky complexion. Her hair was back in a ponytail that fell between her shoulder blades and a shade blacker than a moonless night, and her blue eyes sparkled like chips of sapphire.

The girl's tone made it clear, at least to Spenser, that she wasn't there to ask her to donate to her school fundraising drive but had something serious on her mind. Something that she needed Spenser's professional help with. Disappointed at the intrusion, she cut an apologetic look at Ryker who offered her a gentle smile of understanding in return. The sheriff was never off duty. Not really. She reached and squeezed his hand before turning back to the girl with an "all business" expression on her face.

"And you are?" Spenser asked.

"Aspen," she said. "Aspen Gilchrist. You might know my mom, Wendy?"

Spenser racked her brain quickly. She'd heard the name, of course—the Gilchrist name was all over town. They were one of the richest and most influential families in town, but Spenser had never met the matriarch of the family. All she knew was that the Gilchrist family made their money in timber and were, in fact, one of the biggest timber companies in the continental US.

"I'm afraid I don't know your mom, but what can I do for you, Aspen?" Spenser asked.

"It's my mom… she's missing," she replied, her voice thick with emotion. "Please, Sheriff. I need you to find her."

She looked like she was trying to hold it together, but Aspen's face turned red, and her bottom lip quivered as tears spilled down her cheeks.

"I'm sorry, Sheriff. I promised myself I wouldn't freak out on you," she stammered.

"It's all right," Spenser said. "I'm sure you're under a lot of stress right now."

Aspen nodded. "I am."

"How long has your mother been missing, Aspen?"

"Almost two days," she said.

"Are you sure she didn't just—"

Aspen shook her head, cutting her off. "She wouldn't just leave and not tell us. That wasn't her, Sheriff. She wouldn't just not tell us she was going somewhere."

"Okay, okay," Spenser said soothingly. "I believe you."

"Please, Sheriff Song. We need your help."

Spenser frowned and gave Ryker an apologetic look. He nodded and squeezed her hand.

"Go do your thing," he said softly.

She mouthed "Thank you," then turned to Aspen. "Honey, let's go down to my office and we'll see if we can't sort this all out."

CHAPTER THREE

"Can I get you some water or a soda maybe?" Spenser asked.

"Water, please," Aspen replied.

"You got it."

Spenser walked out of the conference room that sat next to her office and closed the door behind her after getting Aspen calmed down and settled at the table. With most of her deputies working the festival, the office was being manned by Victor Shenn and Miguel Bustos, and of course, her steadfast receptionist Alice Jarrett, who'd been with the department for more than two decades. Truth be told, with her experience, firm hand, and "take no crap from anybody" demeanor, Alice pretty much ran the office. And that was just fine with Spenser.

She walked into the break room and pulled two bottles of water out of the refrigerator. She turned and was headed back to the conference room to talk to the girl when Young stepped into the break room.

"Hey, Sheriff," she said. "I ran into Ryker and he told me about Aspen."

"Yeah, I've got her in the conference room. I was just about to talk to her," Spenser replied.

"I'd like to sit in… if you don't mind. I'm pretty familiar with the family, so I might be able to help you navigate those waters. The Gilchrists can sometimes be… prickly."

"Is everything okay at the festival?"

She nodded. "All quiet. I left Woods in charge."

Darren Woods was an experienced deputy and the head of Spenser's makeshift SWAT team. He was good at his job, had a steady hand, and was respected by everybody in the department. She trusted the man.

"Great. I could probably use your knowledge," Spenser said. "How familiar are you with Aspen and her mother…?"

"Wendy. Wendy Gilchrist," Young replied. "I'm a few years older than Aspen and her sister Dallas, and a few years younger than their brother, Brendan."

"What can you tell me about Wendy?"

"Emerald Timber has been in Wendy's family since the mid-1850s. It was passed down to her about fifteen years ago when her father retired. He passed away about five years ago," Young said. "She divorced her husband right around the same time. He'd been working as the company's CFO at the time, but the word was, he was lazy and more interested in living off the Gilchrist name than being a contributing member. That didn't go over well with Wendy who's got a Midwestern work ethic. She kicked him to the curb and by all accounts, the kids don't have anything to do with him after that, either."

"Wow. The kids cut their own father off, too? That's brutal," Spenser said.

"The rumor was that was Wendy's doing—a condition she imposed on her children. Though, I can't verify that. You know town gossip can be malicious."

"Yeah," Spenser said. "But still, it seems odd that she'd divorce her husband over a lack of work ethic. It just seems like—"

"You don't know Wendy Gilchrist."

"That's true," Spenser said. "But humor me. Were there ever any infidelity rumors? On either side. Any other reason she might have sent her first husband packing?"

Young shook her head. "Shockingly enough, no. None that I ever heard. As far as I know, there was no infidelity—and I like to think I'm pretty plugged into the town's rumor mill," Young said. "It sounds unbelievable, but Wendy Gilchrist is such an exacting taskmaster, it's very believable that she would have sent her first husband packing because he didn't eat, sleep, and breathe work."

"How about Emerald Timber? Hear of any trouble with the company?"

"None at all," Young said. "I mean, they've gone through layoffs and whatnot with downturns in the economy, like everybody else. In fact, they went through a round of layoffs about a year and a half ago. But I've never heard of any shady dealings with the company."

Spenser nodded and absorbed the information. She twisted the cap off the bottle and took a long swallow as she processed everything Young had told her.

"What about the kids?" Spenser asked. "What do you know about them? Do they ever get into trouble or anything like that? Anything that might have been glossed over or…"

"Not that I've ever heard of. I mean, the girls go to UW and they've got a bit of a reputation as party girls. I've heard they can get a little wild, but I think that's to be expected of kids their age getting their first taste of freedom at college," Young said.

Spenser laughed quietly. "You say that like you all aren't around the same age."

"Yeah, maybe. But my life experience is a lot different than theirs. My worldview is vastly different," she countered.

"Fair enough," Spenser replied. "Anyway, go on."

"Well, Brendan is kind of the black sheep of the family. He's a computer savant—maybe even better than my brother, but don't you dare tell Jacob I said that," Young said with a smile. "He's back east at MIT and from what I've heard, he's got zero interest in taking over the family business when Wendy steps down. Timber's just not his thing, I guess."

"Money is everybody's thing."

"I'm sure he'll still get a fair share of it. Families like the Gilchrists tend to take care of their own," Young said.

"This is true," Spenser replied. "Have you ever known Wendy Gilchrist to just up and leave like this? Is she impulsive?"

"The opposite, actually," Young said. "She's rigid. Strict. Very disciplined. It wouldn't surprise me if she scheduled her bathroom breaks in advance."

"So, not the type to just drop off the grid."

"Definitely not the type. Plus, she's got a keen mind for business," Young replied. "It's probably why her father put her in charge of the company rather than her brother."

"That cause any tension?"

"I don't know, to be honest," Young admitted. "The Gilchrists tend to close ranks and keep internal strife—if there is any—internal."

"Okay, that's all good stuff, Amanda. Let's go talk to Aspen and see where we're at."

"Let's do it."

Spenser led Young across the bullpen and into the conference room. Young closed the door softly behind them and joined Spenser at the table, sitting across from Aspen. The eldest Gilchrist daughter sat slumped in her chair, her eyes red and puffy, her cheeks flushed and still wet with tears. Half a dozen damp, crumpled tissues sat on the table in front of her.

"Aspen, I think you know Undersheriff Young," Spenser said as she handed the girl a bottle of water.

She nodded. "Hi, Amanda."

"Hi, Aspen," Young replied gently.

Spenser laid her palms flat on the table and leaned forward. "Okay, can you tell us what happened and why you believe your mom is missing?"

"Me and Dally—that's my sister, Dallas—we came home from school and mom wasn't there," Aspen said. "We didn't think anything of it at first, but it's been almost two days now and we haven't seen or heard from her. She's not returning our calls or texts—it's just radio silence."

"And I take it that's unusual?"

Aspen nodded. "She never does this. She always makes sure we know where she is. If she doesn't tell us verbally, she's got it marked in her calendar," she said. "I checked and there's nothing in her calendar about going away. I've asked around the office and the mill and nobody's seen or heard from her."

"Okay, well, did you notice any signs of foul play at the house? Anything that might indicate she didn't leave of her own free will?" Spenser asked.

Aspen shrugged, a look of disgust crossing her face. "How would I know what to look for, Sheriff? I'm not a cop. I don't know what might indicate she didn't leave of her own free will."

Aspen looked down as her cheeks flushed and she wiped her eyes with the tissue in her hand. She drew in a long, shuddering breath and held it for a moment then let it out slowly, seeming to be doing her best to compose herself. After a couple of moments, she looked up.

"I'm sorry, Sheriff. That was uncalled for."

"That's all right. Nothing for you to be sorry about," Spenser said. "I mean no disrespect and I don't want you to think I'm taking you lightly."

"We just need to gather as much information as we can right now, Aspen," Young added. "So, bear with us if we're asking what might sound to you like stupid questions."

"I understand," she said.

"I have to be honest with you here. We'll do a little digging around, of course, but you need to know that unless we can find evidence of a forcible abduction, there isn't much we can do," Spenser said. "Your mother is an adult and as difficult as it is to hear, she has the right to disappear without a word if she chooses."

"She didn't just choose to up and leave, Sheriff. Something happened to her," Aspen said, her tone bitterly acidic.

"We understand," Young said. "I'm just trying to give you an honest lay of the land here. If we turn up evidence that she didn't just leave, that's one thing. But if we're not able to find anything that points to an abduction, our hands are kind of tied."

"That's not good enough. That's not nearly good enough," Aspen growled. "She didn't just leave. That's not who my mother is or how she does things. She was taken."

"Okay, okay," Spenser said calmly. "Tell me this. Do you know if your mother was having trouble with anybody recently? Any threats you're aware of?"

Aspen shook her head. "No. Nothing that I was aware of," she said. "But you know there are always people looking to take her down. The Green League is always harassing her—"

"The Green League?" Spenser asked.

"Local environmental group," Young answered. "They've been known to be a little militant and have butted heads with Emerald Timber in the past."

"Aspen, what about your uncle?" Spenser inquired. "I understand your grandfather gave the company to your mother instead of him. Was there any bad blood between them because of that?"

"We don't see Uncle Baker very often," she replied. "I don't think there was any bad blood between them, but my mom was usually pretty private, so I can't say for sure."

"What about your stepfather?" Young asked. "How was their relationship?"

The girl shrugged again and looked down at the table. "I don't know. Me and Dally are up at school so much, but when we come home for break or whatever, we've heard them fighting. Like all the time. My mom didn't say much about it—like I said, she is a private person. But I didn't get the feeling things between them were all that good."

"What about her relationship with your father?" Spenser asked.

"There was no relationship," Aspen answered. "My father is a lazy bum. A leech. No drive and no ambition and my mother had finally had enough and cut him loose. But that was like ten years ago or something. So, if you're thinking he had something to do with her disappearance, it's unlikely. None of us have had anything to do with him since she kicked him out."

"Did your mom ask you to cut him off?" Spenser asked.

"She didn't need to," the girl replied. "Josh Baden isn't a Gilchrist. He never was and he never will be. He's just… common. He's a bum and offers nothing to society."

"That seems pretty harsh," Spenser said. "I mean, he's your dad."

Aspen shrugged. "Just because he got my mom pregnant doesn't make him my dad. It just makes him somebody who donated some genetic material. If my mom had gone through artificial insemination, would you call the turkey baster my father?"

Spenser exchanged a look with Young. The girl was colder than the Arctic in the dead of winter. If Aspen was the one to judge by, Young was right—the Gilchrists were an odd bunch. Aspen seemed to lack feeling and emotion. At least, for her father. She seemed to be suffering an overabundance of emotion when it came to her mother. But then, because her father was kicked out of the house when she was about eleven, Wendy Gilchrist had been her only role model growing up. It shouldn't have been surprising Aspen formed such a bond with her mother.

"Okay, good, Aspen," Spenser said. "That gives us a place to start. Thank you. And we will keep you in the loop—"

"You're going to find her, right? You're going to find my mom?"

"We're going to do everything in our power to figure out where she went," Spenser replied.

"And again," Young said. "Just to reiterate what the sheriff said, it's possible your mom just took off to blow off some steam. So… try to keep from worrying yourself too much."

"I'll try," she said. "Thank you, Sheriff. Thank you, Amanda."

Spenser nodded. "Of course. We'll look into things and will be in touch."

Taking her cue, Aspen stood up and offered them a weak, shaky smile before leaving the conference room. When the door closed behind her, Spenser leaned back in her seat and ran her fingers through her hair as she blew out a long breath, letting everything Aspen said bounce around in her head for a minute. She finally turned to Young.

"Wow. That is one cold girl," Spenser said.

"The Gilchrist clan is odd," Young said. "But it tracks. If you're not part of the clan, you're not worth thinking about. They're very big on loyalty and making sure people are doing things their way. And if you can't do that, you're never going to be part of their clan."

"Still. To cut your father off like that, just because your mom asked you to—brutal," Spenser said. "Anyway, what do you think?" Spenser asked.

"I'm thinking if something did happen to Wendy Gilchrist, at least we've got some solid places to start," Young replied. "We've got her ex, her current husband, and the leader of the Green League to look at."

"It's a start," Spenser said. "And we'll start looking into them all first thing in the morning."

CHAPTER FOUR

Spenser was back in the office the following morning, still a little grumpy about having her evening with Ryker ruined. But that was the job. And if there was any chance that Wendy Gilchrist hadn't left of her own accord, then it was her duty to look into it. She glanced at her watch and saw it was just after eight in the morning and figured she'd give it another hour before she went out to the Gilchrist home to poke around. She had enough paperwork to keep her busy until then.

She stifled a yawn and then took a drink of her coffee before turning back to her computer. The mountain of reports she had to file weren't going to write themselves. She also needed to draft a revised request to the City Council for funding to hire an additional six deputies. Her last request had been for twelve and that one had been summarily dismissed. The council said they simply didn't have the money for it, nor was there a need for that many deputies. Spenser had argued she had eighteen deputies, which was inadequate for a town the size of Sweetwater Falls. She was hoping that if she split the difference, she might win them over.

A knock on her door pulled Spenser away from the computer screen. "Come in."

The door opened and Mayor Dent walked in with a smile on her face. Holding a pair of coffee cups from Ryker's shop, Maggie slipped in and nudged the door closed with her ample hip. The mayor walked over and set one of the cups down in front of her then dropped into the chair behind her, cradling her cup between her hands.

"Good morning, Spenser," Dent chirped.

Spenser eyed her cautiously. "*Timeo Danaos et dona ferentes.*"

Dent laughed. "I didn't know you knew Latin."

"That's the only phrase I know. But it's one I live by."

"Well, I'm not Greek. And this is a cup of coffee. Not a giant wooden horse."

A grin curling the corner of her mouth upward, Spenser eyed the mayor. "I think the principle remains the same."

"You're always so suspicious of people's motives."

"It's an occupational hazard," Spenser said. "So, then you're just here for a cup of coffee and a pleasant conversation then?"

Dent looked at her with a sly smile touching her lips. "There was something I wanted to talk to you about."

"And there it is," Spenser said with a laugh.

"Okay, okay, so I've got some ulterior motives," she said. "But it is still just a cup of coffee. No strings attached to it."

"Fair enough."

"Now, if I'd brought you a scone..."

They shared a laugh and Spenser pushed her mug of coffee aside in favor of the cup from Ryker's shop, Higher Grounds, which was far superior to the break room swill. She took a sip and her chair creaked as she leaned back in it. Dent took a drink as well then sat, her back straight, hands cupped around her coffee, and an expectant look on her face.

"So, what can I do for you, Maggie?"

"I heard about Wendy Gilchrist going missing—"

Spenser held up her hand. "We don't know that she's missing. We haven't even started looking into it just yet," she said. "We only spoke to Aspen last night."

She wasn't surprised that Dent knew. Spenser figured by now, the story and a thousand competing theories—most of them of the tin-foil hat variety—were buzzing around town. In places as small as Sweetwater Falls, gossip seemed to spread faster than chickenpox in an elementary school classroom. Nothing ever stayed secret in places like Sweetwater Falls. Not for long.

"I've known Wendy for a long time, Spenser. She's never been one to just up and leave without a word. She rigidly schedules everything."

"That's what Amanda told me. But that doesn't mean that she wasn't having a bad day and decided to bail for a few days," Spenser said.

"It would be the first time she ever did anything like that."

"I get that. But even so, it's still a possibility."

Dent looked down at her cup. "It is. I understand that. But you need to understand Wendy and how disciplined she is. How rigid she is. If you knew that, you'd know this is so far out of character for her that it seems unbelievable."

"I understand that, Maggie. I really do. But no matter how rigid and disciplined a person is, everybody's got a breaking point. A point where they do something so wildly out of character, we have a hard time believing it. I've seen it more times than I can count," Spenser said. "We don't know what was going on in Wendy's life and until we have conclusive evidence that she was abducted, we need to proceed with all options on the table—even if we don't necessarily like or agree with them. That's the nature of police work, Maggie."

She sighed and sat back in her chair as Spenser studied her. It was rare that Dent took an interest in active cases or how Spenser did her job. It was almost unheard of. She usually let Spenser do her job how she saw fit and never interfered. The fact that she was sticking her nose into this and trying to steer Spenser's investigation was interesting.

"You and Wendy are friends," Spenser said, not a question.

She nodded. "We're pretty close, yes."

"I was under the impression Wendy didn't have many close friends," Spenser said. "That she held people at an arm's distance."

Dent laughed softly. "A story perpetuated by people who don't know her. Wendy is indeed guarded. She's aloof with most people. But a woman in her position has to keep some boundaries. People are always trying to take advantage of her," she said. "But beyond those walls, Wendy is one of the kindest, sweetest people I know. Yes, she's rigid and yes, she's a taskmaster. She's a highly organized, type-A person. But that's just her public face."

"And privately?"

"Privately, she loves to laugh. She loves wine—maybe a little too much. But she has a million jokes and stories and when she lets her hair down, she's one of the funniest people you'll ever meet," Dent said. "Ninety-nine percent of people never see that side of her. But I have and I know what kind of person she is. She's a great friend."

Spenser bit back the words sitting on her tongue. That was all great background information and gave her a more complete picture of the woman herself, but none of it changed anything. It was still just as possible Wendy Gilchrist, needing to get away from it all, blew town on an impromptu trip as it was that she was taken by somebody with nefarious motives.

But Spenser also knew that when emotions were involved and somebody was personally connected to a case, logic was usually the first thing to go out the window. She could see that Dent was worried about her friend. She knew this case was going to impact her deeply until it was brought to a conclusion one way or the other. Spenser knew she was going to need to tread lightly.

"Maggie, you need to know that there may be very little we can do," Spenser said. "If it turns out Wendy decided to just blow town, no matter how unlikely you believe that to be, then we can't do anything about it. Walking away from your life isn't a crime."

"I know she didn't just leave, though. I know something happened to her," Dent said, her voice thick with emotion. "I can feel it. I know it deep in my bones, Spenser."

Spenser frowned and looked down, running the tip of her finger around the plastic lid of her coffee cup. Dent believed what she believed, and Spenser knew there was nothing she could say or do at that moment to dissuade her from that position. She believed Wendy Gilchrist had been taken and to her, that's all there was to it.

"Tell me something. Let's assume you're right and something did happen to her," Spenser said. "Who would you suspect? The ex? The current husband? The brother?"

She shook her head. "Any and all of them, to be honest. None of them are any good. They're all dirtbags, in my opinion. Joshua is lazy and still bitter that Wendy cut him off the Gilchrist teat. Her brother Baker is still angry she was given control of the company instead of him—but he would have run it straight into the ground," Dent said. "And Brock, her current husband... he's an idiot. He's a bona fide idiot. He works as the company's Marketing Director but it's an honorary position. Nobody takes him seriously. Wendy is very quietly drawing up divorce papers to serve him. If he got wind of that..."

Her words trailed off, but the implication was clear. He had a motive. All the men in Wendy's life seemed to have a motive. But motive didn't always translate to violence and murder. Spenser was thinking about explaining that to Dent, but in her current state she wasn't going to hear her. Thinking about the men in her life, though, raised a question in Spenser's mind.

"If Brock is such an idiot, why did Wendy marry him in the first place?" she asked. "I mean, from what little I know of her, Wendy Gilchrist is a strong, intelligent woman who doesn't seem to suffer fools."

A small smile quirked the corner of Dent's mouth. "Deep down, we all crave connection and companionship, Spenser."

"It has to be more than that."

Dent looked away and seemed to be uncomfortable. Spenser figured Dent didn't feel right about airing out her friend's business, but it couldn't be avoided. The mayor frowned and ran a hand through her tangled brown hair.

"Maggie, I know this is difficult, but if you and Aspen are right and something did happen to Wendy, then I need to know everything I can," Spenser told her. "I'm not here to judge. I'm just here to figure out if we have a missing woman or not."

"Okay, look, Brock is quite a bit younger than Wendy. She's forty-eight and he's thirty-seven. He's young. He's a very good-looking man and he paid attention to Wendy. Believe me, Spenser, when you get to be our age, the attention of a young, pretty man is intoxicating," she said. "And like I said, he's not very smart and easy to control. I'm sure that factored into their relationship as well."

It did factor in. If Brock was tired of being controlled and manipulated, that might add to a potential motive to do something about it.

"Listen, I'm not here to tell you how to do your job," Dent said. "If I'm coming across like I am, I apologize. I'm not trying to be heavy-handed here. It's just that I know Wendy. Better than most. And I know she wouldn't just up and leave without a word."

"Aspen believes that as well," Spenser added. "And it's not that I'm doubting you. But like I told Aspen, I want you to prepare yourself for the possibility that she did."

Dent nodded, but Spenser could see her words were falling on deaf ears. She was going to keep believing what she'd said until she was given incontrovertible proof to the contrary. Perhaps not even then.

"Please, just look into this, Spenser. Closely," she said softly. "Look at everything—and everybody—closely. Please, Spenser. Find my friend."

"I'll do my best, Maggie. I'll give you my word."

"There's something else you should know. Or at least, keep it in the back of your mind."

"And what's that?"

"The Gilchrist family is powerful. They're very influential. Hell, I probably wouldn't be mayor if Wendy hadn't thrown in for me. I mean, it was her idea in the first place, but I only won because of her," she said. "Like it or not, this is going to have political implications. The Gilchrist family can either make or break you. And your job is a political one. Not too far down the line, you are going to have to run for your job."

"I'm aware of that. What's your point?"

"My point is that you want the Gilchrist seal of approval. You want... no, you need their endorsement if you want to keep this office."

"Remember what you were just saying about not wanting to strongarm me?"

She shook her head. "I'm sorry, Spenser. I'm not trying to. I'm just laying out the reality here. Just as you need me to accept the possibility that Wendy blew town, you need to accept the reality that you need their endorsement if you hope to win."

Spenser gritted her teeth and stifled the growl that rose in her throat. She was resentful of the fact that politics were once again being injected into her job. That her job was being threatened if she didn't appease the Gilchrists. Dent was right. That was the reality of her position. And pointing it out was the mayor's way of trying to help open her eyes to what was on the line. She would want the Gilchrists as allies. Not enemies.

"Message received, Mayor Dent," Spenser said. "I will put my all into it... like I always do."

CHAPTER FIVE

"Is this spread still within town limits?" Spenser asked.

"Just barely," Young replied.

The gates were open, and Spenser piloted the Bronco between a pair of tall, red brick pillars that were already festooned with garish holiday decorations and down the long driveway that led to the main house. A stone fence surrounded the Gilchrist compound, which was a vast swath of land that held a main house, and from what she could see, a riding complex and three smaller houses on the grounds behind it. And all around the property, Spenser saw a veritable army of people putting up lights and other Christmas decorations.

"You weren't kidding—people go all out for Christmas around here," Spenser said.

"Tis the season to outdo your neighbors," Young replied. "I don't even want to imagine the electricity bill some of these people rack up this time of year. Probably more than I make in a year."

"I hope that's not you bucking for a raise," Spenser chirped with a snicker.

"Bucking? No. But if you wanted to get into the holiday spirit and put a little something extra in my stocking…"

"I think the Grinch known as the City Council will be putting coal in all our stockings."

"Bah humbug," Young said.

Spenser followed the narrow road into the circular driveway and parked near the front of a massive three-story house. In the center of the circular drive stood a giant tree that was flocked white and laden with red and green bulbs. All red brick with white trim, the Gilchrist home—as well as the other houses on the property—were constructed in a Georgian Colonial style with high peaked roofs and a portico that extended from the front door, supported by tall, white columns. Dark shutters flanked all the windows with a front door that matched.

"Nice place," Spenser remarked.

"Right? I could get used to a house like this."

As she and Young climbed out of the Bronco, the front door opened and Aspen walked to the edge of the porch and waited for them, her arms folded over her chest, a look of upset on her face. With Young following close behind, Spenser climbed the half dozen steps to the top of the porch where the girl waited.

"Good morning, Aspen," Spenser said.

"I'm glad you could make time in your busy schedule to come out, Sheriff."

The girl's gaze was as biting and acidic as her tone, but her expression immediately softened as she ran a hand over her face and shook her head.

"I'm sorry," Aspen said. "I didn't sleep much last night and didn't mean—"

"It's fine," Spenser said. "I don't suppose your mom has called or texted since yesterday?"

"Nothing," Aspen replied.

"Okay, well what we'd like to do is come in and take a look around," Spenser said. "We'd like to get a feel for your mom and see if anything stands out to us."

"Please," she replied. "Look around. Take whatever you need—whatever you think might help you find her."

"Thank you."

Spenser led Young into the house with Aspen trailing behind. They stepped into a round foyer that was done up in off-white paint on the walls and dark wood flooring. A tall Christmas tree that matched the one in the driveway stood in the center of the foyer, white lights twinkling. Softly curving staircases lined with garland and holly to the left and right led to the second-floor landing. Doorways on either side of the foyer opened into what looked like formal sitting rooms and the hallway in front of them led deeper into the house.

Though elegant and beautifully furnished and decorated, the house was surprisingly restrained. It was obvious the people who lived there had money, but it wasn't ostentatious and didn't beat a person over the head with their wealth. Aspen frowned.

"My mother loves Christmas," she explained, sounding slightly embarrassed.

"Nothing wrong with that," Young said. "It's a wonderful time of year."

"Yeah," she replied awkwardly.

"Aspen, would you mind showing Amanda your mother's bedroom?" Spenser said, breaking the sudden and strained silence.

She nodded. "It's on the second floor. Follow me."

"I'm going to have a look down here if that's all right," Spenser said.

"Yes. Please," Aspen replied. "Do whatever you need to do."

"Thank you, Aspen."

Spenser watched as Aspen silently led Young up the staircase on the left. They turned into a doorway at the top of the landing and disappeared. Spenser took a moment to poke around the two formal sitting rooms, which were virtually identical in almost every way from the rugs to the furniture and how it was arranged. The only difference she could see between the two rooms was that different pieces of art hung in each room—one more modern in style and the other filled with paintings—or at least, very fine replicas of the masters.

Not finding anything of interest in the sitting rooms, Spenser headed down the long hallway. The walls were all done in white wallpaper with pale blue paisley designs. Photos of the family—mostly two girls—hung on the walls at various stages of their lives. She noted there were only a couple of pictures of the son and those when he looked to be eight or nine. Other than that, it was almost like he didn't exist. It was an odd omission.

Spenser passed a pair of closets, a bathroom, and a door that led to a basement. She was going to head downstairs but heard somebody moving around at the back of the house. Curious, Spenser walked down the hall and stepped into the kitchen. To her right was a long table of light oak that looked like it could seat eight. Four large French doors were set into the wall behind the head of the table and looked out into the expansive rear grounds of the house that included a large pool and jacuzzi set in an enclosed glass building.

Beyond the table was an informal and comfortable-looking living room with a pair of cushy recliners flanking a deep, plush sofa centered on an oversized fireplace. Blankets and throw pillows dotted the sofa which looked like somebody had been sleeping on it. Above the fireplace was a mantle that held more family photos—again, mostly of the girls—and above that, a mammoth flatscreen TV hung on the wall, currently tuned to one of those trashy reality shows Spenser despised. It looked cozy and she suspected this was where the family spent most of their time.

To her left was the kitchen. There was a large, marble-topped center island with a double sink in the center. The large space was lined with white shaker cabinets, stainless steel, state-of-the-art appliances, and marble countertops all around. It was a beautiful space and if Spenser was a cook, it was the kind of kitchen she would have liked. But she could barely make Pop-Tarts without nearly burning the house down so a kitchen like that would go to waste in her house.

Leaning against the other side of the center island and staring at her with a petulant expression on her face was a girl who looked exactly like Aspen. She had the same midnight black hair, crystalline blue eyes, smooth, porcelain skin, and petite, curvy body. If they weren't separated by a year, they could be twins. The only difference between them that Spenser could see was that Aspen was an inch or two taller than her younger sister.

Holding her phone in one hand, the girl spooned some yogurt from a small container into her mouth with the other, her eyes never leaving Spenser. She hit send on her text then dropped her phone into the handbag sitting on the counter next to her. Spenser didn't know much about high-end, designer bags—she didn't understand the idea of spending hundreds, if not thousands of dollars on a handbag—but she knew enough to know the one sitting at the girl's elbow was pricey. Very pricey.

"Good morning," Spenser said. "You must be Dallas."

"Yeah. But most people just call me Dally."

"I'm Sheriff Song, Dally," she responded. "You can just call me Spenser."

"My mom is dead, isn't she?"

"Why would you say that?"

The girl shrugged. "Just a feeling. She doesn't just up and take off without telling us," she said. "She's strict. Organized. She is the least impulsive and spontaneous person in the world. The woman schedules her bowel movements. So, no. I don't believe that she just took a trip on a whim."

Her tone was oddly flat and unlike her sister, Dallas seemed cold. Emotionless. Spenser wasn't sure if the girl was just trying to control her emotions and that flatness was an effect of that, or if she was genuinely just that way.

"What do you think might have happened to your mom?" Spenser asked.

The girl frowned and her face clouded over, and Spenser saw a mix of emotions pass through her eyes. She quickly stifled it though and adopted that cool, unaffected posture once more. Dallas raised her gaze to Spenser, a frown on her full, vibrantly

THE LIES IN THE FALLS

red lips. Like Aspen, Dallas was well put together. She wore high-end clothes. Her makeup was immaculate and expertly applied. It seemed to Spenser that Dallas and her older sister might be what some considered to be high-maintenance girls.

"I don't know," she said. "But if something did happen to her, you should be looking at her husband. Brock."

"Why do you say that?"

"Do you know what a Lothario is, Sheriff?"

"I do."

"That's what he is," she replied. "He wormed his way into her life, charmed and seduced her, all for the purpose of getting his hands on her money."

"I take it you don't like your stepfather."

"Don't call him that. Aspen and I don't consider him our stepfather," she growled. "He's a leech. A user. He's just sucking off the Gilchrist family teat. He's a dirtbag. The only reason my mother married him is because he's pretty and she was lonely. For being such a smart woman, she made the stupidest mistake."

"Well, loneliness and a desire for connection can sometimes make us do irrational and inexplicable things," Spenser offered diplomatically.

"To say the least."

The vitriol in her voice was unmistakable. It was more than clear to Spenser that Dallas hated her stepfather. Though she wasn't quite as vocal about it, she'd said enough to make Spenser think Aspen probably did, too. That, of course, made Spenser wonder if they were pointing the finger at Brock Ferry out of anger and their dislike of the man. He made for a convenient target for them since they were already predisposed to think the worst of him.

Just as it was with loneliness and a longing for connection, strong emotions like anger could lead a person to do irrational and inexplicable things—like fingering an innocent man for a crime he didn't commit. Spenser knew, though, that she was getting ahead of herself. She didn't even know if a crime had even been committed.

"Where is your stepf—Brock?" Spenser asked.

"No idea. I don't keep up with his comings and goings," she replied dismissively.

"He's out of town on business," Aspen said.

Spenser turned to see Aspen and Young walk into the kitchen. Aspen joined her sister on the other side of the center island while Young stepped over to where she was standing. It was like looking at a pair of twins. And yet, they were very different in their manners of expression. Aspen wore her heart on her sleeve while Dallas was more self-contained and hid her emotions behind the high, thick wall she kept around herself.

"Do you know where he went on this business trip?" Spenser asked.

"I think he's in California maybe," Aspen answered.

"And when did he leave on this trip?"

Dallas shrugged. "About a week ago, I guess. Like I said, I don't keep track of him."

"It was four days ago," Aspen added.

Aspen seemed to take after their mother in terms of being organized and perhaps a little bit Type-A about things. She seemed to have a firm grip on things. Dallas just seemed disinterested in everything that was going on around her. As for the stepfather's trip, if Brock was out of town, it seemed to suggest he couldn't have had anything to do with their mother's alleged disappearance, making their insistence he was involved a non-starter.

But neither girl seemed to see the fallacy in their argument. And until she knew what they were dealing with, Spenser decided to not bring it up.

"Do you know if your mother has been having problems with anybody lately?" Young asked. "Any threats?"

Aspen shook her head. "No, not that I'm aware of. But she usually didn't share that kind of stuff with us anyway."

"What about your father? I've been told the divorce was acrimonious," Spenser asked.

Dallas laughed. "Please. That man is too much of a coward to do anything. Not to mention he's too lazy. Abducting our mother would require him to get off the couch."

Spenser exchanged a look with Young. The venom in Dallas' voice for her father was biting. She seemed to like him even less than she liked her stepfather. Aspen gave her sister a pointed look then turned back to Spenser, a more even expression on her face.

"Our father gets a monthly stipend from the company," she explained. "Doing anything to our mother would jeopardize that and he doesn't like to work, so I doubt he would run that risk just because they didn't part on good terms."

"What about your uncle?" Spenser asked. "My understanding is that he's upset he was passed over and didn't get control of the company."

Dallas opened her mouth to undoubtedly deliver another biting commentary, this time of her uncle—she didn't seem to have anything nice to say about anybody in her life—but Aspen put her hand on her little sister's shoulder. Dallas closed her mouth and looked away, her words dying on her tongue. It was clear who the alpha in their relationship was.

"Our uncle is always looking for his next get-rich-quick scheme. He's poor with finances and his judgment is equally as bad," Aspen said. "Grandfather was afraid that he would use the company as an ATM and run it into the ground. It's why he groomed our mother to take over instead—he wanted to protect the company as well as our family's legacy."

"Have you ever known him to be violent?" Spenser asked.

"Me personally? No. Not at all. He was always really nice to Dally and me," Aspen replied. "But I know he has some things in his past—a few run-ins with the police and all. I think he's been arrested a few times for things like assault and domestic violence. Stuff like that."

"Okay, good—"

"Are you going to find her, Sheriff?" Dallas asked, her tone impatient.

"Dally," Aspen cut her off. "Stop. Let them do their job."

Dallas frowned at Spenser. "She doesn't even think Mom is missing. I can see it in her eyes," she said. "Do you think she's going to do a damn thing?"

"Dally," Aspen hissed. "Stop. Now."

"I promise you that I am taking this seriously and we are looking into this," Spenser said. "I give you my word that if—"

"If. If," Dallas snapped. "She's going into this doubting that she's missing. That's what I'm talking about, Aspen—"

"Dally, be quiet. You're not helping. There's a process she needs to follow," Aspen said. "Let. Them. Do. Their. Job."

"I can assure you that we are not assuming anything right now, Dallas," Spenser told her. "We are taking this seriously and as I was saying, if there is something for us to find, we will find it."

"Yeah. Whatever," she growled.

Dallas snatched her bag off the counter and stormed out of the kitchen. Aspen turned and gave Spenser a watery smile.

"I'm sorry about her. It's not you. She's just taking this all pretty hard," she said. "She just tends to show it… differently. Anger is easier for her to express."

"I understand," Spenser said. "And I promise you that we will get to the bottom of this, Aspen. We will find out what's going on."

"Thank you, Sheriff," Aspen replied. "I know you will."

Aspen put a better mask on her words and emotions than her sister did, but Spenser saw the same doubts in her eyes she'd seen in Dallas'. She supposed she couldn't blame them. They seemed genuinely terrified of the idea that their mother had been taken and Spenser felt bad that she wasn't convinced Wendy had been taken. She didn't want the girls to think she was minimizing their fears or downplaying what they thought.

And as much as Spenser hated to admit, the political implications of this case had her wanting to stay in the good graces of the Gilchrist clan. It bothered Spenser to no end that she would even have to factor that into her thinking or considerations about a case, but that was the reality of her situation. Her job might depend on their endorsement. As political as it was when she worked for the Bureau, it was never that overt.

The problem with all of this was that there wasn't a whole lot to indicate Wendy had been taken in the first place. She knew Aspen and Dallas weren't ready to accept that answer. They might never be. And if Spenser wasn't able to find Wendy and the girls never got around to accepting the possibility that she'd left of her own accord, the impact on her career could be dire indeed. It could perhaps even be fatal to it.

Spenser hated politics.

CHAPTER SIX

"**W**HAT DO YOU THINK?" YOUNG ASKED.

"I'm still processing," Spenser replied.

She sat at the table in the conference room back at the office after finishing their tour of the Gilchrist compound and coming up empty. Young stood at the whiteboard. She taped a picture of Wendy Gilchrist at the top of the board, writing her name just beneath it in her neat script. Beneath that, she taped pictures of the uncle, Baker Gilchrist, the ex-husband, Joshua Baden, and the current husband, Brock Ferry. To the right of Wendy's photo, Young put up pictures of Aspen and Dallas then took a step back and studied her handiwork for a moment.

"All three of our guys here have a motive to make Wendy disappear," Young said and tapped on the whiteboard. "I looked into it and Aspen was right about Uncle Baker. He's taken collars for domestic battery—twice. He tuned up his girlfriend after a night of drinking, according to the complaints. He was also arrested for assault—also twice. The latter two were bar fights."

"Okay, so Baker has a history of violence and isn't afraid to put his hands on a woman," Spenser said. "But did you find any threats of violence or anything that involved his sister? Did he show up at the company HQ and threaten her? Hit her? Anything like that?"

"No, nothing like that," she admitted. "But that sort of thing might not show up in any official reports. The Gilchrists tend to keep things in-house, after all."

"Right. But typically speaking, that sort of violence tends to escalate," Spenser said. "It usually doesn't come out of the blue. Most of the time, we're going to see an inciting event of some sort that leads up to something like an abduction. There would have been signs that Baker was ramping up to this."

"We'll need to dig into this deeper then," Young said. "There may be something floating around out there—rumors at the very least. Somebody may have seen something. I'll ask around and put out some feelers."

"That's good. That's a good place to start with the uncle," Spenser said. "Tell me about the ex. What's Joshua Baden's story?"

"He doesn't work often—hasn't been able to hold a job and seems content to live off the monthly stipend he gets from Wendy. The girls were right about that," Young answered.

"I'm kind of surprised Wendy didn't have an ironclad prenup that precluded him from getting any sort of alimony."

"If I remember right, at the time, the rumor was that he had some sort of kompromat on Wendy and negotiated a settlement. Wendy agreed to the deal to avoid any bad press," Young said. "Now, bear in mind, that's just a rumor and I have no idea if it's true or not. People do sometimes like to sensationalize things."

"It's a curiosity, though. If Wendy is as hard of a woman as they say, and divorced Joshua because he was lazy and shiftless, I can't see her paying him to allow him to continue being lazy

THE LIES IN THE FALLS

and shiftless unless there was some incentive," Spenser said. "It's something else we're going to want to dig into a little deeper."

"Copy that," Young said.

"And how about bachelor number three?"

"Brock Ferry. He's a piece of work," Young replied with a grin.

"Thirty-seven years old—"

"Wait, he's thirty-seven?"

"Yep."

"And Wendy is... forty-eight if I recall correctly?"

"Yep again," Young said.

Spenser nodded. "Okay, then. To each their own," she said. "Tell me about him."

"Born in Southern California, did some modeling in his twenties, and apparently tried to establish himself as an actor. That didn't work out," Young said. "Moved to Seattle where his work history is best described as spotty. I found some suggestions he was a male escort, but that's not confirmed. But then he married Wendy and has been living on Easy Street ever since."

"I would love to hear the story of how those two met."

"It would probably make our skin crawl."

"Possible," Spenser said. "It might be an interesting tale, though. Or if nothing else, it could be somewhat enlightening."

"I'll look into it."

Spenser looked at the whiteboard, studying all the faces looking back at her. A thousand different things were firing through her mind simultaneously. The one thing that kept pushing its way to the forefront of her mind was wondering if she'd be jumping through all these hoops if the person who was supposedly missing wasn't named Gilchrist. Spenser tried to tell herself she would. She tried to tell herself that she took every crime seriously and that a person's last name, socioeconomic status, or political influence didn't matter.

But she also knew that if it was any other person—any other adult person specifically—she probably wouldn't be investigating their disappearance like a crime. Not unless they had some piece of evidence or compelling reason to believe it was, in fact, a crime... neither of which they had in the case of Wendy Gilchrist. As Spenser had said a thousand times already, it wasn't a crime to walk away from a life you wanted to leave behind. Adults could make that choice—even if their loved ones didn't understand it.

She was in a position, though, where she felt she had to investigate Wendy's disappearance until they found an answer. Even if that answer was one Aspen and Dallas would ultimately refuse to accept. Spenser felt caught between the proverbial rock and a hard place and she wasn't sure that any outcome was going to either satisfy anybody or be good for her, career-wise. If Wendy was trying to not be found, she was going to be pissed if Spenser found her. But if Spenser kicked the can down the road, the girls would crucify her. She was starting to see that there was no winning in this situation. Not for her.

But it was her job. And she would work it as hard and diligently as she worked any other case that came across her desk—motivations and ramifications be damned. And when they arrived at an answer, whatever that answer might be, she had no choice but to let the chips fall where they ultimately would.

"Okay, this is all good background, but we're getting a little over our skis here," Spenser said. "We need to establish that Wendy was in fact, taken. Once we figure that out, we can then pivot to start figuring out who took her."

"Fair enough. And how are we going to figure that out?" Young asked.

"What did you find at the house?"

She shook her head. "Not much. Her car was gone. Aspen said that a bag, some clothes, and a couple of other personal items were missing."

Spenser sat back in her chair, her eyes still fixed on the board. "A bag, some clothes, and some other personal items," she said. "Kind of sounds like somebody leaving for a few days rather than somebody being abducted, doesn't it?"

Young nodded. "Unless that's what the person who took her wanted us to think."

Spenser laughed. "You really should stretch out before you make those kinds of stretches and leaps. I'd hate for you to pull a muscle, Amanda."

She grinned. "Yeah, maybe. But it could be true."

"Why are you so invested in Wendy being abducted?" Spenser asked. "Why do you seem to want there to be a crime here?"

"I just… I guess I feel bad for Aspen and Dallas. I just want to get some answers for them."

It wasn't often that Spenser was reminded that her undersheriff was still very young and had a lot of growing to do, but in that moment, the reality that she was still just twenty-five smacked her in the face. She still needed a lot of seasoning. Still needed a lot of experience. And she needed to learn to set personal feelings and relationships aside when it came to working a case.

"So do I. But we can't just make up answers out of whole cloth," Spenser replied. "We have to follow the evidence and apply logic—even if it leads us somewhere we don't want to go. That's the cornerstone of any investigation. You should know that by now."

"Yeah, I do. It's just hard seeing those two girls hurting like they are."

Spenser's mind drifted back to Aspen and Dallas Gilchrist. Though almost identical in appearance, their personalities—and their reactions to all this—couldn't be more different. They were both intelligent and articulate, but Aspen seemed to be a bit more emotionally mature than her little sister. But they both still seemed very young. All the politics and other garbage aside, Spenser came to realize at the heart of the matter, this was simply a matter of two girls worried for their mother and couldn't necessarily blame Young for sympathizing with them.

"Okay, we need to get some answers," Spenser said. "The first thing I want to do is get a line on Brock. We need to find out where he is and what he's been doing. I want to know how long he's been on this business trip."

"Absolutely."

The door to the conference room opened and Young's brother and Spenser's tech genius, Jacob, walked in. He set his bag down at the table as he took a seat.

"Afternoon," he said.

"How fortuitous," Spenser replied. "I was just going to call for you."

"I picked up on your vibes, Sheriff. You and I are on the same wavelength."

"I somehow doubt that. I'm pretty sure the sheriff doesn't live in the dork zone like you do, oh brother of mine," Young teased.

"Children, behave," Spenser said. "Jacob, I need you to run two sets of financials for me. First, I want you to look into Brock Ferry. I want to know where his paper trail leads. And I also need you to find out the same thing for Wendy Gilchrist."

"On it, Sheriff."

Jacob opened up his laptop and went to work. Spenser listened to the tap-tap-tap of his keys for a few minutes, her eyes drifting back to the photos on the whiteboard. She kept playing and replaying everything Aspen and Dallas had said and kept coming back to the vitriol they'd expressed for their stepfather. It made her wonder what was going on inside that family. Was their hatred for him based on something more than just his relationship with their mother? Or were they genuinely that protective of her and as they'd told Spenser, didn't like seeing her being taken advantage of?

From seemingly cutting their father out of their lives with such ease to being so dismissive of their relationship with their uncle, to their loathing of their stepfather, to the lack of their brother's presence in their lives, the girls seemed to have issues with men, while rallying around their mother. It might not mean much. It might not mean anything at all. But it was one of those curiosities that was lodged in the back of Spenser's mind.

Jacob cleared his throat and drew Spenser's attention. "Okay, according to his charge receipts, it looks like Brock Ferry checked into a hotel down in San Francisco four days ago. It looks like he's due to fly back tomorrow," he said. "But he must have paid for a lot with cash down there because outside of the first two days, there isn't any activity on his cards."

Spenser frowned. She thought it strange there was no activity on his cards for the latter half of his business trip. But it wasn't outside the realm of possibility that he was paying cash for things outside the hotel. He would hardly be unique in that practice. She'd found that men, for whatever reason, preferred to use cash. Also, if he wasn't due to fly back until tomorrow, it seemed to take him off the hook for Wendy's disappearance. She knew Aspen and Dallas weren't going to like that answer, but it was what it was.

"Well, that sucks," Young said with a frown. "I would have bet money it was the husband. It's, like, always the husband."

"You watch too much *Dateline*," Jacob remarked.

Young shrugged. "Yeah, maybe."

"Believe it or not, stranger murders are relatively rare. The vast majority of murders are committed by somebody the victim knows," Spenser said. "What can you tell me about Wendy? What's the activity on her cards? We can end all the speculation here and now."

"One moment," Jacob said.

His fingers flew over the keys and his face was screwed up in concentration as he searched out the information. A few moments later, he sat back and pursed his lips.

"What is it?" Spenser asked.

"Well, the day she disappeared, Wendy Gilchrist bought a train ticket to Connecticut," Jacob said. "But there is no further card activity after that."

"Connecticut?" Young asked, sounding disappointed.

Her brother nodded. "That's what I said."

"And no further card activity, huh?" Spenser asked.

He shook his head. "Not so much as a cup of coffee."

"That would make sense if she really was trying to go off the grid, I guess," Young offered.

"Yeah, maybe," Spenser said, her tone thoughtful as she got to her feet. "Come on."

"Where are we going?" Young asked.

"The train station."

CHAPTER SEVEN

"This is definitely Wendy's car," Young said as she looked at her tablet. "The tags trace back to Wendy Gilchrist."

Spenser walked around the black Lexus SUV, peering in the windows; however, they were tinted too dark to see through. It was parked at the far end of the lot, well away from most of the other cars. It was also behind a tall screen of bushes and trees that lined a median in the lot which made it difficult to see. If Spenser hadn't been looking for it, she might not have seen it.

It seemed like Wendy—or whoever drove the car—was trying to hide it, which didn't make a lot of sense to Spenser and started the first red flags in her head waving. If it had been Wendy who drove to the train station, why would she try to conceal her car? On the other hand, if it had been the person or persons who abducted her, why go through the charade of buying a train ticket and parking here at all? Things were not lining up in Spenser's mind. And she didn't like it when things didn't line up.

"What do you think?" Young asked.

Spenser walked around to the passenger side door and on a whim, gave the handle a try. It was unlocked. She looked over at Young who looked back at her with a frown.

"Don't we need a warrant to go poking around in there?" she asked.

"Exigent circumstances," Spenser replied. "We're looking for a missing woman."

"You're the boss."

"Just make sure you glove up," Spenser said.

Spenser pulled a pair of black nitrile gloves from her coat pocket and put them on as she watched Young do the same. Together, they searched the car, starting from the back and working toward the front, Spenser on the passenger side, Young on the other. When they were done, they stood at the front of the Lexus, stripping off their gloves. By that time, they'd drawn the attention of the few people who happened to be at the train station who cast curious looks their way. Spenser turned her back and tried to ignore them.

"Nothing," Young said.

Spenser shrugged. "If she really hopped on that train, she wouldn't have left anything behind for us to find, though, right?"

"You suddenly sound skeptical."

"There are just a few things that aren't lining up in my head," Spenser replied. "Things that all might have an easy and benign explanation, don't get me wrong. But right now, those things aren't quite squaring up for me."

"Like what?"

"The car being way out here, the lack of use of her credit cards—small things. And like I said, things that might have a simple explanation," Spenser replied thoughtfully. "At the same time, all these small things are adding up to a bigger picture I'm not crazy about. But again, the answers we're looking for might be simple and benign."

Young looked away and seemed to be pondering Spenser's words. She was invested in this being an abduction and in finding the answers for Aspen and Dallas. But she couldn't deny reality or the facts. Young thought it over for a moment then turned back and gave her a nod.

"Okay, so what's our next move?" she asked.

"We go in and speak with the station manager. I want to look at their records and surveillance footage," Spenser said. "Do me a favor and call Arbery. Get him and his team out here to process the car. I want to know if they find any prints, fibers—anything. When they get here, if I'm not already done in there, join me in the manager's office."

"Copy that, Sheriff."

Spenser had poached Noah Arbery from Seattle PD and he was her only full-time forensics tech—and the City Council had fought her on the funding to hire him. His team, Vanessa Ortiz and Anthony Price, were grad students and assisted him for credits and experience. Because the City Council wasn't willing to kick loose the funding for a proper forensics department, Spenser had cobbled together these working relationships.

In her more truthful moments, Spenser had to admit that a full forensics department in a town the size of Sweetwater Falls was probably a bit of overkill. But Arbery's skills had proven invaluable on more than one occasion already, so that wasn't something Spenser was going to admit to anybody else anytime soon. And she would always keep fighting to do right by her deputies. She wanted them to be modernized, streamlined, and to be on the cutting edge of law enforcement.

Spenser had inherited a broken and dysfunctional department. Most of the deputies made Barney Fife look competent in comparison. She'd culled her ranks, weeded out the bad apples, and had spent a lot of time properly training those who were left. And she liked to think she was running a tight, sleek department. Sweetwater Falls was growing, and Spenser was determined that when her time as Sheriff was done, the department, the town, and the people would be safer and better off than when she'd arrived.

That was her goal. That was what drove Spenser. It was why she did everything she did and pushed for everything as hard as she pushed. Marley had been right when she urged Spenser to come west—she'd come to love her adopted town. It was exactly where she needed to be as she reset her life and Spenser wanted the people of Sweetwater Falls to be able to sleep easy at night knowing the department she was building was there to protect them and keep them safe.

"Good afternoon," Spenser said as she stepped into the office and over to a chest-high counter. "May I speak with the station manager, please?"

A middle-aged man sat behind a desk behind the counter. His brown hair was thin and his hazel-colored eyes looked magnified behind a pair of glasses as he glanced up from his crossword puzzle book. He got to his feet and offered her a smile. A good three or four inches shorter than her five-nine frame, the man was portly and had a kind, almost boyish look about him. His cheeks were round and rosy, and he had a thick, bushy mustache on his upper lip.

The man wore what looked like the standard company uniform—a dark blue sweater vest with the train company's logo on the left breast, a light blue button-down beneath that, and a pair of gray slacks. The man, like the office around him, was neat and tidy and he seemed like the sort of person who took pride in his job.

"Afternoon, Sheriff," he replied as he shook her hand. "James Muncy. I'm the manager here. What is it I can do for you?"

"I need you to access your records. I need to see if the ticket Wendy Gilchrist bought was used," Spenser said.

He frowned. "Wendy Gilchrist? I figured somebody like her would take a private flight."

"Her financial records show she bought a train ticket. To New Haven, Connecticut, specifically," she said. "I just need to see if she used the ticket."

"Yeah, sure. No problem. Come on back," he said.

Spenser stepped through the swinging half-gate to her right and walked over as Muncy sat down at his desk again and started plugging away at his keyboard. She stood behind him, watching him input the information. A moment later, he read off the screen.

"Yeah, it looks like the ticket was used," he told her.

Muncy pointed to a line on the screen and Spenser leaned down and followed his finger. The ticket had indeed been used. That would seem to prove Wendy had boarded the train and simply blew town without telling anybody and closed the case. But something was nagging at the back of Spenser's mind. She couldn't say what exactly. Not yet. But those red flags that had started waving when she'd found the car at the far side of the lot hadn't gone away. If anything, they seemed to be waving even harder.

"Mr. Muncy—"

"James," he corrected. "Or Jim is fine. Either is good."

"James then," she said. "Do you have security footage of the platform when Mrs. Gilchrist boarded the train?"

"Yeah, of course," he said. "Follow me."

He got to his feet and led Spenser through a door behind his desk and into the small room beyond it. There were four computer screens mounted to the wall and a desk sitting beneath them. The images on the screens in front of her were black and white and grainy. The pictures weren't very sharp or clean, making Spenser frown.

"Are there any cleaner pictures?" she asked.

Muncy shook his head. "The company feels the equipment we have is adequate, so they won't cough up the cash," he said. "Believe me, I've tried."

Spenser chuckled ruefully. "I feel your pain, my friend," she said. "Okay, can you show me the footage from the date and time Wendy Gilchrist boarded the train?"

"You got it."

Muncy's fingers quickly pecked at the keys as he plugged in the parameters for the video footage Spenser wanted. A couple of moments later, he snapped his fingers.

"Here you go," he said.

"Great. Let it play, please."

"Yes, ma'am."

The video rolled and Spenser watched the mostly empty platform—Sweetwater Falls was a minor stop on the line and wasn't a bustling hub of activity which was probably why the company didn't want to invest a lot of capital into the station. There were only half a dozen people standing on the platform waiting for the train's arrival and none of them was Wendy Gilchrist.

"Fast forward a bit please?" Spenser asked.

Muncy did as he was asked, and Spenser watched the footage scroll by. It was a couple of minutes before a new person appeared on the platform.

"There," she said. "Stop."

The footage stopped, that moment frozen in time as Spenser leaned closer to the screens and studied the newcomer. The woman, dressed in a bulky coat, wide-brimmed, floppy hat, and oversized sunglasses, stood near the edge of the platform and checked her phone. Between the glasses, hat, and the quality of the footage, Spenser couldn't make out the face. Given the bulkiness of the coat the figure was wearing, it was hard for her to say it was even a woman standing there.

"Roll the film, please?"

Muncy nodded and tapped a few keys. The footage resumed rolling and Spenser watched as the figure in the hat walked around the platform with movements seeming to Spenser to be more feminine than masculine. She was comfortable saying it was a woman on the platform. What she couldn't say, though, was whether or not it was Wendy Gilchrist.

She and Muncy watched in silence as a few minutes later, the train rolled into the station and the woman in the coat and hat boarded. Five minutes after that, the train departed and Wendy Gilchrist, or whoever that was, hadn't been seen or heard from again. Spenser had him roll it back and freeze on the image of the woman standing on the platform, her face obscured by the hat and glasses she was wearing. She stared at it for a long moment and frowned.

"Can you make me a copy of this footage?" Spenser asked.

"Of course," Muncy replied. "Did you find what you were looking for, Sheriff?"

"I'm honestly not sure."

CHAPTER EIGHT

"**M**ORE WINE?" RYKER ASKED.

"Yes, please," she replied.

After wrapping up at the train station and getting a little paperwork done at the office, Spenser punched out. On her way home, Ryker had sent her a text, asking her to come over for dinner. She'd been planning on take-out, so when Ryker sent the invitation, she jumped on it. And she was glad she did. He'd gone all out.

"That's the thing—the height is the same. And from what I can see of the build, that matches, too," Spenser said. "But I can't swear under oath, in court, or anywhere that the woman on that train platform is Wendy Gilchrist."

As she continued to rant and rave, Ryker poured her another glass of wine then sat back in his chair and listened to her. It was one of the things she appreciated most about him. He was always willing to let her scream like a banshee without judgment. And he listened to her wail... often. Spenser picked up her glass of wine and took a swallow, taking a moment to savor the deep, rich flavor. Between the wine and the company, Spenser felt the tension that had built up in her shoulders all day begin to melt away.

"This is really nice," she said, holding the glass up.

"I thought it might go well with dinner."

"As usual, you are right," she said. "I think you missed your true calling. You would have made a fine sommelier."

He chuckled. "Good to know I've got a fallback option."

Spenser took a bite of the Beef Wellington he'd made for dinner and groaned appreciatively then washed it down with another swallow of wine.

"And if you ever get tired of being a coffee mogul and decide to pass on a career as a sommelier, you can always be a five-star chef," she commented. "I seriously don't know how you can be so good at so many things."

"I've got nothing but time on my hands and an endless supply of YouTube tutorials," he replied. "You'd be surprised how much you can learn to do online."

Spenser laughed and took another bite of her meal before pushing the plate away, stuffed to the gills. She took another sip of her wine and set the glass down.

"My God, that was amazing," she said.

"Glad you enjoyed it."

"Thank you. I appreciate you going to so much trouble."

"It's no trouble at all. Besides, it's nice to have some company," he said.

Spenser looked at him and smiled warmly. When his chocolate brown eyes settled on hers, Spenser felt her heart swell and a feeling of warmth blossom in her belly.

"We've come a long way, haven't we?" she asked.

"Yes, we have."

They sat across the table from each other, small smiles playing across their lips and the air between them crackling with a sense of anticipation. Spenser soaked in the moment. Relished it. After Trevor's murder, she never thought she would feel so comfortable in another man's presence. Never thought she could feel what she was feeling. After she watched Trevor die that night, she thought the part of her that held her ability to care for somebody else had died along with him. It was a pleasant surprise to find that part of her was, in fact, alive and well.

Ryker cleared his throat and took a sip of his wine and the moment gently passed, but he offered her a smile that told Spener he'd not only felt it also but relished it as much as she did. And a wave of emotion swelled within her.

"Did your forensics team find anything in Wendy's car?" he asked.

"Nothing out of the ordinary."

"And you said there's been no activity on her credit cards?" Ryker asked.

"Nothing. Not so much as a cup of coffee," she replied.

"Not to play Devil's Advocate or anything, but that doesn't necessarily mean anything," he said. "I like to use cash when I'm traveling. And it makes even more sense if she's going off the grid and doesn't want to be found."

"Yeah, I had the same thought."

"Pinged her phone?"

"She has it shut off," Spenser replied.

"Also makes sense if she's off the grid."

"Figured that, too," she said with a laugh. "And you're right, it all makes perfect sense. If she doesn't want to be tracked down, it's logical. But Aspen and Dallas insist Wendy would never do something like that. They insist it's out of character for her."

Ryker made a face. "That's not exactly true. She's gone off the grid before."

"Has she?"

He nodded. "It was before the girls were born, but Wendy disappeared for a while. It was a big deal and had people all over town talking. I was just barely a teenager myself, but I remember it because the way people were acting, it was like somebody kidnapped the Lindbergh baby again. But she was gone for a few weeks... maybe a month?"

"And where was she?"

"Nobody really knows to this day. The Gilchrists kept a tight lid on it," he replied. "Scuttlebutt around town said she was in rehab. Others thought maybe she had a psychotic break and was in some sort of mental health facility—it's all still a mystery."

"What do you think? If you had to speculate, that is."

Ryker shrugged. "I think being a Gilchrist in this town comes with a hell of a lot of pressure. And from the little I know, old man Gilchrist was grooming Wendy to take over from an early age, which adds an even thicker layer of pressure. I only met the guy a couple of times, but I can tell you that Wendy's father was a hard man," he told her. "I honestly haven't spent a lot of time thinking about it, but if you asked me to speculate about what happened to her back then, I'd say it's probably likely she went to some facility to get her head right."

It was an interesting piece of information and sort of put all the other bits of information Spenser had into a different context. Being the matriarch of a powerful, wealthy family as well as the owner of a company like Emerald Timber had to be difficult and come with a lot of pressure. Was it possible Wendy Gilchrist needed a mental break, checked herself into a facility to decompress, and that was why she left town under a shroud of secrecy? Yeah, it was possible. As she thought more about it, Spenser thought it might even be likely. That wasn't the sort of information a woman as tightly controlled as Wendy Gilchrist would want out there for public consumption.

It also raised a thousand questions, but it brought one important question to the forefront of her mind: Why would she not tell her daughters something? Anything? Why not make up some story about a business trip or something to that effect? Why make them wonder about what happened to her? Why make them jump to all sorts of conspiracy theories about her husband murdering her? Why would she leave them hanging in limbo like that when, by all the accounts she'd heard, Wendy was very close with Aspen and Dallas and doted on them? Why put them through that sort of hellish uncertainty?

"What's going through that big brain of yours, Spense?"

"Nothing. Everything," she replied with a wry grin. "I just have so many questions right now and don't know how to go about answering them. I keep flashing back to the video footage at the train station. The hat, the big glasses—it all felt like a disguise to me."

"That might fit with somebody wanting to make a low-key exit out of town."

"Yeah, maybe," she said. "But why the train? Why not hop on a plane?"

He shrugged. "Maybe a relaxing rail tour across the country is a way for her to start decompressing," he said. "Or... maybe it just makes it easier for her to get off somewhere between here and Connecticut and not leave a paper trail."

Spenser nodded. She had to admit, it made sense. But something about the video footage—about the person who was supposedly Wendy Gilchrist—nagged at her. It was relentless and wouldn't let go. It was like an itch, just under the skin that no amount of scratching was going to satisfy. Not until she identified what was causing it.

"You're still not convinced," Ryker said.

She pursed her lips. "I don't know. There's just something that still feels off to me. Something that just doesn't feel quite right."

Ryker sipped his wine and then breathed heavily. "Then I think you should trust your instincts and follow your gut. If something feels off to you, then it probably is off."

"Yeah. Maybe," she replied, unsure if what felt off in all this was her instincts.

CHAPTER NINE

"Okay, so what is your gut telling you?" Young asked.

Spenser paced in front of the whiteboard in their conference room staring at the photos. Her eyes kept drifting back to the DMV picture of Wendy Gilchrist and then to the still image taken from the security camera at the station of the woman on the platform in the wide, floppy hat and oversized sunglasses. And no matter how many times she tried to make them match, she just couldn't quite make them fit. It was like the old square peg and round hole conundrum.

"My gut is telling me that's not Wendy Gilchrist on the platform," Spenser said.

Jacob frowned. "I don't know. I mean, it could be. It's just hard to say because the security footage is so grainy and pixelated."

"Can you clean it up at all?" Spenser asked.

He shook his head. "I tried but the equipment they're using is pretty dated," he replied. "Unfortunately, it is what it is."

Young leaned back in her chair with a smug grin on her face. "So, you've come around to believing Wendy was taken, huh?"

Spenser laughed. "Settle down, now. All I'm saying is I've come around to thinking we need to look into things a little bit deeper here."

"I'll take what I can get."

"So, you think somebody is impersonating Wendy Gilchrist and that this imposter, whoever they are, is who got on that train?" Jacob asked.

Spenser frowned. "It sounds goofy, I know. But… yeah."

"Okay, so somebody wanted us to think Wendy left town," Young said. "But why?"

"To think that she's just off somewhere living her best life or whatever," Spenser replied. "Somebody perhaps doesn't want us looking into Wendy too closely."

"So, you think somebody killed her and is trying to throw us off the scent," Young said.

"Maybe," Spenser said then turned to Jacob. "I need you to put those skills of yours to use on something. You're probably going to need to dig deep and shine some light in what are going to be some really dark corners."

"That's my specialty," he replied.

"Good. Because I heard a story that a long time ago, Wendy disappeared like this. There were a lot of rumors at the time but one of the most prevalent was that she had some sort of an episode and was checked into a mental health facility," Spenser said. "I want you to see if you can find anything to corroborate that. And if you can, I need the name of the facility. It's entirely possible nothing nefarious happened to her and she just went off the grid to get a mental tune-up. I want to make sure we're covering all bases here and aren't keying in on a mystery that doesn't actually exist."

THE LIES IN THE FALLS

"Got it. I'll do what I can, Sheriff. But you know how tricky it can be with medical information—especially psychological information," Jacob said.

Spenser smirked at him. "I know your bag of tricks is deep. I don't need records or specific information about diagnoses or whatever. I just need to know if it's true. So, just do your best."

"Aye, aye, Captain. I'm on it," he said.

"Good. Thank you."

"And what about us?" Young asked.

"We are going to go talk to Brock Ferry and see what he has to say for himself."

Young rubbed her hands together and grinned. "Excellent."

"Mr. Ferry, I'm Sheriff Song, this is Undersheriff Young," Spenser introduced them.

"Hey. Yeah. Come on in," he said.

Spenser noted the suitcases near the bottom of the stairs as they followed him through the house to the kitchen at the back. He offered them chairs at the center island then walked over to the refrigerator. His demeanor was relaxed. Casual.

"Can I get you guys something to drink?" he asked.

"No, we're fine," Spenser replied. "Thank you."

Brock was wearing long shorts, a Hawaiian print shirt, and flip-flops, and his blonde hair was pulled back into a ponytail that fell to his shoulders. He was about six-one with cornflower blue eyes and a toned, taut physique. His chiseled jawline was dotted with stubble and Spenser had to admit that Dent was right, he was a good-looking man. He had that classic Hollywood leading man look about him. Not that she was shallow, but it was easy for Spenser to see why it was easy for Wendy to soak up the attention she got from him. Especially if she was feeling lonely and vulnerable.

"So, Mr. Ferry—"

"Brock," he said. "Just call me Brock."

"All right, Brock," Spenser said. "You are aware that nobody has seen or heard from your wife in several days, correct?"

"Yeah, Aspen and Dallas made sure to tell me—after accusing me of burying her in a shallow ditch somewhere," he grumbled and rolled his eyes.

"When was the last time you heard from Wendy?" Young asked.

He sighed loudly and dramatically. "Hell, I don't know. I think it was before I left for my trip."

"And what was the nature of your business in California?" Young asked.

"I was meeting with a couple of clients. We were discussing an advertising campaign that I want to roll out," he said, his voice soft but deep.

"Was it normal for you and Mrs. Gilchrist to not communicate with each other like that?" Spenser asked.

"We communicated just fine when we needed to," he said, his voice tight.

"Are there problems in your marriage, Brock?" Spenser asked.

A wry grin twisted his lips. "I see what you're doing."

"And what are we doing?" Spenser asked.

"You're trying to drum up problems in my marriage so you can pin whatever happened to Wendy on me," he said.

"Do you think something happened to your wife?" Spenser pressed.

"How should I know?" he replied. "Like I said, I haven't spoken to her since I've been out of town. As far as I know, she's out somewhere on a bender."

"Has that happened often?" Spenser asked. "Wendy just up and disappearing and going off on a bender somewhere?"

"From time to time. You have to understand she carries the weight of the world on her shoulders. She's always under an immense amount of pressure and sometimes, she just needs to get away and blow off some steam. We all have our ways of coping with stress. That's hers and I'm not one to judge or demand she explain herself to me," he said.

"And how is it that Aspen and Dallas don't know where she is?" Spenser asked.

"Because Wendy is very careful to manage her image. She's never wanted them to know about her little vacays and has always blown town when they've been gone," he replied. "They came home from school unexpectedly this time and naturally freaked out when they thought their mother had disappeared. Understandably so."

Spenser exchanged a look with Young. The man had an answer for everything. The trouble with it was that his answers, to that point, were all entirely plausible. It was certainly a far different picture of the woman than had been painted for her. Young gave her a subtle shrug.

"I was given to understand that Wendy isn't an impulsive sort of woman," Spenser said.

"Yeah, well, you don't really know her, do you, Sheriff?" he replied. "She's got a face she wears in public and one she wears in private."

"As do we all," Young said. "And I couldn't help but notice that you've very smoothly dodged one of our original questions, Brock."

He sighed and ran a hand over his face. The stubble on his chin and cheeks made a dry scratchy sound that made Spenser cringe.

"Look, we had our ups and downs. We had good days and bad days. And yes, we had our fair share of arguments—like every married couple," he replied, his tone dripping with irritation. "Wendy could be hard. She could be unyielding and unreasonable at times. At the end of the day, she's my wife and I love her. With all my heart I love her."

Spenser leaned forward and locked eyes with him. "So, you had nothing to do with her disappearance then?"

"No, of course not," he growled.

"And you didn't do anything to her?" she pressed.

"Why would I do something to her, Sheriff?"

"You're part of the Gilchrist clan, Brock," Young chimed in. "There might be a lot of money at stake if something happened to Wendy."

"Yeah, and I'm not entitled to the Gilchrist fortune or any part of the company. I signed an ironclad prenup. In the event of divorce or Wendy's death, I get a one-time payout of one hundred grand and sent on my way. I don't even get to keep the house," he said. "So, I ask you again, why in the hell would I do something to Wendy? What would be my motive, Sheriff?"

Spenser and Young shared another look. It was possible he was lying, but he had to know that would be simple enough to verify, which suggested to Spenser that he was telling the truth. She'd learned long ago, though, it was always best to be sure.

"If you wouldn't mind, I'd like you to send me a copy of your prenup, Brock."

"Yeah, fine. Whatever. I'll get it over to you ASAP," he grunted. "Are we done here? I'm pretty beat and would like to take a nap."

"Are you really not worried about your wife?" Young asked. "I mean, forgive me for saying so, but you just seem so nonchalant about your wife being missing."

"Like I said, there's nothing to worry about and she's not missing. She's probably just blowing off steam somewhere," he said testily. "She'll probably be back in a day or two. Just like all the other times she's disappeared."

"All right, that's all we have for the moment. Thank you for your cooperation, Brock," Spenser said as she got to his feet. "But I'd appreciate it if you let me know if you hear from your wife or she turns up."

"Yeah, sure. No sweat."

"We'll show ourselves out," Spenser said.

As they walked out of the house, she thought some questions had been answered but even more cropped up that hadn't. Spenser leaned into her gut feeling, since it was the only thing she had to guide her. And at the moment, her gut was telling her that Brock Ferry was hiding something. That he hadn't been entirely forthcoming with them. She thought he was a sleaze but didn't think he had anything to do with Wendy's disappearance.

CHAPTER TEN

"**G**OOD MORNING. I'M SHERIFF SPENSER SONG."

The dark-haired, darker-eyed woman sitting behind the desk looked up at her and offered Spenser a professional if somewhat chilly smile. The nameplate on her desk identified her as Cynthia Hall, the woman Spenser was looking for. Her desk sat atop dark gray industrial carpeting and was surrounded by walls that were a couple of shades lighter. The credenza behind her was a dark, polished wood, as were the two bookcases that flanked it. A pair of chairs sat near the wall across from her desk, beside the door, and fake plants stood in the corners.

"Yes, good morning," she said. "How may I help you?"

"I was told that you're Wendy Gilchrist's personal assistant."

"That's right," she said. "But Mrs. Gilchrist isn't in this morning."

"Oh, I know," Spenser said. "I was hoping to have a word with you, actually."

The following morning, the first thing Spenser did was check in at the office, handle roll calls, and hand out assignments for the day. Jacob had no new information on Wendy's stay in a facility when she was younger, but he said he had a few leads and would keep digging. She'd also had him constantly monitoring Wendy's phone, hoping to get a ping. But that, too, had yielded no new results. Her phone was still shut off, her cards still hadn't been used, and nobody had heard from her. She was still a ghost.

Spenser had put Young in charge of following up with Brock. She wanted a copy of that prenup and had left her with a few more subtle, probing questions she wanted Young to ask him. Her gut still told her Brock wasn't involved with Wendy's disappearance, but she'd been wrong before. And with so many variables in play and so much uncertainty, Spenser thought it was best if she double-checked her own work.

While that was going on, Spenser took a trip down to the corporate offices of Emerald Timber. She wanted to get a feel for Wendy Gilchrist that wasn't shot through a prism of the emotions of those closest to her. Spenser was hoping Wendy's PA might be able to shed some light on a few questions she had.

"All right, well, what can I do for you, Sheriff?" Hall asked.

"Listen, I know that Mrs. Gilchrist hasn't been into the office in almost a week now," Spenser said. "Her daughters have not heard from her and are getting worried. They've asked me to look into things and see if I can figure out where their mother is."

"I honestly don't know where she is."

"Have you ever known her to disappear like this before?"

Her face went blank, and she looked down at her desk for a moment. Spenser's experience told her the woman was about to lie to her.

"I need the truth, Ms. Hall," Spenser said.

"Please, call me Cindy," she said.

THE LIES IN THE FALLS

"Very well. I need the truth, Cindy, and I'm sure Mrs. Gilchrist appreciates your discretion," Spenser said firmly. "And I don't need the details. I'm not looking to invade Mrs. Gilchrist's privacy. But I need to be able to look Aspen and Dallas in the eye and tell them honestly that there's nothing to worry about. So, please. Whatever you can tell me would be appreciated because those girls are terrified for their mother's safety."

She frowned and remained silent for a long moment. Hall finally got to her feet then crossed the small office and closed the door. She turned back to Spenser, her expression solemn.

"Okay, listen, I've worked for Mrs. Gilchrist for a little more than a decade now and I keep her calendar. It's not common knowledge—in fact, I may be the only person who knows—but she sometimes takes what I refer to as sabbaticals," Hall said. "She'll usually have me block out a few days on her calendar and list it as something innocuous—usually inventory or supplier meetings. Something simple like that. But she'll go off grid to decompress for a while and she's completely out of touch during that time."

Spenser nodded. It lined up with what Brock had told them. But it still didn't answer all the questions that continued to nag at her.

"Do you know where Mrs. Gilchrist goes during these sabbaticals?"

"I don't. It's not my business, so I don't ask," she replied. "If she wanted me to know, Mrs. Gilchrist would tell me. She's always under a tremendous amount of pressure so nobody should begrudge her a little time away."

"That's fair," Spenser said. "How often does she go on her sabbaticals?"

"Usually, a couple of times a year," Hall said.

"Okay, so, can you tell me if she is on one of her sabbaticals right now? Is that why she's dropped off the radar?" Spenser asked.

A frown crossed Hall's face and her expression darkened. Spenser could see the concern for her boss etched into her features.

"Not that I know of," Hall admitted. "She didn't block anything out on her calendar. But when she didn't come in, I just kind of assumed she took a spur of the moment sabbatical. But… she's usually not gone this long."

"Have you tried contacting her?"

"I've left messages, of course," she said. "But like I said, she's totally unreachable when she's off on a sabbatical."

An ominous feeling pressed down on Spenser as a thousand thoughts, each one darker than the last, scrolled through her mind.

"Cindy, would you mind if I took a look at Mrs. Gilchrist's calendar?"

She shook her head quickly. "I'm afraid not. There is private information on her calendar that I simply cannot let you see," she said. "But trust me, I have looked at it myself—quite a few times, in fact—and there is nothing there. She didn't block out any time for herself and everything is business as usual. Or rather, it's supposed to be."

"I understand your protectiveness and I appreciate it," Spenser said. "But I really need to see that calendar. I'll get a warrant if I have to, but I hope it doesn't come to that."

"I'm sorry, Sheriff. I can't. If you can get a warrant, I'll let you see it, but because of the private information, I can't just open it up for you."

Spenser frowned. She'd been hoping she could strongarm and/or guilt Hall into letting her look at Wendy's calendar simply because there was no way any judge in their right mind would give her a warrant for it. It didn't look like she was going to get a peek at it, so Spenser had to be satisfied with Hall's statement that Wendy was likely on a sabbatical. At least, she'd have to be satisfied with it for the moment since there wasn't anything she could do about it.

"Okay, maybe you can tell me this then," Spenser said as she switched gears. "Has Mrs. Gilchrist received any threats recently? Anybody giving her a hard time? Anything like that?"

"She's received plenty of threats from that local environmental group, the Green League," Hall replied. "They're a nuisance and do nothing more than cause trouble. They act as if Mrs. Gilchrist is responsible for every environmental catastrophe in history. They're ridiculous."

"Have they made any specific threats that you can recall?"

Hall scoffed. "This I'll show you without a warrant."

She walked around to her desk and sat down then spun around in her chair. She opened a drawer in the credenza and fingered through the files, pulling one out from near the back. Hall turned back around and handed it to Spenser.

"Take a look," Hall said.

Spenser opened the file and began flipping through the letters that had been stacked inside. They went back more than three years and each one seemed more threatening than the last. There was no outright threat of violence or anything like that, but the tone was ominous, and the threats were vague and suggestive rather than overt. The person who'd written these letters was smart. They knew exactly where that line was and knew better than to cross it. She looked at the signatures and saw they were all signed by the same person: Max Carter, President of the Green League.

"Why haven't you come to us about this?" Spenser asked.

"Because Mrs. Gilchrist didn't want to raise a fuss about it," Hall replied. "This Max character is a lot of bluster and bravado but that's about it. We've never taken him very seriously, Sheriff. His threats, if that's what you want to call them, are idle—"

"Until they're not."

Hall opened her mouth to respond but closed it again without speaking as Spenser's words seemed to sink in. Her eyes widened and she looked at Spenser with an expression of horror on her face.

"Y—you don't think this man did something to Mrs. Gilchrist, do you?" Hall asked. "I mean, his threats are vague. I hesitate to call them threats at all. But… Oh, dear God. If he did something to her and we haven't been taking his threats seriously all this time…"

"We don't know that he did anything to her, Ms. Hall. Or that he's involved in this in any way," Spenser said. "I mean, we don't know for sure that Mrs. Gilchrist is anywhere but off on one of her sabbaticals. Now I'm going to do everything in my power to figure out what's going on," Spenser said and tapped the file in her hand. "May I take these? I'll make sure to get them back to you."

"Of course," Hall replied.

"Thank you," Spenser said. "And I'll touch base with you if I have any follow-up questions."

"Please do."

Spenser turned and walked out of the office and headed for the Bronco, questions firing through her mind as a dark sense of dread grew thicker in her belly. Although not much had changed, Spenser felt more certain than before that something had in fact happened to Wendy Gilchrist. She was increasingly certain Wendy was not the woman in the security video who'd boarded the train to Connecticut. But if not Wendy, who was it really?

She hoped that Max Carter, President of the Green League, might help provide some of the answers she was looking for.

CHAPTER ELEVEN

S PENSER STOPPED BY THE OFFICE TO CHECK IN AND monitor progress, which was simple since there hadn't been a lot of progress to that point. Wendy's phone still hadn't been turned on, her cards were still inactive, and finding out if she had, in fact, stayed at a mental health facility was proving to be more difficult than Jacob had thought.

After touching base with him, Spenser updated Young on what she'd learned from Wendy's PA. She gave the younger woman the file of threats, which were mostly from Max Carter and the Green League, but they'd found a couple of other unknown person's names sprinkled in along with his missives. Once they'd sorted them into piles of "Max" and "Others," Spenser tasked Young with running down the other people and doing a quick threat assessment on them, weeding out the cranks from the real threats.

Once that was done, Spenser climbed back into the Bronco and headed across town to the headquarters for the "Pacific Northwest Chapter of the Green League." Though, in the brief bit of research she did on the organization, she had not found any other chapters. Anywhere. As far as she could tell, the Green League was a one-branch, one-issue operation. They had an office in Sweetwater Falls and their main mission—their only mission really—was to be a wrench in the works of Emerald Timber.

Spenser parked in a lot beside a dry cleaner's shop and looked up. The Green League office sat on the second floor of the multi-use building that housed a couple of different small businesses and happened to correspond with Max Carter's home address. She found a door on the side of the building with a staircase that led to the second floor. Spenser climbed the stairs and at the top, found herself at the end of a long hallway that was thick with the odor of marijuana.

There were four apartments on the second floor—two on a side. Carter's place was at the end of the hall on her left. When she reached his door, Spenser knocked. She heard music coming from inside and was sure the reek of pot was coming from his place. Somehow, it didn't surprise her. Spenser knocked again, harder and louder this time, and a moment later, she heard shuffling footsteps approach the door and then it opened, the expression on the face of the man in front of her quickly morphing from irritation to panic.

"Max Carter?" Spenser asked. "I'm Sheriff Song."

Eyes wide and mouth falling open, the man staring back at her looked like he was about to soil himself. He looked like Spenser had expected—five-ten and rail thin with limp, shaggy brown hair that hung to his shoulders, thin lips, with stubble covering his gaunt cheeks and long, pointed chin. He was in his mid-to-late thirties, standing there barefoot and sporting a pair of blue jeans with no shirt covering his narrow chest.

"Max Carter?" Spenser repeated, more forcefully this time.

"Yeah—yeah, that's me," he stammered.

"May I come in?"

"This isn't a good time—"

"We need to talk, Max," Spenser said, her voice low and menacing. "Now, may I come in?"

He glanced behind him, and Spenser could see his mind spinning, trying to figure a way out of what he had to believe was going to be a drug bust. Spenser rolled her eyes and sighed.

"I couldn't care less about your weed right now, Max," she said. "I'm not here about that."

He looked at her suspiciously. "You're not?"

"No. I'm here on an unrelated matter."

"Umm... you give me your word?"

"Do you want me to pinky swear?" Spenser growled impatiently.

Still uncertain and looking like he was thinking about bolting, Carter stepped aside and let her into his apartment. Spenser stepped across the threshold and grimaced.

"Can you like, open a window?" she asked. "Or two."

"Yeah, sure."

He closed the door and darted across the room, quickly opening the pair of vertical sliding windows that overlooked the rear parking lot. She watched as the cloud of smoke that hugged the ceiling quickly drifted out. With the sudden flood of light streaming in through the windows, Spenser looked around at Carter's shabby, rundown apartment. A green flag bearing the "Green League" name and symbol hung on the wall to her right along with a collection of bumper stickers and flyers for past events his group hosted.

A ratty, beat-up-looking couch sat atop a threadbare rug in front of her, and on the battered and scarred wooden coffee table sat a tray that held a bong and a moderately sized bag of weed. He had enough that Spenser was certain he was supplementing his income by selling the stuff. Carter quickly snatched up the tray and hauled it into the kitchen, believing it was a case of out of sight, out of mind. But, she had given him her word, so she wasn't going to hassle him about it. A large TV sat on a small nightstand in the corner of the living room and was tuned to a nature documentary. The whole scene seemed too cliché to be real.

Having pulled on a t-shirt, Carter stepped out of the kitchen and folded his arms over his chest. He tapped his bare foot and chewed on his thumbnail nervously. Spenser let the heaviness in the air between them hang for a moment. She allowed the silence between them to linger to put the man back on his heels. It was a power play. She's always believed that having a potential suspect on the defensive from the jump made it more likely they would slip up and say something incriminating.

"So, um... What can I do for you, Sheriff?" he asked, his voice trembling.

"I'm curious about something, Max," she said and pointed to the Green League flag that hung on the wall. "You boast of having an army at your disposal. But looking around your place—your organizational HQ, mind you—it seems more like an army of one."

"What? What are you talking about?"

"The letters you wrote to Wendy Gilchrist and Emerald Timber," she replied. "When you were threatening her, you referred to your army and alluded to acts of violence you were willing to commit against her."

He licked his lips nervously and his face blanched as he shifted on his feet. Carter shook his head and ran a hand through his hair. It wasn't hard to see his mind spinning.

"That—I didn't make any threats," he said defiantly. "I never said a single thing that can be construed as an actual threat."

"You were very careful and precise in your language. That's very true," Spenser said. "You walked right up to that line without actually crossing it. I take it you learned that from the law classes you took down at Oregon State?"

A sardonic grin pulled a corner of his mouth upward. In the surface dive she did before coming to see him, Spenser had learned that Carter had taken and passed the bar. He did a little work in environmental law, which was probably where his inspiration for founding the Green League stemmed from. His career in law, like his organization, though, seemed to have fizzled out.

"I see you've done some homework," he said.

"I believe in being prepared," she replied. "Why'd you stop practicing law?"

He shrugged. "Let's just say I was disillusioned. I realized I was doing nothing more than treading water and wasn't making the difference I wanted to make. The corporations have all the money and hold all the power and until we have some leaders in office with the backbone to actually make some changes, nothing ever will. If we want change, we have to take action ourselves."

"So, you set your sights on Emerald Timber and Wendy Gilchrist… why exactly?"

"I'm originally from Sweetwater Falls. I've seen the deleterious effects Emerald Timber is having on the land around us," he said. "They are the reason the natural beauty of this town is going to be a thing of the past. They're going to turn our town into nothing more than just another concrete jungle sooner, rather than later."

"So, you figured what, taking Wendy Gilchrist out was cutting off the head of the snake? And that if you did that, the body would die?" she asked. "Did you think that Emerald Timber would fold up without her?"

He cocked his head, an expression of confusion on his face. "What are you talking about?"

"Did you do something to Mrs. Gilchrist, Max?" Spenser asked. "Did you make good on those veiled threats?"

He shook his head, his expression shifting from confusion to horror. "Did something happen to her?"

"You tell me."

"I have no idea what you're talking about. I really don't," he stammered. "If you're telling me that something happened to that woman, you're barking up the wrong tree. I didn't do anything to her. I swear to God."

"But you see my problem here, don't you, Max?" Spenser pressed. "I have dozens of letters written by you that are vaguely threatening, promising that you have an army of people at your disposal and that they'll not tolerate her—and I'm quoting here—continued raping and pillaging of the Earth. Does that sound familiar?"

"Well, umm, yeah, I wrote those letters. But I didn't do anything to her. I would never hurt her. I'd never hurt anybody. Never. That's just not who I am," he said quickly.

"Those letters, though—they tell a different story," she said. "In those letters, you sound pretty strident. Militant. You sound like a man ready to take action against a woman you've painted as evil. Somebody you see as your arch enemy."

He shook his head again. "Sheriff, those letters were just me trying to intimidate her. That's it. I was never going to follow through with them. Never. I just wanted to scare her into listening to me. Into thinking about what she was doing to this planet," he argued.

Spenser listened and watched him closely, studying him for any tells, searching for the slightest hint of deception. But she saw none. She hadn't expected to, anyway. The minute she laid eyes on Carter and saw his place, she just had the feeling he was more of a talker rather than an action taker. But she had to play it all out anyway because one never truly knew. Even so, she'd pushed him and didn't see anything that would have led her to believe he had the spine to follow through on his threats.

"What about the other members of your… army?"

"I don't have an army."

"There are other members of the Green League, aren't there?" Spenser asked. "Perhaps some of them are more militant than you are? Maybe they'll take action where you won't?"

He frowned and his face clouded over with a blend of emotions—embarrassment being the most prominent among them."

"I used to have more members. But they didn't feel like I was taking enough action. That I wasn't committed enough to the cause to do what needed to be done," he admitted glumly. "They called me 'Max the Mouth' and left the Green League a couple years back. It's just been me ever since. But if something happened to Wendy Gilchrist, you might want to look at them."

"I'm going to need names."

"Yeah," he replied. "I know."

She could see he was conflicted about giving up his former compatriots, but she could also see he was the type who wouldn't hesitate to do what he needed to do to save his own skin.

"I may have some follow-up questions, so be sure to stick around town," she said, making her tone sound threatening.

THE LIES IN THE FALLS

Carter's shoulders sagged and as he let out a breath of relief so heavy, his legs nearly gave out beneath him. He managed to stay upright, however.

"Yes, ma'am," he said.

"And do not talk to anybody about Wendy Gilchrist. Nobody, Max," Spenser said. "I don't want you discussing our conversation with anybody. Especially your former friends. Am I clear?"

He nodded eagerly. "I understand. We're clear."

"See that you remain that way," she said. "Or I will take a real interest in your dope and whatever else you have going on. I'll make your life really uncomfortable, Max. Got me?"

"Yes, ma'am."

She let her eyes linger on him for a long moment just to impress the point. He seemed to get it. More satisfying, he seemed too afraid of Spenser to break his word to her. She mentally put him on the back burner and didn't think he had anything to do with Wendy's disappearance, but she wasn't willing to cross him off the list entirely. Not just yet.

"Have a good day, Max."

CHAPTER TWELVE

"So, where are we at?" Spenser asked as she took her seat at the conference table.

"Well, the good news is I was able to confirm that Wendy Gilchrist did, in fact, spend time at the Morley House in Montana," Jacob said. "It's a low-key mental health facility that caters to the wealthy who require discretion. She's been there a few times in her life."

"Do I want to know how you confirmed that?" Spenser asked.

"You really don't."

"Fair enough," Spenser said.

"Now for the bad news," Young chimed in. "I contacted the facility and tried to get them to tell us whether Wendy was there or not. Obviously, they can't tell me outright. But after I explained that she was missing and we were searching for her, the person I spoke with all but told me that she's not there."

Spenser sat back in her chair and rubbed her chin as she absorbed the information. "Are you sure that's what she said? I mean, if discretion is their stock in trade—"

"No, I'm sure. She was telling me without specifically telling me," Young cut her off with a shake of her head. "She was deliberately vague, of course, but it seemed very clear that she was saying Wendy was not there. I'm one hundred percent on that, Sheriff."

Spenser nodded. She trusted Young's instincts. If she was sure the woman she'd spoken to was telling her Wendy wasn't there, Spenser was going to trust her at her word. She just hoped it wasn't a case of confirmation bias since Spenser was starting to make that turn and come around to believing that Wendy's disappearance was a case of foul play. She couldn't get that image of the person on the train platform out of her head.

Nor could she stop believing the woman in the floppy hat and oversized sunglasses was not Wendy Gilchrist. Somebody wanted people to believe it was. They'd gone to a lot of trouble to make people believe it was Wendy.

"Okay, so, she's not at this facility," Spenser mused. "Where the hell could she be?"

"What sort of hit did you get off Max Carter?" Young asked.

"He's not involved," she replied. "He's a jellyfish. Talking a good game and writing vaguely threatening letters to Wendy is the extent of his activism. That frustrated the former members of the Green League enough that they left the group—after apparently dubbing him 'Max the Mouth.'"

Young and Jacob chuckled. Spenser pulled the sheet of paper Max had given her out of her pocket and slid it over to Jacob. He picked it up off the table and read the names scrawled on it in Carter's shaky hand.

"Those are the former members of the Green League. Max says they're a lot more strident and militant and might have the spine to do something to Wendy," she said. "Do me a favor and run them down. I want to know what they're all about."

"I'm on it," he said.

"Before you get into that, though, I want you to do a quick dive on the ex-husband," Spenser said. "We need to have a talk with him, and I'd like to know what we're walking into."

"On it."

His fingers flew over the keys on his laptop and a moment later, the screen on the wall next to the whiteboard lit up and a man's DMV photo popped up. Joshua Baden was listed at five-ten and two hundred and ten pounds, with black hair, eyes, and a thick, bushy beard. There was a ruggedly handsome look about him, but he seemed to be the polar opposite, lookswise, from Wendy's current husband, Brock Ferry. It was as if after divorcing Joshua, Wendy went looking for somebody as far away from him as she could possibly get.

"Joshua Baden," Jacob said. "He's got no priors. But he's got a very spotty work history. He is currently working as a part-time teacher over at Taft—a tutor, mostly. It looks like the majority of his income comes from the monthly stipend he gets from the Gilchrists."

"Yeah, that jibes with what Aspen told us," Spenser said.

"He's more comfortable suckling off the Gilchrist teat than putting in an honest day's work is how I believe they put it," Young said.

"Wow. Family get-togethers at the Gilchrist house must be wild," Jacob chimed in.

"Pretty sure Joshua isn't invited to family get-togethers, big brother," Young replied. "Not a lot of warm fuzzies in that family."

"Yeah, speaking of warm fuzzies, did you happen to notice they've got almost no pictures of the brother in the house?" Spenser asked. "It's like he doesn't exist."

"That's because he's a computer genius and doesn't want to be part of the family company," Jacob said. "He's doing his own thing out at MIT and Mama Gilchrist is apparently none too pleased with that."

"Do you know the son? What's his name? Brendan?" Spenser asked.

"I knew him a little bit, yeah. We ran in some of the same circles," Jacob replied. "I wouldn't say we're best friends or anything, but we were acquaintances."

"They were in the same nerdy gamer group," Young clarified. "They spent more Friday nights playing D&D than I can count."

Jacob frowned and looked away, his cheeks flushing, but didn't fire back at his sister. That told Spenser what she'd said was probably spot on. Spenser turned to Jacob.

"You think he can give you any insight into the Gilchrist clan?" I ask. "Any inside information on the ex and current husband?"

"I doubt it. Like I said, we're not close," he replied. "But I'll reach out."

"Thank you," Spenser said.

"You know, I have to be honest, I think we're spinning our wheels here," Jacob said. "I'm almost positive that the woman on the train platform is Wendy Gilchrist. The height matches and the facial structure—what we can see of it anyway—seems to match. Also, if she was trying to slip out of town unnoticed, it stands to reason that she'd wear a getup like that."

"A getup like that seems more likely to draw attention," Young said. "A big hat, those glasses—those scream, 'look at me, look at me.' That's not the sort of thing somebody would wear if they were trying to keep it low-key. To me, it looks like somebody wanted to make sure people would see her and if they looked into it, would assume it was Wendy Gilchrist."

Jacob sat back, his eyes on the still photo of the woman on the platform. He didn't look convinced. And the trouble was, Spenser couldn't definitively say he was wrong. They might very well be tilting at windmills. Just because Wendy wasn't at the Morley House didn't mean she wasn't at another facility somewhere else. For all they knew, she could be tucked away in a hotel enjoying some room service, a spa day, a bottle of wine, and some peace and quiet.

Spenser was finding that increasingly unlikely, though. The longer Wendy went without contacting anybody, without so much as turning on her phone, using her cards, and maintaining radio silence, the more she believed something about the whole situation smelled.

Spenser sat forward in her chair. "Okay, in any murder investigation, the first question we ask is, who stands to benefit from a person's death."

"Not to point out the obvious, but this isn't a murder investigation," Jacob said.

"No, but I want to work it like it is," Spenser replied. "So, who stands to benefit?"

Jacob shrugged. "The obvious answer is Brock—"

"Not according to that prenup," Young said. "He only gets a hundred grand."

"A hundred grand is a lot of money to some people. There are people out there who've killed for a lot less," Jacob replied.

"That's a fair point," Spenser said. "We also shouldn't discount the possibility of him trying to get more through legal action. Aspen and Dallas might throw him a bone just to get him out of their lives once and for all."

"Speaking of Aspen and Dallas, I'd imagine they'd stand to inherit quite a bit if their mother was no longer in the picture," Jacob said.

"Except for the fact that they're the ones pushing us hard to find their mother," Young said. "It doesn't track that they'd be pushing us as hard as they are if the trail will lead back to them."

Spenser drummed her fingers on the table. "How about insurance?" Spenser asked. "Can we find out if she currently has any insurance policies out on her? And if so, I want to know who took them out and in what amount?"

"That's a good question," Young said.

"And fortunately, I might be able to find an answer to that," Jacob said. "One moment."

Jacob banged away at his keyboard as Spenser and Young waited in a tense silence. Having an insurance policy wasn't necessarily ironclad proof of somebody's guilt or even their intent to harm Wendy Gilchrist. It could, however, be considered a motive. It could be a signpost that might point them in a direction they should be looking.

"Okay, so it looks like Wendy Gilchrist has a policy on herself worth two million dollars," Jacob said. "She lists Aspen and Dallas as her beneficiaries on the policy."

"Wow," Spenser said. "She doesn't list her son as a beneficiary?"

"Not that I see here," Jacob said.

"That's cold-blooded," Spenser remarked. "I guess she takes that whole loyalty to the family business thing seriously."

"That's what Brendan used to say," Jacob offered.

"Reminds me of how the mob operates," Spenser replied.

Jacob tapped away at his keys and watched his screen, his brow furrowing as he read whatever it was he'd pulled up.

"What is it?" she asked.

"There's another policy for another two million. It's older, but it's still active—the premiums have been kept up with," Jacob explained.

"And who holds that policy?"

Jacob looked at her, his expression serious. "Joshua Baden."

CHAPTER THIRTEEN

Joshua Baden lived in a small Craftsman-style house in a working-class neighborhood just off the main square in town. The house was green and trimmed in white, the paint showing a bit of wear. The deep red porch was also worn, some of the individual stones cracked and chipped. A pair of faded white wicker chairs sat on the porch, an ashtray on the matching table between them filled with cigarette butts and the trash can beside it was overflowing with crushed beer cans.

Wood blinds were drawn over the windows, keeping Spenser from seeing in as she mounted the steps that led to the porch. She crossed to the doorway and pulled open a screen door that was pocked with small holes and tears. Spenser rapped on a front door made of a hard, solid wood that had four small stained-glass windows set in a diamond pattern in the upper half. She stood there for a moment and waited but heard nothing inside. Spenser glanced at the driveway and saw the black GMC Yukon in the driveway.

It was Baden's vehicle, which suggested to her that he was home. Spenser was picturing him inside, hunkered down, hiding, and waiting for her to leave. She knocked again, harder this time.

"Joshua Baden," she called. "Sheriff's department. Please come to the door."

She gave it another minute and when he still didn't come to the door, she knocked again, even harder, and called out his name and her office again, even louder. She spoke so loudly, her voice echoed around the quiet street. A moment later, the door opened, and she found herself staring at the man from the DMV photo Jacob had pulled up earlier. His hair was mussed, his eyes red and rheumy, and even with several feet between them, she could smell the alcohol wafting off him. More than that, she could see the telltale residue of white powder around his nostrils.

"Keep your voice down," he hissed. "I don't need my neighbors knowing my business."

"Then maybe you should open the door the first time I knock."

"I was... indisposed."

"Flushing your stash?" she asked. "Pro tip, Joshua. If I was here to search for narcotics, I wouldn't stand at the door knocking. I would have a warrant that allowed me to kick in your door, so you probably just threw a lot of money down the toilet for nothing."

His face darkened and a frustrated scowl crossed his lips. He quickly composed himself and tried to subtly wipe at his nose, doing his best to rub the evidence away.

"So, how can I help you, Sheriff?" he asked.

"We should have a chat," Spenser said. "Mind if I come in?"

"Uhh yeah. Sure."

Joshua stepped aside and let Spenser into his house. He closed the door then led her into the living room, where a pair of large, plush recliners sat atop a beautifully patterned area rug in front of an even larger television, currently playing sports highlights from the night before. A round table made of dark wood was set between the recliners and a fireplace sat to their right. The walls were a pale shade of green that was soothing and trimmed in white with crown molding around the top and tastefully artistic prints hung all around.

Given the smell of booze and evidence of drug use, Spenser had expected Baden's home to be an absolute pigsty. She had anticipated the place being filled with piles of beer cans, pizza boxes, and fast-food wrappers. So, it surprised her to see the place was immaculate. Everything was neatly ordered, the wood polished to a glossy sheen, and she couldn't see a speck of dust anywhere. Even the air in the room carried the faint lemony scent of cleaner and polish. It was a bachelor's pad, but it was spotless.

It was an odd juxtaposition from the image of the slovenly layabout the girls had painted their father to be. But he wasn't working in the middle of the day and looked awfully comfortable sitting in front of his television, so Spenser wasn't going to discount what they'd told her either.

Baden dropped heavily into his recliner and gestured to the other. "You're welcome to have a seat, Sheriff."

"I'm fine, but thank you," Spenser said. "I understand you work as a tutor over at Taft?"

"Yeah, it's a good gig. I do SAT tutoring a couple of days a week."

"I guess the monthly stipend you receive makes it easier to work part-time."

"Yeah. It does. But as far as I'm concerned, I earned every penny of what I get. So judge me as harshly as you want, it doesn't bother me," he replied defensively. "Putting up with that woman for all those years was the worst job I've ever had."

Spenser walked over to the fireplace and looked at the photos in silver frames that stood on the mantle. She immediately recognized Dallas and Aspen. And unlike Wendy's home, there were also photos of Brendan—recent ones. Given the placement of the photos, it was clear to Spenser that Baden was incredibly proud of his children. That also contrasted with the image of him that had been painted by Aspen and Dallas.

"I met your girls. They're intelligent and articulate," Spenser said, gesturing to one of the pictures of them. "They're pretty remarkable young women."

"That they are. They take after their mother in most ways—that's both a good thing and a bad thing," he said gruffly. "I just wish they'd stop focusing on partying and status and get their heads on right. They can do anything in this world."

Spenser turned toward him and hooked her thumbs behind her gunbelt. Baden's shoulders slumped and the pallor of sadness that painted his face was unmistakable. He looked tired. More than that, he looked like a man who felt defeated and lost.

"If you don't mind me asking, why was your relationship with your daughters so strained?" Spenser asked.

"Strained? That's an understatement. Fractured beyond repair is probably the more accurate way to describe it," he said, his voice flat and emotionless.

"What happened, Mr. Baden?"

"The divorce happened," he said simply. "Wendy, being the control freak she is, made them choose sides. They wanted to stay in her good graces, so they made their choice."

A few things were starting to fall into place and Spenser felt like she was starting to gain a better understanding of the Gilchrist family dynamics. She suddenly thought she understood why Brendan was a non-entity in the household.

"I take it Brendan didn't make the same choice the girls did," she said.

"No, he made a different choice," Baden said. "He chose himself. He's off doing his own thing back east and doesn't have much to do with us. Any of us."

"That has to sting."

"It all stings, Sheriff. There is nothing about any of this that feels good," he said testily.

"You must harbor a lot of resentment for Wendy," Spenser said. "For making your kids choose between you and fracturing your relationship with them?"

"Yeah, that's a fair statement. If not for her…," his voice trailed off and he shook his head. "It doesn't matter. But yeah, I guess it's fair to say I hate that woman with every fiber of my being."

Spenser watched him closely. His disdain for Wendy was more than plain. And the fact he was so open about it caught her somewhat off guard. If he had done something to Wendy, Spenser had to wonder if he would be so vocal about his dislike for her. Then again, a cunning man might be willing to be open about disliking somebody for the simple fact it would make an investigator ask the very question she just posed to herself.

It was a risky gambit to play since it would cast a spotlight on a strained relationship. However, he likely had to know she already knew their relationship was fractured and by addressing it up front, free of her having to press him about it, Baden might think it made him look more forthcoming and helpful, ergo innocent. The real question Spenser needed to answer was: how clever was Joshua Baden?

"Mr. Baden, I understand you are still the beneficiary listed on a rather sizable life insurance policy taken out against Wendy Gilchrist," Spenser said.

He chuckled. "I think you better check again, Sheriff. When I signed off on our divorce, I was cut out of all investments and everything else we held jointly. I settled for the monthly alimony—mainly so I didn't have to deal with Wendy ever again."

"And yet the premiums are still being paid monthly. Are you really going to tell me you know nothing about it?"

Something in Spenser's tone made Baden sit up straighter in his recliner. His face clouded over, and he looked at her the way a small rodent might look at an owl sitting on a branch above it. He ran a hand over his face and tried to compose himself.

"What's going on here? Why are you asking me all these questions about Wendy?"

"Tell me about the life insurance policy."

He shook his head. "Like I said, I don't know a damn thing about it."

"Then how do you explain the monthly premiums being paid?'

"I can't. I mean… I don't know," he said, his voice tight. "All my bills are paid automatically because I don't want to be bothered. If there's an insurance premium being paid on Wendy, you're going to want to talk to her because she must have forgotten to cancel it."

Spenser narrowed her eyes and looked closely at him. "I'd love to ask her about it. Do you happen to know where I can find her?"

He stared back at her, not seeming to understand what she was getting at. But then his eyes widened, and an expression of surprise crossed his face as Spenser saw comprehension finally dawn on him. He shook his head and wagged his finger at her.

"I don't like what you're implying here, Sheriff."

"I'm not implying anything. I'm just asking a few questions," she replied. "Do you happen to know where I can find your ex-wife?"

"Why would I know that? It's not like she runs her calendar by me anymore," he spat. "What's happened? Is she missing or something?"

"It doesn't sound like you'd be overly concerned if she was."

"Why would I be? I can't stand the woman. The best thing she ever did was divorce me. She set me free," he said. "But if you're implying I did something to her, you're way off base. Why would I? I get a fat monthly check from her. That was a gift. Yeah, I had to relinquish all my other claims, but so what? I'm living a pretty good life right now. Why in the hell would I screw with that? Especially after all these years. If I was going to do something to her, don't you think I would have done it long before now? It makes no sense."

"People often don't make sense, Mr. Baden," Spenser replied. "The trouble I'm having is with that insurance policy. That would be one hell of a payout."

"Again, I don't know anything about that. I think we took out policies on each other when we were married, but I assumed she canceled them after we split up," he said.

"But you didn't bother verifying that?"

"Why would I? She handles all that stuff," he said. "Wendy is such a control freak, I just let her do her thing. If there's an active policy, I assume she overlooked it, but once you bring it to her attention, I'm sure she'll cancel it right away."

"Did you ever know your ex-wife to take off on unplanned… sabbaticals?" Spenser asked.

He chuckled. "No. That woman is the least spontaneous woman on the planet. She schedules everything. Literally everything."

Spenser found that interesting. Wendy either didn't tell Baden about her sabbaticals or Hall was lying to her. She assumed the former was more likely. But why wouldn't she tell her husband about her need to take a break now and then? It was another interesting insight into the dynamics within the Gilchrist clan.

"Mr. Baden, do you know of anybody who might want to hurt your ex-wife? Anybody she had problems with? Anything like that?"

He grinned and shook his head. "The list of people who hate Wendy Gilchrist is long and lengthy. She's not a very likable person, Sheriff. You haven't been in town long enough to know that, but she is a very deeply unlikable person."

"As you keep saying."

"All I'm telling you is that if somebody did something to her, she probably deserved it for something she did to them," he said. "I don't wish anything bad on her, but I'm not going to shed a tear if something did."

The more Spenser talked to Baden, the more she thought he wasn't involved in anything that might have happened to her. It was clear that he despised Wendy, but she wasn't getting any sort of hinky hit off him. He didn't put off that vibe. But like Max Carter, although she mentally moved him to the back burner, Spenser wasn't going to cross him off the list. Not just yet.

"Just out of curiosity, where were you last Thursday?" she asked.

"Right here in this very chair watching TV," he replied.

She eyed him for a long moment then nodded. "Okay. Thank you for your time, Mr. Baden. And I'd appreciate it if you kept our conversation confidential for now."

"Sure thing. Not like I have many people to tell anyway. But whatever," he said then perked up. "Say, how much is that insurance policy worth—"

"No," Spenser called over her shoulder as she headed for the door. "Just no."

CHAPTER FOURTEEN

"Oh dear, God. The Christmas virus seems to be spreading," Spenser remarked.

The corners of Ryker's eyes crinkled as he flashed her a smile that sent a flutter through her heart. He stood in the center of his coffee house and held his arms out wide. Garland and bows lined the counters and pastry cases, and strings of colored lights hung from the exposed beams. A large, full tree that was flocked and lighted stood in the corner, the pair of plate glass windows that overlooked the street had been painted with a snowy, holiday motif, and Mariah Carey's Christmas songs issued from the speakers mounted in the corners of the store.

"Behold, Ebeneezer. Christmas has come to Higher Grounds," he intoned.

Spenser rolled her eyes but laughed. "I didn't take you for the big holiday kind of guy."

"He's not. He's the OG Grinch. This is all my doing," Kelli called out with a laugh.

Kelli was his manager and longtime confidant. She was intelligent, confident, and had a great sense of humor, and Spenser liked her from the start—mostly because she didn't put up with Ryker's crap. But Kelli had been there for him when he had nobody else. When he was busy isolating himself from the world. She had helped get his business off the ground and Ryker owed her practically everything for its success. Without her driving it forward, Ryker would just be a guy growing beans on his land.

But Ryker's coffee shop, Higher Grounds, had become a town favorite. Early on, most people came in hoping to catch a glimpse of the reclusive and enigmatic Ryker Makawi. He'd once been more myth than man and people had spread stories far and wide about him. Stories he'd never attempted to dispel. He didn't care what people thought or said about him. He was changing, though, and had won them over with the quality of his product and it was now consistently one of the most popular coffee shops in town. More than that, people were warming to him. Ryker was starting to become more man than myth, which was good to see.

"It looks like Santa Claus threw up in here," Spenser said.

"Thank you," Kelli replied cheerily. "I have always loved Christmas. I never took you to be such a Scrooge, Spenser."

"I find Christmas about as enjoyable as a colonoscopy," she remarked dryly.

"Wow," Kelli said. "Bah humbug indeed."

"Sorry," Spenser replied. "I've just never been big on Christmas. It always just felt contrived and forced to me."

"I suppose I'll forgive you," Kelli said.

"I won't," Ryker chimed in. "Christmas is a great holiday."

"Maybe it'll grow on me," Spenser said.

"I certainly hope so," Kelli added.

"It will," Ryker said.

"Anyway, what can I get you, Spense?" Kelli asked. "We've got the toasted white mocha ready to go. How's that sound?"

"That sounds fantastic."

"Comin' up."

Ryker led her to a table in the corner and sat down with her. He reached across the table and took her hand, squeezing it before he sat back and smiled at her. Spenser felt her heart swelling and had to suppress a giggle. She already felt like an idiotic, giddy schoolgirl, and didn't need to embarrass herself by sounding like one, too.

"One toasted white chocolate mocha for you," Kelli chirped as she slid the mug down in front of her.

Spenser leaned forward and inhaled the sweet aroma. "Bless you, my child."

Kelli smiled at her. "You're very welcome."

A few people filtered in through the front door, so Kelli tipped her a wink then turned and trotted off to help them, leaving her alone with Ryker. He scooped a bit of the green and red sprinkles whipped cream off the top and laughed as he dabbed it on the end of her nose. Spenser laughed and wiped it off then picked up her mug and took a sip, savoring the rich flavor. It was similar to the regular white chocolate mocha they had all year, but the toasted flavoring added just a little bit extra to it that Spenser loved. It wasn't a unique drink. She'd had it many times before back in New York, but something about the way Kelli made it was just better.

"I love this drink," she said.

"See? There's one redeeming quality for the holidays."

"Yeah, there's one."

"You're going to love Christmas by the time I'm done with you, Spenser Song."

"Good luck with that," she said but grinned.

"So, how are things going with the case?" he asked. "I mean, do you have a case?"

Spenser took another drink and set the mug down, her smile slipping into a frown. She shook her head and shrugged.

"Honestly, I'm at a loss. I think there's a case. I think she's missing," Spenser said. "But I can't prove anything. All I have right now is my gut feeling."

She caught him up to speed on everything they'd found about Wendy's trips to Morley House, the sabbaticals she took from the office Cindy Hall had told her about, and everything else she could think of. Sometimes, talking things out and listening to herself speak sparked an idea. Nothing was coming to her, though. She hoped that after listening to her, Ryker might have some brilliant insight about it all to share with her.

"So, what do you think?" Spenser asked.

"I honestly don't know what to think," he replied.

"That's not helpful. I was counting on you to crack this," she teased.

"Sorry, I'm just a coffee bean slinger," he said.

"Oh, I think you're a bit more than that."

They gazed at each other for a moment and Spenser smiled as that familiar warmth crept into her cheeks. Ryker returned her smile and they sat quietly, enjoying the moment—a moment broken when a figure stepped over to their table.

"Good morning, Sheriff Song."

Spenser looked up. "Mayor Dent. Nice to see you."

"Love what you've done with the place, Ryker," Dent said. "I like how festive it is."

Ryker grinned. "Just trying to keep up with everybody else in town."

Dent smiled and gave him a nod. She held her cup of coffee in hand and looked at Spenser with a gleam of anxiety in her eyes, her unspoken question more than clear. She was worried about her friend and for that, Spenser's heart went out to her. Dent's eyes pointedly shifted from her to Ryker and back again. She offered the older woman a soft smile.

"You can talk in front of Ryker," Spenser said. "Since he's more familiar with town history than I am, he's been advising me."

"History," Maggie said with a gruff chortle. "That's an unusual word for gossip."

"Hey, information is information. You'd be surprised how much truth there is in gossip," Spenser said. "And at this point, I'll take whatever I can get."

"And what have you found? Anything?"

"We're still talking to some people, Maggie," Spenser said. "We've got multiple lines in the water but so far, no bites."

"So, nothing then."

"At the moment, no. I can't prove something happened to Wendy right now. I can't prove she's not just off on one of her sabbaticals… as she is apparently known by some to do," Spenser said pointedly.

Dent frowned but stood firm. "This isn't that, Spenser. Believe me, it's not. Wendy always made sure to tell me and Cindy when she was going—"

"Why didn't you mention it to me earlier? That seems like useful information."

Dent's expression darkened. "As I said, this isn't that. She never told me or Cindy she was going," she said. "And that has never happened."

"Just because it hasn't happened before doesn't mean it didn't happen now."

"Trust me, this isn't that. She would never just disappear," Dent pressed.

"I'm going to keep looking and digging into everything I can, but, like I told the girls, you need to be prepared to accept the idea that maybe the stress in her life got to be too much and Wendy decided to just walk away," Spenser said.

Maggie frowned and gave her a nod but the expression on her face told Spenser she was never going to be able to accept that answer. She reached out and gave Spenser's shoulder a squeeze.

"I know you're doing your best, Spenser."

"I'll keep you looped in," she replied.

With a wave to Ryker, Maggie walked out of the coffee house. Spenser turned and watched her go, feeling a sense of helplessness that was uncommon to her. She finally turned back and looked down at her mug. The whipped cream and sprinkles were melting, leaving a white, red, and green residue over the top of her drink.

"Do you believe Wendy just up and walked away?" Ryker asked.

"I don't. I'm ninety-nine percent sure something bad happened to her. I'm sure she's out there right now, just waiting to be found where she was left," Spenser said with a shake of her head. "But I'm not finding anything yet that points to anything else so the possibility she walked away is still alive. I just don't want to give anybody false hope or wind up contradicting myself later, so I'm trying to play both sides right now."

"That's understandable," he replied.

"I just wish I had something that pointed in one direction or the other," she said.

"That would be too easy. You always need a challenge."

"A challenge is one thing. This is like trying to understand quantum mechanics problems written out in Aramaic," she groused.

He offered her an encouraging smile. "I know you're going to get the answers. One way or another, you're going to figure out what happened. Mostly because you're just too damn stubborn for it to go any other way."

Spenser laughed. "Thanks," she said. "I hope you're right."

"I know I am. Just trust your gut and believe in yourself," he said. "Like I do."

She couldn't keep the smile from her lips. Even in the face of the uncertainty that gripped her, Ryker made her feel cared for. Made her want to believe in herself. It was a nice feeling. It was one she could get used to.

CHAPTER FIFTEEN

"Dear God, I can't escape it," Spenser said. Young had a wide smile on her face as she walked over to where Spenser stood, singing, "It's beginning to look a lot like Christmas…"

And it was beginning to look a lot like Christmas indeed. A couple of her deputies were putting a tree up on the far side of the bullpen, stringing lights and ornaments all around it. Ropes of tinsel and garland were being hung, and blue and white stockings—each bearing one of their names—were being hung on the wall beside the tree.

"I didn't authorize this," Spenser said. "Why is this happening?"

Young simply pointed at Alice Jarrett. The department's receptionist was busy stringing ropes of garland and bows on the desks in the bullpen.

"Aside from Alice being a big-time Christmas lover, we've run a 'toys for tots' type program out of the office for a while," she said. "You know, we take donations then send everything out to needy children in the community. It's tradition."

Spenser pulled a face but couldn't argue with the worthiness of the tradition. She might be a Scrooge, but she wasn't a cold, unfeeling jerk.

"Did you want to tell Alice to stop?" Young asked.

"God no. That woman scares me."

"Wise choice."

"If I hear Christmas music playing, though, I'm firing everybody," Spenser said.

As they walked across the bullpen, headed for the conference room, she could hear Bing Crosby's warm, friendly voice as Little Drummer Boy emanated from a portable stereo set up in the corner. The deputies working with Alice to decorate the office laughed and sang along, adding to the festive atmosphere. Spenser didn't care for the holidays, but she did enjoy the building sense of morale and camaraderie that was starting to filter through the department. It had been a long road that was filled with pits and potholes when she took over, but they were starting to round into the form she had envisioned when she took the job.

"You better get to work on those pink slips, Sheriff. It's going to take you all day to get them all filled out," Young said with a snort.

Spenser grumbled under her breath as they walked into the conference room and she quickly closed the door behind them, shutting out the music.

"Hey," Jacob said. "I like that song."

"Better stow it, big brother, or Sheriff Scrooge might put a pink slip in your stocking."

"Well, bah humbug," he replied.

Spenser laughed as she took her seat at the table and Young took her place.

"Okay, so, where are we at with the other eco-warriors?" Spenser asked.

"I ran backgrounds on them all and didn't find anything alarming," Jacob said. "None of them have records and aren't connected to any other open cases. Although, I heard they don't like Christmas music, so we should keep them on the suspect list."

"You're playing with fire, big brother," Young teased.

"You might say I enjoy roasting chestnuts over that open fire," he replied.

Spenser laughed. "Oh my God, stop it. Both of you."

The siblings shared a snicker that left Spenser shaking her head. Their laughter eventually tapered off and Spenser's eyes were drawn back to their whiteboard, looking at the faces in the pictures taped to it.

As the silence in the room stretched on, Spenser's gaze fell on the photo of the figure at the train station again and she felt that now familiar niggling in the back of her mind. She stared at the picture, racking her mind, and tried to figure out what exactly was bothering her about it. As with every time she looked at it, though, it wouldn't come.

"What are you thinking?" Young finally asked.

"Just trying to figure out what we have on our hands here," Spenser replied.

"I assume you have a theory," Young said.

Spenser nodded. "Yeah. I'm pretty convinced somebody killed Wendy Gilchrist and disposed of her body. I'm equally convinced this mystery killer had an accomplice—a woman. And that woman masqueraded as Wendy at the train station to make us all think she boarded the train and simply disappeared," she explained.

"That's a complex theory," Jacob said. "If I'm being honest, it's kind of bordering on tin-foil hat territory, Sheriff."

"And you believe Wendy just walked away from her life and away from her children without a word to anybody?" Spenser asked.

"Let's not pretend the Gilchrists have a warm and fuzzy family relationship. I don't know if that's what happened for sure, but I wouldn't be surprised if she did just decide to chuck it all and start over somewhere," he countered.

"Okay, let's play that theory out," Spenser said. "If she wanted a fresh start, she would need money. A large sum of money, I would assume. Search her finances and see if you find any large sums of money being moved around."

Jacob turned to his laptop and started banging away at his keys. His brow furrowed and the pink tip of his tongue protruded from the corner of his mouth as he worked. Spenser kept her eyes on the whiteboard. She let her mind spin out her theory a little more. It made sense to her. But Spenser couldn't deny that Jacob was right in that it did sound a little bit like she was crossing into tin-foil hat territory. But that didn't make her wrong.

"Okay, so, a cursory look at her finances doesn't show big sums of money being moved around," Jacob said. "But that doesn't mean it didn't happen. She's got investments and other accounts I can't look into—"

"Ever hear of Occam's Razor, big brother?"

"Just because I don't see money being moved around doesn't make that the likeliest answer," he said. "If she was determined to start a new life somewhere, she would have been discreet in how she went about moving that money. She probably used shell companies, private, offshore accounts… things like that."

"As far as I know, Wendy Gilchrist isn't an accountant or a money person," Spenser said. "I don't know if she's got the skill set to do that without leaving a trail."

"Okay, but she could have hired somebody off-book to do it for her," Jacob countered.

"Now who's crossing into tin-foil hat territory?" Young chimed in.

"Dig into it," Spenser told him. "See if you can find anything definitive."

"I'm on it."

"In the meantime, I want to play with my theory a bit," Spenser said. "And that means finding out who the woman on that platform is."

"And how are we going to do that?" Young asked.

"Well, if my theory is sound, then that means she was working in concert with somebody who wanted Wendy dead and out of the way," she replied. "So, we start by looking at the three men who theoretically stood to gain the most if she was gone—Joshua Baden, Brock Ferry, and her brother, Baker Gilchrist—"

"But none of them were going to gain financially if Wendy was gone, right?" Young asked.

"Let's not blind ourselves by assuming the motive was financial. It might have been something else entirely," Spenser said. "People kill for a lot of different reasons. One thing we do know for sure is that there was a lot of animosity floating around between all those people. Anger and hate are often every bit as powerful a motive as money is."

"Fair enough," Young said. "So, where do we start?"

"You and I are going to have a conversation with Baker. I want to get a feel for him and lock him into a story," Spenser said. "Jacob, I want you to dig into Joshua and Brock. I want you to see if you can poke holes in their stories and dig up some dirt on them. I need something we can go at them with."

"Ten-four, Sheriff," Jacob said.

"Great. Thank you," Spenser said as she got to her feet. "Okay, let's roll out and see what Baker has to say for himself."

"Right behind you... pa rum pum pum pum," Young said in a sing-song voice.

Spenser cast a withering glare at her. "You do realize I'm armed right?"

"I like to live on the edge."

Spenser harrumphed and headed out of the conference room, chased across the bullpen by the sound of Young and Jacob laughing together which was somehow even more grating than the Christmas music filling the rest of the office.

CHAPTER SIXTEEN

"Wow," Spenser said. "Are you sure this is the right place?"

"This is the address that popped up in the system for him," Young replied.

"Wow," Spenser said again.

To say Baker Gilchrist didn't live like the rest of his family would have been an understatement. Spenser piloted the Bronco along the narrow, dusty lanes that cut through the Pine Vista Mobile Estates. They passed aged mobile homes that were faded, rusty, and looked to be on the verge of falling apart.

"This is a far cry from the Gilchrist estate," Spenser said.

"That family seems to have no problem eating on their own if they don't toe the company line," Young observed.

"Right?" Spenser replied. "What was his offense, anyway?"

"Booze and drugs," Young said. "He racked up quite an impressive rap sheet when he was younger for drinking and drugging. Lots of bad decisions in his life."

"Must be why Papa Gilchrist cut him off," Spenser said.

"I've heard he was a teetotaler and didn't tolerate drinking and drugs," Young said. "From everything I've heard about him, he was a hard, mean man. Still, it's kind of surprising that he'd cut his own son off."

Spenser drove along, looking at the numbers on the homes as they passed, searching for the one that belonged to Baker Gilchrist.

"Up there," Young said. "The blue one on the right."

Spenser pulled to a stop in front of the long, narrow mobile home. The fence that surrounded the lot was a rickety, waist-high job that looked like it might fall over in a stiff breeze. The yard behind it was mostly dirt and rocks, the few patches of grass were long dead and dry. The double-wide home sat on a red brick base, the blue paint on the siding was faded, cracked, and peeling and the roof over the porch sagged, looking perilously close to falling in completely. Sheets covered windows and along the side of the home were boxes of old newspapers and other trash. The entire place was dim and dingy.

As Spenser and Young climbed out of the Bronco, she noticed one of the sheets over the windows move. Baker Gilchrist was watching them. A chill ran down her spine as she imagined he was watching them from the other side of a shotgun.

"Heads up," she muttered to Young. "He knows we're here."

Moving calmly but purposefully, and with her hand near the butt of her Glock, Spenser led Young up the cracked and pitted walk that led to the porch. The tension in the air was thick. She motioned for Young to stay at the bottom of the small set of stairs that led to the front door. Moving her hand down, she gripped the butt of her weapon, ready to pull it as she ascended the six steps. Not knowing what was on the other side of it, Spenser stood to the side of the front door then reached out and knocked.

"Baker Gilchrist. Sheriff's department" she called. "Can you come on out here, please? We'd like a word with you."

"What the hell do you want?" he roared from the other side of the door.

"We just want to talk, Mr. Gilchrist," Spenser called back. "Can you please come on out?"

She cast a look back at Young who was standing close to the wall, her eyes wide and a nervous look on her face. She had her hand on her weapon, ready to pull at a moment's notice like Spenser had taught her. Beyond Gilchrist's lot, she could see other residents of the mobile home park starting to take notice. They were coming out to watch what was going on with expressions of curiosity but also anger and disdain on their faces. They clearly had no love for cops.

"I have nothing to say to you people," Gilchrist called back.

"Please, we just need to have a word. That's all," Spenser called.

"You got a warrant?"

"We're not here to arrest you, Mr. Gilchrist. We just want to talk," Spenser said. "Now, please, don't make this harder than it has to be. All we want is a quiet word. That's all."

The silence from the man inside the mobile home stretched on. Spenser's belly roiled as she felt control of the situation starting to slip away. Her entire body was as taut as a bowstring and beads of sweat trickled down her back, tickling her uncomfortably. She licked her lips and started mentally running through contingency plans. Her body was so tight that when the heavy click of the door being unlocked sounded, Spenser flinched. She recovered quickly and crouched down as she pulled her weapon. Behind her, Spenser heard Young gasp, obviously as startled as she was, but pulled her weapon as well.

The door opened a crack and Spenser crouched lower, waiting to see the barrel of a weapon sticking out of it. But that didn't come.

"Okay," Gilchrist called. "I'm opening the door. I don't have a weapon so don't shoot."

The door opened wider, and Gilchrist stepped out with his hands up to his chest, palms facing them. He wore blue jeans and a dingy tank top she thought might have been white at one point but was now an off-yellow color. He was a heavyset man, about an inch taller than Spenser's five-nine frame, with limp, greasy brown hair that fell to his shoulders and the same cappuccino-colored eyes his sister had. His cheeks and chin were covered in stubble, though it wasn't an attempt to look stylish. It simply looked slovenly.

Spenser holstered her weapon and backed down the stairs, allowing Gilchrist to come down unimpeded. The pungent odor of decay and filth flowing from his mobile home made Spenser think the conversation would be better had outside in the fresh air. Spenser stepped back and stood beside Young, who had also holstered her weapon already as Gilchrist stopped at the foot of his stairs. He eyed them both closely for a moment then pulled a pack of cigarettes out of his pocket and shook one out. Slipping it between his thin lips, he tucked the pack back into his pocket then lit the one in the corner of his mouth. Spenser gave him a moment to take a drag.

"So? What the hell do you want?" Gilchrist grumbled.

"What was all that about?" Spenser asked. "Why didn't you just come out?"

He scoffed. "As I'm sure you know, I don't have the best history with cops. Been roughed up by more than a few—"

"Well, maybe if you didn't resist as hard or disobey lawful orders, you wouldn't have that kind of trouble," Young snapped at him.

"Maybe if you cops didn't think you could beat people with impunity—"

"Stop," Spenser said gruffly. "Both of you."

Young clamped her mouth shut and looked down at the ground. Gilchrist sneered at her. He took another drag off his cigarette and blew a thick plume of smoke her way, but a soft breeze kept it from reaching her.

"What do you want?" he repeated. "I've got things to do today."

"I'm sure you do. We'll do our best not to take up too much of your time, Mr. Gilchrist," Spenser said, her tone dry.

Not missing her sarcasm, Gilchrist frowned as he puffed on his cigarette angrily. Spenser noticed the people who'd been curiously watching events unfold earlier were drifting away, looking disappointed there was no gunplay or bloodshed to be seen. She turned back to Gilchrist.

"Mr. Gilchrist, when was the last time you spoke with your sister?" Spenser asked.

He scoffed. "I haven't spoken to that woman in a while. We've got nothing to say to each other," he growled. "She dropped me in this hellhole and hasn't given me a thought since."

"Your sister bought this home for you?" Spenser asked.

"It was the least she could do after she stole my life," he spat. "I'm the one who should be running our family's company. Not her. No, definitely not her. But because she sucked up to our father, she's the one who got the keys to the kingdom."

"You sound angry about that."

"You're damn right I'm angry about it. She got everything. I got nothing," he howled. "You've seen the spread she's living in and now you've seen what I'm living in. You'd be pretty pissed if you were in my place, too."

"Has your relationship with your sister always been contentious?"

"It was by design," he said. "Our father pitted us against each other. He treated earning his affection, respect, and favor like a damn reality show. She obviously won..."

His voice trailed off as he stared at us closely, his expression darkening. Gilchrist drew off his cigarette as Spenser watched the wheels in his mind turning. Smoke trailed out of his mouth and drifted away on the breeze.

"This isn't about me at all," he said.

"I never said it was," Spenser replied.

"Then, what in the hell is this all about?" he asked. "Why are you standing here asking me so many questions about Wendy? What's really going on here, Sheriff?"

"Mr. Gilchrist, I know you have a few assault convictions in your past, so I know you have a temper," Spenser said, ignoring his questions. "I also know that your sister can be... difficult—"

"That's putting it mildly," he grumbled.

"Did you and your sister ever fight? What I mean is, did you and she ever get physical with one another?" Spenser pressed.

"Nah. As much as I might have wanted to, I've never laid a hand on my sister," he said. "I'm not built like that, Sheriff. I don't hit women."

Young opened her mouth, undoubtedly, to raise the domestic violence collars he'd taken. Spenser gave her a subtle shake of the head. It wasn't the time to bring those up. Not while he was talking. Spenser would raise those arrests later if needed.

"So even with this reality show circus around your childhood, you and your sister never got physical with each other?" Spenser asked.

"No," he replied. "Now, what is this about?"

"And the last time you saw your sister was... when again?"

"I'm done answering questions until you tell me what this is all about," he said.

Spenser frowned for a moment, debating with herself whether to tell him what was going on or not. She knew, though, he'd get the story with a phone call to his nieces after she left, so keeping it from him was pointless. If nothing else, she might be able to provoke a reaction from him that might tell her something about his involvement—or lack of involvement.

"Mr. Gilchrist, your sister is missing. For almost a week now," Spenser said.

"And you think I had something to do with it," he replied.

"We don't think anything right now. We're gathering facts—"

"Lining up suspects, you mean."

"You can see it however you'd like to see it," Spenser said. "But we're simply trying to figure out what's happened to your sister."

He shrugged. "Don't know. Don't care."

"This is your sister," Young said, her tone aghast.

"By blood, yeah. I have no say in that matter. But if she got hit by a truck on the highway, I wouldn't lose a wink of sleep over it."

Spenser eyed him closely. "You do realize you're not making yourself sound very good right now. If we were lining up suspects, you're putting yourself at the top of the list."

"Investigate me if you want. I don't care. I didn't have anything to do with her disappearing," he said. "You want my opinion, she's off on a bender somewhere. Either that, or she's back in that loony bin Dad threw her into when she was younger. My sister isn't exactly mentally stable. She's fragile. That's just another reason she shouldn't be running the show."

He took another pull of his cigarette then dropped it and ground it out under his shoe. As he blew out the smoke, he raised his eyes to Spenser again.

"And if you're looking for a motive, I don't have one," he said. "Even if she's dead, I don't get any slice of the company pie. I was cut out. Completely. She saw to that."

Spenser could feel the man's hatred for his sister radiating off him like heat from the sun. She could see him doing something to her. She could see it very easily.

"I will say this," he said as a smile crossed his face. "If somebody did something to her, she deserved it. In fact, I hope somebody did take her out. That'd brighten my day more than you can possibly imagine."

"Mr. Gilchrist—"

"Nah. We're done here," he said. "Unless you're going to drag me down to the station and charge me? If that's the case, you might as well go ahead and get a public defender down there because I will have nothing further to say to you."

Spenser and Young exchanged a look of disgust. The man was smart. And he'd been in trouble with the police enough that he knew the ins and outs of the system. If he'd been able to beat his demons when he was younger, he might have done a pretty good job running the family company. But he couldn't get his head on straight and his act together. And as a result, there he was, living his life at the Pine Vista Mobile Estates.

"No, we won't be taking you in, Mr. Gilchrist," Spenser said. "Not at this time."

"Good."

He turned and walked back into his mobile home, slamming the door behind him hard enough that Spenser was half-afraid the thing was going to collapse in on him. He certainly had enough anger that it would have given him the motivation to kill his sister. But Spenser wasn't sure he had the will to do it. He would have delighted in reliving the tales of somebody else taking his

THE LIES IN THE FALLS

sister's life, but Spenser didn't know if he had the backbone to do it himself.

"So? Where to now, Sheriff?"

"Back to the drawing board, I'm afraid."

CHAPTER SEVENTEEN

"So, this is us. Back at square one. Of course, being back at square one implies we got off square one at some point," Young groused.

"Most investigations are a marathon, not a sprint, Amanda," Spenser reminded her. "Patience, Grasshopper."

Jacob laughed. "Wow. You dropped a kung-fu reference. I'm impressed."

Spenser looked at him. "What's *Kung Fu*? I thought that was a *Star Wars* thing."

Jacob rolled his eyes. "I'm so much less impressed now."

"Anything on Wendy's electronics or financials?" Spenser asked with a laugh.

"Afraid not," he replied. "Phone's still not on and no activity on any of her cards."

Spenser leaned back in her chair and looked at the whiteboard again. She understood Young's impatience. Understood wanting this to be a sprint and not a marathon. With time passing without any sign or signal from Wendy, it felt like the clock was ticking and nothing good was going to happen when the alarm went off.

"What about the rest of her finances you were looking into?" Young asked. "Did you find any big money transfers or anything?"

He shook his head. "No, not yet. I'm still looking, but so far, I haven't found any big sums of money being moved around. Certainly not enough to start a new life on."

"So, are you finally coming around to thinking something hinky is going on here, big brother?" Young asked.

He shrugged. "There are still a few things I want to look into," he said, then added slowly, "But yeah, given what we've found—mostly what we haven't found, I should say—it's looking like maybe something hinky is going on. Oh, and I looked into Joshua Baden a little more like you asked," Jacob said as he turned to Spenser. "And he wasn't at home the day Wendy supposedly disappeared."

"No?" Spenser asked.

He shook his head. "According to his credit card, he was over in Greenfield. At the Evergreen Hotel, to be precise."

Greenfield was a neighboring town that was a little larger than Sweetwater Falls but not quite as affluent. It wasn't a poor or rough town but was solidly working class. It was also fairly quiet and a nice place to live and raise a family. What Spenser wanted to know was what Joshua Baden was doing there… in a cheap hotel of all places.

"So, he lied to us," Young said.

"Seems that way," Spenser replied. "The question is why?"

"I can only think of one reason for a guy to take a room at a seedy hotel," Jacob said. "And it has nothing to do with sleep."

"So, he had some company," Young said.

Spenser's mind immediately flashed to the woman on the train platform who she thought was cosplaying as Wendy Gilchrist. It fit the narrative she was building. It also put that insurance policy he'd claimed to know nothing about back in play. Although Jacob had confirmed that Baden paid his bills automatically and electronically, that didn't mean he wasn't aware he was still paying on that insurance policy.

"He never mentioned having a lady friend to you, did he?" Young asked.

"No, but I didn't specifically ask him, either. I don't recall seeing anything at his place that indicated he had one," Spenser replied. "But I'd like to know why he's meeting her in a hotel the next town over when he's got a perfectly serviceable home at his disposal."

"That's a good question," Young stated.

"Have you done any digging into his life, Jacob? Any leads on who this mystery woman might be?" Spenser asked.

"Nothing that stood out to me. No jewelry or anything you might normally associate with a romantic relationship. I didn't even find any charges for nice, romantic dinners out," he replied.

"Well, to be fair, he didn't strike me as the flowers and romance type," Spenser said.

"He does, however, have regular charges to the Evergreen Hotel… usually once every couple of weeks, although I did note it's sometimes every week," Jacob said.

"So, a set, regular meeting in a neighboring town," Young said. "Sounds like somebody's having an affair with a married woman."

"Sounds like it to me," Spenser said.

"Should we go have a chat with him? See what he has to say for himself?" Young asked.

"Not yet. We need to get some solid information first—like who this mystery woman is," Spenser replied. "Without some facts to drill him with, he's just going to lie to us again and I'd rather not play the back-and-forth game with him. I want to know who she is first and find out if Baden had her play dress up for the cameras at the train station."

"And how are we going to do that?" Young asked.

Spenser looked over at Jacob. "How far do these regular charges to the hotel go back?"

"Hang on, let me filter by the charge," he said as he tapped away at his keys. "Okay, it looks like he's been going there regularly for a little over a year."

Spenser nodded. "Somebody who works there has to have seen him and his lady friend. We're going to lean on the staff and keep squeezing until somebody gives it up."

"Giving them the old-school rubber hose treatment, huh?" Jacob said with a grin. "I like it. I like it a lot."

"Something like that," Spenser said. "Amanda, who's the sheriff over in Greenfield?"

"Jessica Syler," she replied. "A bit stiff and rigid, but a good one. Smart. Reasonable."

"Okay, good. Do me a favor and give her a call. Let her know we'd like permission to come into her jurisdiction to question the employees over at the hotel," Spenser said. "Tell her she's welcome to join if she wants to or would be more comfortable overseeing us while we're there."

"Copy that."

Young grabbed her phone and got up then walked out of the conference room to find a quieter place to make the call. They probably could have been in and out of Greenfield without Syler ever knowing they were there. Spenser liked to extend that sort of professional courtesy to her peers, though. She wanted to foster cooperation between her department and the departments in the towns that surrounded Sweetwater Falls.

There would be times they had to help one another and she believed it would be better handled with that spirit of cooperation already in place between them, rather than a contentious rivalry. Antagonism between the departments was counterproductive and hindered them all from doing their jobs or operating effectively—especially when they needed it most.

Spenser got to her feet. "Jacob, I know I've heaped a lot on your plate, but in addition to your other projects, if you could keep digging into Baden, I would appreciate it."

"Worry not, for I am a multi-tasking machine, Sheriff."

She smiled at him. "Thank you."

Spenser walked out of the conference room to collect Young and head off to Greenfield. It was the first solid lead they had to follow up on since this whole affair started, and she didn't want to squander it. Especially given that the sound of the ticking clock in her mind was growing ever louder and more insistent.

CHAPTER EIGHTEEN

"THIS IS NOT WHERE I EXPECTED US TO END UP," Spenser said.

"That makes two of us," Young replied, her tone dripping with disgust.

They sat in the Bronco at the curb in front of a large, Colonial-style home in one of the ritzier neighborhoods of Sweetwater Falls. Made of white siding with dark trim and accents, a pair of chimneys sat at either end of the main box of the house which was flanked by large wings that had been added on. Spenser guessed there were at least eight bedrooms in the place. Shutters the same dark color as the trim flanked every window and in the center of the main body of the house was a large red door set back in a round, covered portico.

A concrete walk lined with vividly colored flowers snaked through a lush, beautifully manicured, and expertly landscaped front lawn. The house was one of the largest on a block filled with large houses and screamed of wealth, which wasn't surprising considering who lived there. Just the thought of it made Spenser's stomach churn.

"Are we going to go inside?" Young asked.

"I think you should go in," Spenser replied.

"You're the sheriff. This is why they pay you the big bucks."

"This is why I named you undersheriff—to handle the crap work I don't want to do."

"How about we go in there together?" Young offered.

Spenser frowned. "I suppose that will have to do."

"What has you so unnerved about talking to this guy, Sheriff?" Young asked. "I've seen you stare down gun-toting thugs without flinching. This guy is a... well... he's a geek."

"Zachary Tavares is a giant pain in my butt. He's unreasonable to deal with, thinks he knows police work better than I do, and is always my biggest antagonist whenever I have to deal with the City Council," Spenser told her. "If Tavares had his way, the department would be cut to the bone, and we wouldn't get a quarter of the funding we do now. I just... I don't like him. Don't get along with him. He thinks he's the smartest guy in every room he walks into."

"To be fair, he probably is the smartest guy in every room he walks into."

Spenser rolled her eyes, drawing a rueful chuckle from Young. Spenser felt the expression on her face and knew she looked like she'd just bitten into something sour or rotten.

"Let's get this over with," Spenser said.

They climbed out of the Bronco and headed up the walk. Spenser noted there were two cars in the driveway—a silver Mercedes SUV and a black Range Rover. It looked like both Mr. and Mrs. Tavares were home. Originally from California's Silicon Valley, Tavares made his fortune in tech, developing computer security systems as well as a host of apps that he'd then flipped for millions. Once he'd amassed more wealth than he could spend in one lifetime, he'd settled in Sweetwater Falls, started his family, and began accruing power and influence the way he'd accrued money throughout his career.

Tavares wasn't quite as powerful as the Gilchrists—an outsider would never be as influential as somebody born and bred in Sweetwater Falls—but he was close. As close as an outsider was ever going to get anyway. And he wielded the power he had like a cudgel. He'd used it to batter Spenser in more than one City Council meeting already.

They climbed the steps up onto the porch and Spenser gave Young a look, her face tight, a heavy weight pressing down on her shoulders. Without giving herself more time to think, she raised her hand and knocked on the door.

"Last chance to take the lead on this," Spenser muttered.

The click of the door being unlocked sounded and a moment later, it opened.

"Too late," Young whispered back.

Willa Tavares offered Spenser a warm smile. "Sheriff Song, lovely to see you."

"Mrs. Tavares, it's nice to see you, too," Spenser replied.

"Undersheriff Young, you look well," Willa added.

"As do you, Mrs. Tavares."

With blonde hair and warm golden-hazel-colored eyes, Willa Tavares stood five-six and had a trim, athletic figure with soft, feminine curves. A former lawyer turned housewife, Willa had given up her practice to raise the three Tavares children while also being the president of the town's PTA and doing work on the board of half a dozen other charities. Spenser hadn't had many one-on-one dealings with Willa, but she'd seen enough of her to know the woman was intelligent, clever, and coldly calculating.

While Willa had a warm and inviting smile, Spenser knew the woman was ambitious and could be downright vicious when going after something she wanted. She was somebody Spenser did not want to get on the wrong side of. If Zachary had aspirations above sitting on the City Council of a small town—and Spenser thought that was likely—Willa would be the perfect political wife who had the sort of relatable, easygoing personality that would endear herself to people of all political stripes. And perhaps because of that, Spenser could see Willa leveraging Zachary's successes to build her own political platform.

"How may I help you, Sheriff?" Willa asked.

"Mrs. Tavares, is Zachary home?" Spenser asked.

"Well... yes. Yes, he is," she replied, a flash of concern in her eyes.

"We need to speak with both of you," Spenser said. "Privately."

She hesitated for a moment, the smile on her lips slipping. But she quickly composed herself, putting on her well-practiced, even, neutral face again, and nodded.

"Yes, of course," she said. "Please, come in."

The foyer Willa led them through was elegantly appointed with marble flooring and light, polished wood banisters along the gently curving staircase that led to the second floor. Willa ushered them into a sitting room just off the foyer.

"If you'll wait here, I'll go get Zachary," she said. "Please, make yourselves comfortable."

"Thank you, Mrs. Tavares."

Spenser remained on her feet while Young perched on the edge of one of the sofas. The walls in the sitting room were painted a soft shade of blue meant to be soothing. The wainscoting was white, giving it an elegantly traditional look, and the floor was light oak polished to a glossy sheen. A pair of deep, plush sofas sat across from each other, separated by a wood and glass coffee table, and abstract, modern paintings adorned the walls. To Spenser, it felt very stiff and formal. She wasn't comfortable in that room.

The sound of softly murmuring voices and hard steps on the wood flooring preceded the Tavares' into the room. As they walked in, Young got to her feet and Spenser turned to face them. Standing six-two with a lean, athletic build and broad shoulders, Zachary cut an imposing figure. His skin was warm and tawny, his hair was black, and his eyes were like chips of onyx and seemed just as hard. They were cold and reptilian, underscoring for Spenser just how ruthless the man could be.

"Sheriff," he said. "What is this about?"

"Zachary," Willa said quietly. "Manners."

"Forgive me," he said with a smile that didn't soften that cold gaze. "It is nice to see you."

"We're very sorry to drop in on you like this," Spenser said.

"Not at all," Tavares replied. "Please, have a seat."

Spenser perched on the edge of the sofa next to Young while the Tavares' sat on the sofa across from them.

"As I'm sure you're aware, Wendy Gilchrist's whereabouts are currently unknown," Spenser started. "She's missing."

"Yes, we've heard," Tavares said.

"It's terrible," Willa offered. "Do you have any leads, Sheriff?"

"We're following a few threads, yes," Spenser replied then glanced at Young. "And it's one of those threads that have brought us here."

"Explain. What does that mean?" Tavares asked gruffly.

"We were following up on a person of interest—"

"Who?"

"Joshua Baden. Wendy's ex-husband," Spenser said. "And we traced his movements on the day Wendy disappeared to a hotel over in Greenfield where he was meeting with somebody—the same somebody he's been meeting with regularly for a little more than a year now."

Tavares' eyes narrowed and his jaw clenched. He exchanged a look with Willa who looked back at him blankly before turning back to Spenser, her eyes filled with questions.

"I'm not understanding where you're going with this, Sheriff," Tavares said.

"Councilman Tavares, is your daughter here?" Spenser asked. "Claudia, I mean."

His expression morphed from curious to suspicious. He and his wife looked at each other again and Spenser could see them connecting the dots and as they did, she could practically hear the warning bells going off in their heads.

"What does Claudia have to do with this?" Tavares asked.

"Joshua Baden has been tutoring Claudia, correct?" Spenser asked. "He's been prepping her for the SATs?"

Willa nodded. "Yes. Yes, he has. He came highly recommended."

"I hate to have to tell you both this, but Joshua Baden has been carrying on an inappropriate relationship with Claudia for the last year or so," Spenser said.

"That's impossible," Tavares said. "Claudia is seventeen—"

He bit off his words, seeming to realize how lame the argument sounded as the words left his mouth. He turned to his wife and their expressions morphed into looks of horror. Some bit of silent communication passed between them and as one, they turned back to Spenser.

"That can't be right," Willa said. "There has to be some kind of mistake."

"I'm afraid there's no mistake. We've got video evidence from the hotel's surveillance cameras," Spenser said. "It's definitely Claudia going into Baden's hotel room."

Tavares shook his head. "No. I don't believe this..."

His words trailed off and Spenser could see him continuing to connect the dots in his mind. He ran a hand through his hair then raised his gaze to hers. He looked defensive. Defiant. She could see he didn't want to believe the worst in his daughter. But he was also pragmatic enough to know she wouldn't be there if she didn't have concrete proof. As she watched him grapple with the truth of the situation, though, another light entered his eyes. Spenser knew he'd eventually get around to asking the question—and that the storm would quickly follow.

"Sheriff, what do you think my daughter has to do with Wendy Gilchrist's disappearance?" Tavares asked cautiously.

"We know this is upsetting and we are very sorry for that," Spenser said. "But we need to talk to Claudia about her potential role in Mrs. Gilchrist's disappearance."

"Her role?" Willa gasped. "She has no role in that."

"My daughter had nothing to do with it. You are barking up the wrong tree, Sheriff."

"We're operating under the theory that whoever took Mrs. Gilchrist had a partner. A woman," Spenser said. "And we're not saying your daughter is that woman right now. But we need to talk to her to confirm that."

"You don't need to talk to our daughter," Tavares said. "You won't be talking to our daughter, Sheriff. It's not going to happen."

"Councilman Tavares, this is about ruling her out more than anything," Spenser said evenly. "We're just trying to get to the truth."

"I'm telling you, Claudia had nothing to do with it. Period."

"That's for us to determine, Councilman."

"I'm her father. I would know—"

"With all due respect, you didn't know she's been sleeping with her tutor since she was sixteen years old," Spenser cut him off.

He recoiled like she'd just slapped him. Willa covered her face with her hands and seemed to be taking a few minutes to compose herself.

"We'll do everything we can to cooperate. We will bring Claudia to your office for an informal conversation," she said.

"I would appreciate that. And we will be discreet, Mrs. Tavares," Spenser stated.

"We also want Joshua Baden arrested for statutory rape. We wish to press charges," she said.

"That is your right," Spenser said. "We'll have him picked up and refer the case to the DA."

"We would appreciate that," Willa replied. "Will bringing Claudia down tomorrow suffice?"

"That will be fine," Spenser said.

"Fine. We will see you tomorrow then."

Her tone made it clear their meeting was over so Spenser and Young got to their feet. Tavares remained sitting on the sofa, his eyes lowered to the floor, his face almost purple with rage. Spenser supposed she couldn't blame him. Not after the bombshell she'd just dropped on him.

"Thank you for your time," Spenser said. "And again, I'm sorry to have had to deliver that sort of news. I know it has to be shocking."

When neither of them replied, Spenser gave Willa a nod then silently led Young out of the Tavares house. As they climbed into the Bronco, Young turned to her and grinned.

"I thought that went well," she chirped.

"I suppose in the grand scheme of things, it could have gone worse," Spenser replied.

As Spenser pulled away from the curb, Young turned and looked at the house again. "One thing I know for sure is that I would not want to be Claudia Tavares tonight."

Spenser hummed her agreement. "I would want to be Joshua Baden even less," she said. "When we get back to the office, take whoever's there and go scoop him up and toss him in a cell for the night. I don't want Tavares getting any bright ideas and doing something stupid."

"Copy that," she said then paused before asking, "Do you really think Claudia Tavares was the woman on the platform?"

"Honestly? No," Spenser said. "But who knows? With the way this case is going, I wouldn't be surprised if it did turn out to be her."

As Spenser piloted the Bronco back to the office, she frowned. She felt like she was out on the open ocean and was adrift, with absolutely no idea which direction land might be.

CHAPTER NINETEEN

"No, I wasn't at the train station," Claudia said and sniffed. "He never asked me to dress up or anything like that. We spent the entire day at the hotel."

Both Willa and Zachary Tavares tightened up and their faces grew dark as their daughter spoke. Claudia lowered her gaze immediately and softly cried. Five-five with rich, auburn hair, a pale complexion, and dark, smoky eyes that looked a lot like her father's, Claudia Tavares was a pretty, wholesome-looking girl. But her eyes were red and swollen, her cheeks splotched and puffy, and she looked like she hadn't slept the night before and had instead been up and crying all night. Young was right, it seemed like it had been a very rough night for the eldest Tavares child.

Not wanting to scare Claudia or impart the tension that would naturally come from being in an interrogation room, Spenser had opted to seat them in the conference room. Before their arrival, Young had turned the whiteboard over and removed their investigation materials with the goal of making their war room look like a plain, ordinary conference room again. None of their measures seemed to help, though. Claudia sat between her mother and father across the table from Spenser. Their bodies were taut and tension as well as fear was etched into their features.

Her hands clasped together in front of her, Spenser leaned forward. "Claudia, it's really important that you're honest with us now," she said gently. "This is a very serious matter we're dealing with and—"

"Sheriff, she told you she wasn't at the train station," Tavares snapped.

"Councilman Tavares, please. I need you to let me speak with Claudia freely and without interruption," Spenser said.

"Zachary," Willa said softly. "Let the sheriff do her job."

Tavares sat back in his chair, arms folded over his chest, and a petulant look on his face. Spenser gave Willa a small nod of thanks then turned back to Claudia.

"Do you understand how serious this is, Claudia?" Spenser asked gently. "We're trying to find a missing woman and we need to know the truth. We need to know if Mr. Baden asked you to do anything for him."

The girl wiped at her eyes and nose with a crumpled-up tissue in her hand and nodded. She sniffed loudly as fresh tears streamed down her pale cheeks.

"I do understand," she said. "He didn't ask me to go to the train station or anything like that. He didn't ask me to do anything."

"It's obvious this degenerate took advantage of our daughter," Tavares interrupted. "I want him punished, Sheriff. What he did—"

"We've already arrested him, Councilman," Spenser said. "Now, please. I need you to settle down and let me talk to Claudia."

She turned back to Claudia. "Has Mr. Baden ever mentioned his ex-wife to you, Claudia?" Spenser asked. "Has he ever talked to you about Wendy Gilchrist?"

She shook her head. "No. Whenever we were together, he was focused on me. On us," she said quietly. "We never talked about anybody else. He never even mentioned his ex to me. I had no idea who she was."

Spenser studied her closely, looking for signs of deception. There was some small part of her that wondered if her parents might have leaned on her last night, telling her not to admit to anything. Even if they had, Spenser's experience told her a young girl like Claudia wouldn't be able to lie cleanly. Very few kids her age developed the necessary skills to lie as smoothly as adults. There would be tells. And she wasn't seeing any in Claudia's face or posture. As far as Spenser could tell, the girl was telling her the truth.

Spenser sat back in her seat, never taking her eyes off the girl. Claudia kept her head down and her gaze on the tabletop, unable to meet her eyes. It wasn't guilt or shame Spenser saw in Claudia's face but anger. There was even a glimmer of defiance. Spenser could see she didn't regret being with Baden. Far from it. Regardless of what happened, Spenser believed she would go straight back to Baden when she had the chance.

"Claudia, what Mr. Baden is doing with you—it's not only morally wrong, it's illegal—"

For the first time since arriving in the conference room, Claudia raised her head and glared at Spenser, a snarl curling her lips.

"How can it be wrong, Sheriff? We're in love," she spat.

Tavares grunted in disgust and Willa looked away, an expression of distress on her face.

"Don't be stupid. You're too young to know what love is," the councilman said.

"Zachary," Willa softly admonished him.

"I'm not too young to know. I'm seventeen," Claudia said. "I love him. And he loves me. And no matter what you say, we're going to be together."

"He's going to prison for a very long time, Claudia. And you are never going to see him again," Tavares snapped.

"You can't stop me when I turn eighteen," she fired back. "You can't control my life."

Spenser frowned. She'd gotten what she needed from Claudia and didn't need to listen to the domestic squabble. She would have told Tavares there was no use trying to lay down the law with his daughter because his opposition would only drive her toward Baden even more. She thought it probably would have been better to say nothing, let Baden go to prison, and let those feelings Claudia was all wrapped up in wither and die naturally. He was right, she was young. And when you were that young, feelings were often fleeting. But that was just her opinion and was irrelevant. It wasn't her place to offer up her two cents.

"I think we have what we need, folks," Spenser said. "I want to thank you for coming in and I will be in touch. I'm sure I'll have some follow-up questions at some point."

Spenser got to her feet, giving them the hint that they were done. The Tavares family quickly followed suit, obviously eager to be away from Spenser's office, but Willa paused.

"Thank you, Sheriff. We appreciate you handling this as quietly as you have," she said. "We know you could have made a production out of this, so we appreciate you being delicate about it."

"Of course," Spenser said.

"Yes. Thank you," Tavares added, albeit somewhat grudgingly.

"I'll be in touch," Spenser replied.

Spenser watched them walk out of the conference room, their postures rigid, their faces dark with anger, making a beeline for the front doors. As long as Claudia's night was last night, given the defiance that sparked within her as she talked with them, Spenser had a feeling tonight was going to be even longer for her.

After having him moved from a cell to one of the interrogation rooms, Spenser watched Joshua Baden through the observation window for a moment. He shifted in his seat, fidgeted ceaselessly, looking all kinds of uncomfortable. The expression on his face was one of fear mixed with resignation. He knew he'd been caught with his hand in the underage cookie jar and the consequences could be serious.

"What a disgusting pig," Young said as she stepped up beside Spenser.

Spenser nodded. Just looking at him made her skin crawl.

"Yeah. He makes me sick."

"But did he kill Wendy Gilchrist?"

Her lips were a tight slash across her face. "My gut says no. He's a disgusting child molester, but a murderer? I don't think so."

"At least we know now why he lied to us about where he was the day Wendy went missing."

"Yeah, there's that," Spenser said. "I better get this over with so we can wash our hands and be done with him."

"I'll run the audio/visual equipment."

"Good. Thank you."

Spenser walked out of the observation room then opened the door and walked into the interrogation room. She closed the door behind her then took a seat at the table across from Baden. He eyed her the way a field mouse might look at a hawk circling overhead, dread on his face, and the sense of impending doom palpable in the air around them.

"I suppose it goes without saying that you understand that you're in a heap of trouble, huh?" Spenser began.

Baden didn't say anything. He simply looked down at his hands, which were folded together in his lap, the chain from his shackles locked to the bolt under the lip of the table. Spenser waited for a long moment, but he remained quiet.

"I mean, the one thing I want to know is, what were you thinking? She was sixteen when you guys started up—you were fifty," Spenser said. "And if you tell me she's mature for her age, I swear to God I'll come across this table and choke the life out of you."

"What do you want me to say, Sheriff?" he growled. "I made a mistake."

"No, you made a choice," she spat back. "You made a choice to have an inappropriate relationship with a little girl. She was sixteen and you were fifty, Mr. Baden. Do you know how disgusting and disturbing that is?"

He frowned and glared at her balefully. "It happened. Insulting me and calling me names isn't going to change that," he said. "What do you want from me?"

"She thinks you love her."

"What do you want from me?"

"Do you?"

"What does it matter?"

Spenser sat back in her seat and stared at the man sitting across from her. She wasn't sure her opinion of him could have been any lower after their first meeting, but she'd been wrong. He was a lowly, contemptible piece of filth.

"Did you kill your ex-wife, Mr. Baden?"

He shook his head and took a couple of beats as if trying to catch up and process the sudden shift in topic. Spenser liked keeping people back on their heels and she'd always found that one way to do that was to suddenly and radically shift a line of questioning. She'd found that when they were off balance and reacting to her, truth often followed.

"No, I didn't kill Wendy," he said, his voice colored with outrage. "I hated her, but I didn't do anything to hurt her."

"Did you pull that girl into your plot to murder your ex-wife, Mr. Baden?"

He glared at her. "How many times do I have to tell you that I had nothing to do with whatever happened to Wendy—if anything actually happened to her?" he snarled. "And even if I had done something to Wendy—which I definitely didn't do—I would have never brought Claudia into that. Ever. I wouldn't do something like that to that girl."

"Well, I'm glad to see you have a line you're unwilling to cross," she said. "Especially since preying on a child is one you seem very comfortable crossing."

He opened his mouth to reply then closed it again without saying anything. Instead, he stared at her darkly for a moment. Baden cleared his throat and leaned forward.

THE LIES IN THE FALLS

"I don't appreciate your tone, Sheriff. Nor do I appreciate any of the implications you're making," he said. "I don't think I'll have anything more to say until my attorney arrives."

"That's fine. You're going to need your lawyer because you're facing some very serious charges," Spenser said.

"You don't need to keep reminding me. I understand the situation."

"I hope so," she replied. "And I hope that you're being honest and didn't use her feelings for you to pull Claudia Tavares into this mess."

"I didn't pull her into anything because I didn't do anything to Wendy," he said.

"I hope that's the truth," Spenser said. "I really, really hope it is."

CHAPTER TWENTY

SPENSER WAS BUSY WITH SOME PAPERWORK WHEN THERE was a brief knock before the door to her office opened, and Alice Jarrett stuck her head in. She was half afraid the woman was coming in to Christmas-ize her office, but one look at the serious expression on her face told Spenser Alice was there on business.

"Sorry to bother you, Sheriff," Alice said.

"It's fine. What is it?" Spenser asked.

"Aspen Gilchrist is here to see you and she seems rather fired up. I tried to tell her you were busy, but she can be rather… persistent. Said she'd wait until you were free."

Spenser sighed. She wasn't really in the mood to deal with Aspen since she was relatively certain she knew why the girl was there. She was learning that nothing on Earth moved faster than the grapevine in Sweetwater Falls.

"It's fine, Alice," Spenser said grudgingly. "You can send her in. I'll talk to her."

The girl thanked the older woman then strode in, dressed in a designer pantsuit and looking like a young executive. Spenser thought perhaps she was trying to emulate her mother and was dressed like a professional woman in the hope she'd be taken seriously.

Aspen dropped into one of the chairs in front of Spenser's desk and set her large, designer bag down next to her. They stared at each other in silence for a long moment. This was her show so Spenser was content to sit back and let Aspen guide the conversation.

"I heard you arrested my father," Aspen started.

"We did. And I assume you heard why."

The girl nodded. "I did and I'm disgusted. Not surprised but disgusted all the same."

"Why do you say you're not surprised?"

"My father, as I'm sure you're now learning, is a degenerate," she said simply.

Spenser didn't disagree with the girl's sentiment, but she wasn't going to be so unprofessional as to engage in that sort of trash-talking.

"Did he kill my mother?" Aspen asked.

"We're still running down some leads," Spenser replied.

"Sheriff, please," she said. "Do you think he killed my mother?"

Spenser knew she probably shouldn't discuss the case with the girl but in this particular instance, she didn't think it was going to hurt to throw her a bone. Plus, she thought it might get Aspen off her back and out of her office faster.

"Honestly? No, I don't," she answered. "I don't think he did anything to your mother."

"I didn't think so, either."

She said it with a haughty, imperious tone that set Spenser's teeth on edge. Aspen sounded like she thought she knew better than her and that irritated Spenser to no end. The girl sat looking at her with an expectant look on her face.

"You seem like you have something you want to say," Spenser said.

"I do. I just want to know why you aren't looking at Brock," she said. "Dally and I both told you he's responsible for our mother's disappearance—"

"He was in California at the time she disappeared—"

"Was he?" She cut Spenser off. "I mean, did you verify that?"

"We've got the charge receipts from the hotel," Spenser said. "And I know you and your sister don't want to believe it, but I honestly believe that Brock loves your mother."

Aspen's mouth twisted as she silently stared at Spenser for a couple of moments, anger flickering in her eyes. Without saying a word, she reached down into her bag and pulled out a laptop, set it in her lap, and opened it. She tapped on the keys for a minute then looked up at Spenser.

"If he loved my mother, then why was Brock screwing somebody else?"

Aspen's voice dripped with acid as she set her laptop down on Spenser's desk. She turned it around so Spenser could see the screen then slid it across the desk to her. Spenser looked down at the screen and saw that Aspen had called up her mother's email account, opening a string of correspondence between Wendy and Brock. Spenser took a few minutes to read the exchanges between them then looked up at Aspen.

"See?" the girl said with a sneer.

"It's certainly suggestive, but it's not definitive."

Aspen gasped with exasperation. "Are you kidding me? This is proof he was cheating on my mom, Sheriff. This is proof of motive."

"As I said, it's suggestive, Aspen. But these allegations are unfounded at this point—"

"Are you kidding me? He was cheating on my mom. That gives him motive to want to kill her," Aspen all but shouted.

"Your mother made him sign a prenup. It's ironclad. I can't see it being enough incentive for him to risk going to prison for the rest of his life," Spenser explained.

The girl threw her hands up in the air and groaned loudly. Her expression was etched with frustration and tinged with anger. Spenser understood where the girl was coming from.

"Listen, Aspen, I appreciate you bringing this to me," Spenser said. "And I don't want you to think I'm blowing off your concerns—"

"Aren't you?"

"Not at all. All I'm trying to do is give you a realistic lay of the land. I'm trying to be honest with you. I don't want to promise you something and then have to go back on that later," Spenser replied. "Now, these emails are suggestive, as I said. And I promise you that I am going to look into them. But I don't want to promise that these will lead anywhere. I want you to be realistic and manage your expectations."

Aspen slumped back in her chair, her expression still frustrated, but she nodded. "I guess… I guess I understand that."

"This is all good, though. And I thank you for bringing this to me."

"I just want you to find my mom."

"And I'm doing everything I possibly can to do that," Spenser said. "You have my word that I'm not going to stop until I can give you and your sister some answers."

Aspen's gaze lingered on Spenser's for a moment before she got to her feet. "Thank you, Sheriff. Please… keep me in the loop."

"I will," Spenser replied. "Would you mind if I hung onto this computer for a bit? I want to examine the emails a little further. I'll get it back to you as soon as I can."

"Yeah, sure."

Her shoulders sagging and looking dispirited, Aspen turned and left Spenser's office. She took another moment to read through the email chain again, absorbing the words both Wendy and Brock had written to one another. After that, she quickly texted Jacob and Young, telling them both to meet her in the conference room. That done, Spenser grabbed the laptop then headed in herself and took her usual seat. A couple of minutes later, Jacob and Young came in and sat down.

"So, what did Aspen have to say for herself?" Young asked.

"She doesn't feel like we're taking things seriously enough," Spenser replied. "She still thinks Brock is responsible for Wendy's disappearance."

"But he wasn't even in the state at the time," Young said.

Spenser cringed. "You know, she got me thinking about that."

"Uh oh," Jacob said. "Nothing good ever comes of that."

"What's running around your noodle, Sheriff?" Young asked.

"The fact that we're taking Brock at his word to confirm his alibi," Spenser said.

"Yeah, but we've got the charge receipts," Young said.

"Those can be fudged," Spenser replied. "It might be nothing, but I want to independently verify Brock's alibi just to cover our bases."

"How are we going to do that?" Young asked.

"I want you to call the hotel he was staying at when he was on his business trip," Spenser said. "Talk to anybody and everybody who saw him there. I want to know what they saw and when. And try to get video footage sent up to us to corroborate it all."

"Got it," Young said. "I'm all over it.

"Jacob, do me a favor and see if you can authenticate those emails. I need to know if they're real," Spenser said.

"On it," he replied.

"What's in the emails?" Young asked.

"A possible motive," Spenser answered.

CHAPTER TWENTY-ONE

SPENSER WALKED INTO THE CONFERENCE ROOM TO FIND Young talking on the phone, an excited look on her face. She motioned for Spenser to sit and as Spenser dropped into the chair, Young set her phone on the table and turned on the speaker. A man's voice, somewhat high-pitched and nasally, filled the room. Young hit mute then turned to Spenser.

"This is Matthew Buener. He's the manager down at the Clifton—the hotel in San Francisco Brock Ferry was staying at when he was down in California," she said quickly. "You have got to hear what he's got to say."

"Hello? Are you there?" Buener asked.

Young unmuted the phone. "I'm so sorry, Mr. Buener, the sheriff just walked in," Young said. "Let me get you to repeat that, if you would, please."

"Of course," he replied. "As I was telling you, Mr. Ferry was indeed here, but my records show that he checked out a few days early."

Spenser glanced at Young who was smiling wide. It would seem that those words were the pinprick that burst the balloon of Brock's alibi. But just because it seemed that way, Spenser knew it wasn't always that way. After all, things were not always what they seemed.

"Mr. Buener, this is Sheriff Spenser Song," she said. "Mr. Ferry's charge card shows that he booked the room—"

"Correct," he cut her off, sounding slightly impatient. "However, as I was just telling your undersheriff, Mr. Ferry's room was paid for in advance and he didn't request a refund when he left. Our cancellation policy is clear—"

"And you're certain he checked out a few days early?"

There was a pause on the other end of the line and when Buener spoke again, his voice was tight. Their probing for information was obviously irritating him.

"I'm quite certain, Sheriff Song," he replied. "He stated that he and his wife needed—"

"Wait, wait, wait," Spenser said. "Did you just say his wife?"

"Yes," he said through obviously gritted teeth. "I did."

Spenser exchanged a look with Young and she felt a burst of excitement building inside of her. If what Buener was telling them was true, not only was Brock's alibi a flaming ruin, but he gave himself a motive for getting rid of Wendy. There was a stipulation in the prenup he'd signed that eliminated the hundred-thousand-dollar payout he stood to receive if he and Wendy divorced in the case of infidelity. It was a stipulation Brock had failed to mention to them.

Buener's story seemed to corroborate the emails Aspen had given to her. It was titillating and juicy stuff, for sure. As suggestive as the story was, though, it didn't constitute proof of anything, least of all that Brock had murdered his wife. It put them on the road to it, but they still had a long way to go.

"Can you describe the woman Mr. Ferry was with?" Spenser asked.

"She was about five-ten or so, I guess. Platinum blonde, blue eyes… she was thin and had a pale complexion," he replied.

"You have a very good memory, Mr. Buener," Spenser said.

"She was a memorable woman," he replied. "She looked like a model—like somebody from a Victoria's Secret catalog or something. Yeah, she was pretty memorable."

Memorable and definitely not Wendy Gilchrist. "Did you happen to get a name?"

"No. I never spoke to her directly," Buener said. "Mr. Ferry did all the talking."

"And you're certain about the timeline—"

"I'm positive, Sheriff," he snapped. "I appreciate that you have to do your job, but so do I. Are we done here? Because I really need to see to my guests."

"One last thing," Spenser said. "I'm going to need you to send me the front desk surveillance footage the day Mr. Ferry checked out."

"Of course. I'll have that sent to you right away," he said.

"Thank you for your time, Mr. Buener."

"Good luck, Sheriff."

He hung up so Young disconnected the call then sat back in her chair and grinned, a self-satisfied look on her face. It was a possibility that Buener's story just blew the whole case open and handed them a prime suspect. But that's all it was at the moment—a possibility.

Regardless of how tantalizing his story was, they were still woefully thin on hard evidence. They had nothing yet to tie Brock Ferry to Wendy Gilchrist's disappearance. They also didn't have Wendy Gilchrist's body, which no matter how Spenser tried to downplay it, was still a major hurdle to overcome. It might be one that wound up being too big to overcome. But it gave Spenser a light of hope to focus on. If nothing else, it gave her a viable direction to start running in.

The laptop in front of Young chimed and she sat forward again. She pulled the laptop to her and tapped away at a few keys. Her eyes widened and a look of surprise crossed her face.

"What is it?" Spenser asked.

"Take a look."

Young turned the computer around and Spenser saw it was a still image from the hotel's security cameras, just as Buener had promised.

"That was fast," Spenser said.

"I guess Buener wants us out of his hair."

"I can't say I blame him."

The still image showed footage taken from above and behind the front desk, giving Spenser a clear image of Brock Ferry, presumably at the time he checked out. Spenser looked at the time stamp and saw it was indeed three days before he was supposed to have come home. Standing just behind and to his left was a tall, willowy woman with platinum blonde hair and piercing cornflower blue eyes. Buener had been right, she was stunning.

"Wow. She does look like a Victoria's Secret model," Spenser said.

"Right?"

Spenser clicked on the second attachment to the email Young had received. It was a video clip. She pulled it up and hit play. The video was clear and in color but, unfortunately, didn't have sound. It was the same view of the front desk, and she watched as Brock spoke with the clerk. He slid what looked like a room key across the counter then gave the person he was speaking with a smile. She tried reading his lips but all she was able to make out was him saying "Thank you."

Spenser watched as he turned away from the desk. The blonde woman smiled warmly then slipped her arm around his waist. They looked very comfortable together and it made Spenser believe this wasn't the first trip they'd taken with each other. They had a level of comfort only people who'd been together for a while shared. They walked out of the camera's frame and then the video stopped. Spenser watched the brief video clip a second time then pushed the laptop back to Young when it had finished.

"Well, that's not Wendy Gilchrist," Spenser said.

"That is definitely not Wendy Gilchrist."

"Which means that Brock Ferry lied to us."

"It does indeed," Young replied. "Should we go scoop him up?"

"Not yet. I want to be able to hit him with something solid when we do," Spenser told her. "I want to have him boxed in and give him nowhere to go."

"That makes sense," Young said.

"He lied to us, which also means his alibi is busted, and he possibly wasn't even in California when Wendy went missing," Spenser said.

Young nodded. "That it does."

"It's suggestive, but it doesn't necessarily mean that he was here when she went missing," Spenser mused, mostly to herself. "We need to nail down his whereabouts. The problem with that is we can't ask him because he'll probably lie to us again."

"I wouldn't doubt it."

She drummed her fingers on the table, her mind spinning as she tried to figure out how to get an accurate accounting of his whereabouts. That he ostensibly paid cash rather than use his cards while he was supposedly out of town made that difficult. And then the answer occurred to her and she looked over at Young.

"The woman he's with," Spenser said and snapped her fingers. "You recognize her. You know who she is, don't you?"

Young nodded, a smile stretching across her lips. "I do."

"Is she local?"

"She is."

"Then let's go have a chat with her."

CHAPTER TWENTY-TWO

SPENSER PULLED THE BRONCO TO A STOP IN FRONT OF A large, modern-looking house made primarily of smoked glass and burnished steel. It was all gentle curves and had no sharp lines. The yard was small but neatly trimmed and minimally landscaped. A large concrete fountain that looked like it belonged in front of the Bellagio dominated the front yard. The house was a cold, sterile edifice that seemed built to reflect the wealth of the occupants which seemed to fit with what Young had told her about the man who owned the place.

"This place has all the warmth of an iceberg," Spenser remarked.

"Wait 'til you meet Anderson Collins… it'll all make sense," Young replied.

"It's also the only house on this entire street not decked out for Christmas already," Spenser noted. "I guess we've found the Grinch's secret hideaway."

"Oh, then you should feel right at home here," Young said with a snicker.

"You suck."

Laughing together, she and Young got out of the Bronco and headed up the walk. A very successful stockbroker and money manager, Anderson Collins was one of the wealthier residents of Sweetwater Falls but mostly kept to himself. Although he probably could have been hugely influential, he stayed out of local politics and town business. When he wasn't out of town or at his firm in Seattle, he was holed up here in his fortress of solitude. If not for Young filling her in on all the details, Spenser wouldn't have even known the guy existed.

As they walked toward the front door, Spenser noticed the battery of surveillance cameras hidden discreetly around the property and couldn't help but think Collins seemed more than a little paranoid. Then again, she supposed she couldn't blame him for being a little security conscious considering the fact the world around them seemed to be going to hell in a handbasket. He'd amassed a fortune in his life and seemed well determined to keep anybody from taking any single part of it.

They stepped to a tall, wide pair of doors which, like other portions of the house, was made of burnished steel. Each door had a long, vertical chrome handle and three panes of smoked glass that ran down the center. A camera was built into a keypad set into the wall beside the door and Spenser could feel somebody on the other side of it watching her. She glanced at Young and cleared her throat but then raised her hand and rapped on the door.

A couple of moments later, the door opened and Spenser found herself looking at the tall, willowy blonde from the security video the hotel manager in San Francisco had sent along. Even in a silk robe, with no makeup on, and her hair mussed, looking like she'd just rolled out of bed, the woman looked runway-ready. Spenser felt positively plain standing there in front of her. The blonde's eyes widened in surprise, but she managed to compose herself quickly. The look of trepidation melted away and was replaced by a smile that didn't quite reach her eyes.

"Sheriff," she said. "H-how can I help you?"

"Elayna Collins?"

"Yes, that's right," she said, her voice lightly dusted with an Eastern European accent.

"We need to speak with you about your recent trip."

Elayna's gaze cut to Young then back to Spenser and she licked her full lips nervously. "Wh-what's this about?"

"Can we speak inside, Mrs. Collins?" Spenser asked.

The woman looked behind her, a look of worry flashing across her face. But she quickly regained her swagger and confidence. Elayna turned back to Spenser with a clenched jaw and narrowed eyes, adopting an expression of haughtiness and defiance. She stepped out and closed the door behind her. Spenser had hoped it wouldn't go like that, but she seemed to want to do things the hard way.

"No," she said. "Either tell me what this is about or be on your way."

"Is your husband home, Mrs. Collins?" Spenser asked.

"He's sleeping right now," she said. "He just returned from a business trip."

"I see," Spenser said.

She eyed the woman up and down, trying to match her to the person on the train station video. Elayna Collins was taller than Wendy by a good four or five inches. But Spenser thought it was still possible Elayna was the person on the platform since the footage was grainy and it was impossible to get an accurate height from it. Plus, the bulky coat the person was wearing obscured their actual figure, so for all Spenser knew, it could have been the tall, willowy blonde underneath that hat and sunglasses.

Spenser looked at the house pointedly. "You seem to have a pretty cushy life here, Mrs. Collins. A husband who earns what, seven or eight figures a year? A nice home. Cars. The ability to do whatever you want, when you want to do it?"

"Like go to San Francisco at a moment's notice," Young added.

"Is there a point, Sheriff?"

"What were you doing in San Francisco, Mrs. Collins?"

THE LIES IN THE FALLS

She flashed Spenser a look of irritation. "I was on a trip with a... friend."

"Brock Ferry, right?" Young asked.

Elayna's face froze, a look of fear in her eyes. She shifted on her feet, pushing her shoulders back, and tried to gather her wits about her again. She looked at Young with that air of smug assurance that seemed so common and natural to her.

"What I do is none of your concern," she said. "Now, I don't know what this is about, but I do know I have not committed any crimes, so I don't have to speak with you. I owe you no explanations about anything. Good day."

"You're right. You don't have to talk to us," Spenser said, her voice slightly raised. "And you're also right that adultery is not a crime. I'm not one to judge, but some might say it's tacky and tasteless, but not a crime."

Elayna wheeled around, her face twisted with both fear and fury. "Keep your voice down," she hissed. "Who do you think you are?"

"We're just trying to get some answers to our questions," Spenser replied. "We don't want to involve your husband or cause any undue upset in your life, but we're investigating a missing and possibly murdered woman, so your cooperation would be greatly appreciated."

"Murdered?" she gasped. "Who was murdered?"

"We think you know who we're referring to," Young said.

"I—I don't," she replied.

She shook her head and seemed to be racking her brain, looking genuinely confused. To Spenser, the woman's confusion looked genuine, which was somewhat confounding. But then, as determined to avoid local entanglements as Mr. and Mrs. Collins seemed to be, Spenser shouldn't have been surprised that the grapevine didn't extend to their door.

"I don't have any idea what you're talking about," Elayna stated again. "Who's missing and murdered? And why would you think I know anything about it?"

"Brock Ferry," Spenser said. "You were with him in San Francisco recently, correct?"

She cut her eyes back to the house, that glimmer of nervousness flashing across her face again. Spenser could see the woman was terrified her husband would come out and that the jig would be up. That her entire cushy life would be blown to pieces. Spenser didn't know what the dynamics of Elayna's marriage were. She didn't know if she loved her husband, if this was more of a business relationship type deal, and she didn't care to know. It wasn't her business, and she had no desire to destroy it... whatever it was.

But they were looking for a woman who, for all Spenser knew, was dead and had been murdered by Elayna's side piece. A man who had already lied to their faces once. A man who was looking increasingly guilty, so she was going to do whatever it took to get the answers she was seeking. Even if that meant blowing down the house of cards that was Elayna Collins' marriage to get what she was after.

"Yes," she said quietly. "Brock and I were in San Francisco."

"Did he ever mention his wife to you, Mrs. Collins?" Young asked.

"Of course, he did," she replied. "We talk to each other about our lives quite a bit."

"And in what context did he mention her to you?"

She sighed. "He loves her. But she doesn't seem to love him back. He's sad. Lonely," she said. "He and I met at one of the rare social functions Anderson and I attended and things between us followed naturally from there. We are kindred spirits of a sort."

"Do you love him?" Young asked.

"What? No," she replied. "I love my husband."

"Do you, though?" Young asked, her voice thick with skepticism.

Elayna bristled at the tone of judgment in Young's voice and glared daggers at her. But she stood up straighter and pushed her shoulders back again, doing her best to maintain some shred of dignity now that her double life had been exposed.

"Yes. I do. My marriage is... complicated. He is always gone on business. I, too, am often lonely, and like him, my spouse isn't always the warmest or most loving in return. Brock and I fill a need for each other... physically and companionship-wise," she replied. "That's all we are to each other. There's affection between us, of course. But all we do for one another is fill the voids we have in our lives. That's all. I wouldn't expect you, somebody with such little life experience, to understand."

Young bristled but didn't take the bait. She gritted her teeth and bit back the withering reply Spenser was sure sat on the tip of her tongue. Young hated being reminded of how—well—young she was. She felt it was reductionist and rude. But she held her tongue, and Spenser was proud of her for it.

"Mrs. Collins, did Brock ever ask you to go to the train station in a disguise and board a train?" Young asked.

"What? No. Don't be silly."

"So, he didn't ask you to help him create an alibi?" Young pressed.

"An alibi? What would he need an alibi for?"

"Did Brock Ferry ever ask you to help him get rid of his wife?" Young finished.

Her face blanched and her eyes widened. "What? That's absurd. He would never do anything to her. And he certainly wouldn't ask me to help him. Why would he?"

"To be with you," Young replied simply.

She shook her head. "As I told you, our relationship isn't like that. Neither of us is interested in being with the other in that way. We may be lonely but we're both content in our respective marriages. In our own ways, of course."

"Mrs. Collins, Brock's wife, Wendy Gilchrist, is missing," Spenser said. "Now, Brock has already lied to us. And now we find out that you were together with him in San Francisco. More than that, we also know that you both checked out a few days earlier than you'd booked the room for. Do you see where we're going with this?"

"This is absurd. Brock would never do anything to his wife. Neither would I."

"So, why did you cut your trip short then?" Spenser asked.

"Because Anderson phoned and told me he was coming home from his trip early," she replied softly. "I had to be here when he arrived."

It was plausible. It made sense. It would also be very easy to verify. More than that, Spenser heard the ring of sincerity in Elayna's voice and was certain she was telling them the truth. But while that might cover Elayna's butt and provide her with a solid alibi, it still didn't answer Spenser's lingering questions about Brock. She knew for sure that he didn't go home after coming back from San Francisco early—the girls had verified that for her.

"So, after you came home, you didn't see Brock again?" Spenser asked.

She shook her head. "No. We've spoken—mainly through text, of course—but we haven't been together since coming home. Why do you ask?"

"Do you know where he went after coming home, Mrs. Collins?" Spenser asked. "He didn't go home, that much we know. Can you account for his whereabouts?"

Elayna remained silent for a long moment and Spenser could see the woman's mind spinning. She seemed caught between wanting to lie to protect him and telling the truth, which would be very bad for him. After a quick glance back at the house, a sense of self-preservation seemed to creep into her calculations. Elayna pursed her lips and shook her head, a soft but sad expression flitting across her features.

"I—I can't," she finally admitted. "After we got back here, we parted ways and... I don't know where he went. All I can tell you is that Brock is a gentle soul, and he would not do a thing to harm another person. That much I know for sure, Sheriff."

And there it was. Brock had lied to them and even worse for him, he had no alibi. Elayna believed in his innocence, but that belief and five bucks would buy Spenser nothing more than a cup of coffee. It was hard to take the word of a woman she knew to be a liar and a cheat at face value.

"I think we have what we need," Spenser said with a glance at Young.

Elayna's posture grew rigid, and a look of absolute fear crossed her face when the door behind her opened. A tall, broad man with silver hair and a surprisingly smooth, tanned complexion for a man who looked old enough to be Elayna's father stepped out onto the porch. He wore a dark blue tracksuit and eyed Spenser warily as he stepped forward and slipped an arm protectively around his wife's waist and pulled her close. She turned and gave him a warm smile.

Some might see it as a gesture of protectiveness, but Spenser saw it for what it was—a claim of ownership—and she suddenly found herself feeling sorry for the woman and perhaps, on the fringe of understanding why she might seek comfort in the arms of another man.

"Sheriff, what's going on here?" he asked.

Spenser cleared her throat. "Undersheriff Young and I were just making the rounds, collecting toys and donations for the children's charity the department sponsors."

The lie flowed so smoothly from her lips that Spenser was almost ashamed of herself. But Elayna's eyes filled with gratitude telling her she'd made the right call.

"Oh. Right," he said gruffly. "I'll have a check sent down to your office."

"That would be wonderful, Mr. Collins," Spenser said. "Thank you."

"Uh-huh. Sure thing," he replied.

His arm still around her waist, Collins turned and all but pulled her into the house with him, closing the door behind them with a solid thud. Spenser and Young hustled back to the Bronco and climbed in. Spenser felt that warm glow of excitement building inside of her that she usually got when the momentum of a case began to pick up steam. She felt like they were finally on the verge of getting some real answers and finding out what happened to Wendy Gilchrist.

"So? What now?" Young asked.

"Now, we go scoop up Brock Ferry and have a conversation with the man."

"Excellent," Young said enthusiastically. "Things are about to get good."

CHAPTER TWENTY-THREE

"**W**HY AM I HERE?" BROCK FUMED.

"Because you're a liar, Mr. Ferry," Spenser said as she sat down at the table across from him.

Young stepped into the interrogation room behind her and quietly closed the door then walked over and set a bottle of water down on the table in front of him. She stepped back then leaned against the wall to Spenser's right and crossed her arms over her chest, her eyes fixed on Brock. He squirmed in his seat, clearly uncomfortable beneath their scrutiny.

Brock looked away and seemed to be trying to regain his composure. He sat up, his posture stiff, silently conveying that he wasn't there to help them. That they were now adversaries. It made Spenser want to laugh.

"What the hell are you talking about?" he growled.

"There are some questions that need to be answered," Spenser said. "The first of which is, why you lied to us."

"What is it you imagine I lied to you about?"

"How about the fact that you left California and came home three days early?" Spenser said. "You told us you were in San Francisco the day Wendy went missing."

Brock's face blanched and his mouth fell open. He quickly closed it again and tried to control the look of surprise and fear that had crossed his face. Spenser watched as he put all the pieces together and when he realized that information could have come from only one place, he clenched his jaw so hard, she thought he could have bitten through steel. But then his expression changed and that light of defiance in his face faded. Brock's shoulders slumped and he suddenly looked defeated. Scared. His face was pinched with uncertainty as the fight seemed to have been taken out of him.

"Does Elayna's husband know?" he asked quietly.

"No," Spenser replied. "We were discreet."

He sighed. "Thank you for that."

"We didn't do it for you," Young told him. "It just wasn't our business."

"Well... thank you anyway," he said.

"So, Mr. Ferry," Spenser started. "Shall we try this again?"

He looked down at his hands, his face clouding over with emotion.

"You came home three days early. You were in town the day Wendy went missing," Spenser said. "Did you have anything to do with her disappearance?"

He shook his head. "No. I didn't."

"Mr. Ferry—"

He raised his head, a snarl on his lips. "I had nothing to do with it, Sheriff."

"You lied to us about where you were. You lied to us about having an affair," Spenser said. "Why should we believe you now?"

"Because I'm telling you the truth," he replied.

"You see how difficult it is for us to believe that, don't you? I mean, you're cheating on your wife. A woman you told us you loved," Young added.

"I do love her. But being married to her was often… lonely," he said. "Elayna made me feel not so alone. She was a source of comfort."

"Frankly, I'm not interested in your reasons for cheating—or the fact that you're cheating at all," Spenser said. "All I want to know is, where is your wife?"

"And I'm telling you that I don't know."

"Okay, let's try a simpler question then," Spenser said. "You came back home from your supposed business trip early and you didn't go home. So… where did you go?"

"I have a cabin out on Miller Lake," he said. "I was there."

"Can anybody verify that?"

He frowned and shook his head. "No. I was alone."

"That's pretty convenient, isn't it?" Young mused.

"It's also the truth," he snapped.

"So you say," Young clapped back.

Brock scrubbed his face with his hands, frustration and defeat etched into his features.

"You have to admit it does sound rather convenient," Spenser said. "I mean, you secretly come home from a trip early, your wife goes missing, and you claim to have been out at a cabin all alone with nobody to corroborate your story? How do you expect us to believe that? Especially given the fact that you have a track record of lying to us already?"

"I don't know how to prove it to you. But I didn't do anything to Wendy," he said, sounding miserable. "I'm telling you the truth."

"Where is this cabin of yours?" Spenser asked.

"Off Wilbanks Road," he replied. "It sits on a lot on the edge of the lake."

"Is this a Gilchrist family property?"

He shook his head again. "No, it's mine. It belongs to my family," he said softly. "I never told Wendy about it."

"Had to keep a secret love nest, huh?" Young chirped. "Yeah, you're doing a really good job of convincing me that you love your wife."

"I don't have to convince you of anything. You're either going to believe me or not," he said. "And frankly, I don't care either way."

"Why did you go out to your cabin?" Spenser asked.

"Because I wasn't supposed to be home from my trip," he replied. "I couldn't just show up at home early or Wendy probably would have known something was up."

"So, you holed up in your secret love nest," Young said.

"Can you stop calling it that? It's my family cabin," he growled. "It's where I go when I want to get away and clear my head for a while. It's my safe space and nobody knows about it but me. When she needs to decompress, Wendy goes off to… wherever she goes off to. And when I need to blow off steam, I go to my cabin. Having my own place isn't a crime."

"No," Spenser said. "It's not."

She took a drink from her bottle of water then twisted the cap back on, studying him closely. Spenser didn't see any sign of deception on his face. Nor did she hear it in his voice. She wasn't getting that hit off him she usually got when somebody was lying to her, or when she was sitting in the presence of a killer. She thought he was scum. Lying, cheating scum. She just wasn't sure that he was a murderer.

"I didn't do anything to Wendy, Sheriff. I know you don't understand, and I get why you don't believe me, but I love my wife," he said. "Our relationship is complicated and often frustrating. But I would never hurt her. Never in a million years."

"Okay, Mr. Ferry," Spenser said. "We're going to go check out your cabin. We'll see if we can put you there at the time your wife disappeared. I'll need your consent to search and your keys to get into the place."

"Take whatever you need," he said. "And you have my consent to search whatever you want to. I have absolutely nothing to hide."

"I hope that's true."

"It is."

"We'll see," Spenser said.

CHAPTER TWENTY-FOUR

"It's isolated," Young said. "I don't think he's got a neighbor closer than a mile."

As she climbed out of the Bronco, Spenser looked around the property. It was definitely isolated. That could account for nobody being able to confirm that he was there for those three missing days. Situated at the edge of a large, boggy lake, Brock's small cabin gave off a real Unabomber vibe and was perfect for somebody who wanted to get away from it all. Or for somebody who needed an unverifiable alibi.

A thin layer of mist hung over the surface of the lake and the morning sunlight glinted off the water. It was quiet out there. The silence was so heavy, it felt like it had a physical weight to it.

Spenser led Young to the faux-log cabin and walked up the three steps that led to a long, deep, covered porch. A pair of rocking chairs sat to their right, a small wooden table that looked to have been hand-carved was situated between them.

"It's peaceful out here," Young said. "I could get used to this sort of quiet."

Using the keys Brock had given her, Spenser unlocked the door and pushed it open. The hinges creaked sharply, and the door hit the wall behind it with a soft thump as Spenser crossed the threshold. The ground floor was one large room with an oversized fireplace to the right and a kitchen to the left. A large wooden table surrounded by four chairs sat just off the kitchen area and a large sofa and plush recliner sat on an area rug facing the fireplace.

A door across from Spenser stood part way open, revealing the bathroom behind it and to the right of that, a set of stairs led to a decently sized loft. From where she was, Spenser could see a bed and a giant flatscreen television sitting atop a dresser. The place was rustic but still had plenty of modern appliances and conveniences. It seemed like the sort of place for somebody who wanted to get away and be out amongst nature—but not without their creature comforts.

"So, what are we looking for exactly?" Young asked.

"Proof that he was here like he said," Spenser replied. "I have no idea what that might look like, though, so just keep your eyes peeled."

"Will do," Young said. "I'm going to start upstairs."

"Good. I'll poke around down here."

As Young headed up to the loft, Spenser began rummaging around on the main floor. She opened drawers and cupboards and looked in cabinets. She even went so far as to turn over the cushions on the sofa to see if anything was hiding underneath. But she came up empty. There was nothing to prove or disprove that Brock Ferry had been there recently. Spenser turned at the sound of Young descending the stairs.

"Anything up there?" Spenser asked.

"Porn. Lots and lots of porn," she said. "Magazines, DVDs—"

"I didn't realize they still made magazines," Spenser said. "Who buys magazines and DVDs these days? Doesn't the Internet have everything somebody's deviant heart could desire?"

"It does. But I'm thinking Wi-Fi isn't an option this far out in the sticks," Young confirmed. "So, he probably doesn't have any choice but to go old school."

Spenser shuddered. "I think we've spent far too much time considering this. Let's go ahead and move on to something else."

Young laughed. "There's not much else up there. Nothing out of the ordinary anyway," she said. "The bed's made, everything is tidy and put away. The only thing that suggests to me that Brock was here is the lack of dust. Everything's clean. It seems to me like things up in the loft were cleaned recently."

"That's a great observation," Spenser said, genuinely impressed.

Spenser looked around and saw that Young was right. There wasn't much dust anywhere. Not enough to suggest the cabin had been sitting vacant for a long period of time. The lack of dust and overall cleanliness and order of the place suggested to her that it had perhaps been occupied. Recently. It didn't clear Brock. But it suggested he hadn't lied to them about his whereabouts.

As Young poked around the main room, Spenser walked into the kitchen and opened up the refrigerator. There was beer, a jar of pickles, and other food that had a disturbingly long shelf life but not much else. Likewise, there wasn't much in the freezer other than ice cream and a few bags of vegetables. There was nothing fresh. Nothing to suggest that Brock had been cooking during the time he claimed to have been staying there. That wasn't much of a surprise, though. If he wasn't at the cabin for long stretches of time, there didn't seem to be much sense in stocking fresh food.

On a whim, Spenser walked over to the trash can, pulled the lid off, and smiled. Brock had apparently forgotten to take out the trash. She pulled a pair of black nitrile gloves out of her pocket and snapped them on then pulled the whole bag out of the can. Spenser carried it over to the large table in the dining room area and set it down.

"What did you find?" Young asked.

"Maybe nothing," Spenser said. "Just being thorough."

Spenser grabbed another trash bag from under the sink and laid it out on the table then dumped the full bag out on top of it. Young's nose wrinkled as she grimaced.

"That is quite the pungent aroma," she said.

"Tell me about it."

They picked through the fast-food wrappers and scraps of meat and buns left behind to rot. The fact that the food was still in the process of rotting told Spenser it was more likely than not that Brock was telling them the truth and that he had been there when he said he was. She looked up at Young and saw that she seemed to be coming to the same conclusion. Spenser plucked a receipt that was stained with grease and ketchup out of the mess on the table and looked at the information printed on it.

"Well, I guess this confirms it," Spenser said and handed the receipt to Young.

The date and time stamp on the receipt showed it had been purchased and paid for in cash on the day Wendy had gone missing. Assuming it was Brock who picked up the fast food, and Spenser had no reason to believe it wasn't, the receipt corroborated his alibi. Spenser dug around a little more and came away with a couple more receipts, one from a grocery store and another from a gas station that fleshed out the timeline. Brock had indeed been at the cabin for the three days after he'd left San Francisco.

"Well, damn," Young said. "I was sure he was guilty."

Spenser stared through the window and looked at the woods beyond. The trees were densely packed, their limbs spread out wide and cast the floor of the forest in thick, inky shadows. Her mind raced and she pursed her lips as she looked at the way the trees seemed to stretch on into the distance forever. That's when an idea occurred to her.

"You know, just because he was here doesn't mean he still didn't do something to Wendy," Spenser said. "Both things can be true."

"What are you thinking?"

"Follow me."

Spenser led Young out onto the porch where they paused and looked around. She walked down the three steps to the soft ground and together, they made a slow circuit around the cabin, looking for disturbed ground. Spenser didn't see what she was looking for but when they returned to the spot from where they'd started, she stopped and turned to Young, then gestured to the forest that was all around them.

"What do you see out there?" Spenser asked.

Young looked at her curiously. "Woods? Trees?"

"A lot of places you might be able to hide a body," Spenser replied.

The light bulb went off in Young's head and she nodded. "Brilliant."

"Call the office and have Alice send us a few deputies. Also, have her send Arbery and his team. Also, see if we can get a cadaver dog or two if you can," Spenser said. "Get them out here as quickly as they can."

"On it."

Young walked off to make the call, leaving Spenser standing where she was, staring out at the dimly lit forest floor. Finding anything out there was a long shot. But even a long shot was better than no shot. It was well within the realm of possibility that her team might find a disturbed bit of ground or some other telltale sign of a shallow grave. It was grim work. But it was work that needed to be done.

"I hope you're not out there, Wendy," Spenser said. "But if you are, we're going to find you. I give you my word."

CHAPTER TWENTY-FIVE

"BLESS YOU," SPENSER SAID. "YOU ARE AN ABSOLUTE saint among mankind."

"I'm not sure coffee will qualify me for sainthood," Ryker replied.

He set the cartons of coffee he'd brought on the table in the conference room. From the other box, he pulled out creamer, sugar, and all the fixings he'd brought along as well.

"Coffee might not qualify you," Young said. "But these pastries just might. I'll be sure to write to the Vatican and petition the Pope myself."

Ryker smiled as Young tore into the pastry she'd plucked from the box. Spenser quickly fixed a cup of coffee for herself then sank back into her chair and took a swallow of the hot liquid, sighing contentedly. Ryker dropped into the chair to her right and looked at her with a frown crossing his lips.

"You look tired," he said.

"Tired doesn't quite cover it," she replied. "Exhausted. Worn out. Bone weary—"

"And cold," Young added. "I'm not sure how long it's going to take us to thaw out."

"The coffee is helping," Spenser said. "I also need a shower. I'm filthy and I stink."

Ryker grinned. "I wasn't going to say anything, but since you brought it up…"

She threw a wadded-up napkin at him and laughed. "You suck," she said. "Also, thank you for watching Annabelle these last couple of days."

"Happy to do it. Mocha's been happy to have somebody to play with other than me."

For the last couple of days, Spenser had her team out in the field. They searched the area around Brock's cabin, looking in every bush, under every rock, and every other conceivable place they could think of, but hadn't come up with a body. The last forty-eight hours had been a total and complete bust. A big ol' swing and a miss. They'd suffered out there in the damp, cold forest with almost no sleep, searching for Wendy's body, and had absolutely nothing to show for it.

On the one hand, Spenser was glad they hadn't found Wendy's moldering corpse. It kept alive the slim possibility that she was still out there somewhere living her life. On the other hand, it continued the most frustrating case she'd ever caught in her entire law enforcement career. She was like Schrodinger's Cat—somehow dead and alive at the same time.

"I owe you," Spenser said.

"Nah," he replied. "Like I said, I'm always happy to have Annabelle stay over."

"Thank you," she said.

"You're welcome," he replied. "So, no luck out there, huh?"

"Zero. Zip. Zilch. Nada," Young chirped.

"That about covers it," Spenser replied then took another drink of her coffee.

"So, what's your next move?"

"We have to lay off Brock. We've got nothing on him," Spenser said grumpily. "As for what comes next, I need a shower and some sleep before I can answer that."

"Do you think he did something to Wendy?" Ryker asked.

Spenser frowned and cupped her hands around the coffee cup, leaching the warmth from it.

"Honestly? I don't. He's a lying, cheating scumbag, but in some weird way, I think he actually does love her. And I don't think he'd hurt her," she replied. "But we had to go out there and dig around just to be sure."

"The sheriff is a romantic and a big ol' sap," Young said with a grin. "I don't take as charitable a view as she does. I still think if something did happen to Wendy, we're going to eventually find something that proves Brock Ferry is up to his eyeballs in it."

"Amanda is not nearly as cynical as she pretends to be," Spenser said. "She's just really invested in Brock being our guy—mostly because she doesn't like being wrong."

"That's true. I don't," Young said. "But by the same token, neither do you."

"She's got you there," Ryker said. "What makes you think it's Brock, Amanda?"

"Because I don't believe he loves Wendy. I think he's using her," she replied. "And prenup or not, I think he stands to gain a lot more if she's dead than we know just yet. I'm waiting for my brother to turn something up—and I'm almost positive he will."

"Oh, talk about excellent timing," Jacob said cheerily as he walked into the conference room. "I couldn't have planned that better myself."

Jacob strolled in and set his laptop down on the table then grabbed a pastry from the box and took a bite as he sat down.

"Good stuff," he said. "Thank you, Ryker."

"No problem."

"Okay, so, what did you find?" Spenser asked.

"Right, so, it seems that Brock Ferry, despite his prenup limiting him to that one-hundred-thousand-dollar payout—"

"A payout he was not going to get if Wendy knew about his affair," Young added.

"Right," Jacob said. "Aside from that, it seems he's been building himself a pretty nice payday. He seems to have had an exit strategy all along."

"Explain," Spenser said.

"I found an offshore account in his name. I can't prove it yet, but it feels a lot like he's been skimming off the company coffers and stashing it there," Jacob said.

"How much is in the account?" Young asked.

"A little over three hundred thousand at present," he replied. "But again, I haven't been able to trace back the payments yet, so for all I know right now, it's all above board and legit."

"I somehow doubt that," Young said. "If it was legit, why is it in an offshore account?"

"It's shady as hell," Spenser said. "But Jacob is right. Until we can prove he's skimming and stashing, it's suggestive and interesting, but not actionable."

"If I can pose a question," Ryker chimes in. "If he was skimming off the company coffers and stashing it in some offshore account, why would he put the account in his own name? That seems rather… stupid."

"Brock isn't dumb, but he's definitely not a criminal mastermind. I can see him doing something that stupid simply because he wouldn't think we'd find it," Young said.

"Yeah. Maybe," Ryker said.

Spenser sat back in her chair and pondered the questions swirling around in her head. Ryker and Young were both right. Brock wasn't a criminal mastermind. He also didn't seem stupid enough to do something that obvious. Opening an account in his own name and stashing ill-gotten funds there seemed ridiculously dumb. But then, Spenser had always believed that criminals were dumb and were often prone to making stupid mistakes like that either out of ignorance or hubris. As she thought about it, though, another, simpler question occurred to her.

"How did he get access to the money in the first place?" Spenser asked.

"What do you mean?" Young asked.

"If he's skimming money, how is he getting access to it?" Spenser repeated. "He's not one of the company's money men. He's what, a glorified marketing or PR agent? So, how is he getting access to the money he's skimming?"

"I think it's likely he's got an accomplice," Young said. "Somebody who can move money around for the company who's helping him siphon some off for himself."

"Yeah, maybe so," Spenser said thoughtfully. "Talk to some of the people at the company. Do some sniffing around and see if you can figure out who his accomplice might be."

"You got it," Young said as her eyes widened and a strange look crossed her face. "Heads up. Aspen Gilchrist is coming in hot."

Spenser had just processed what Young said when Aspen burst into the conference room. Her pale cheeks were flushed, her blue eyes glittered with barely controlled rage, and the set of her body was tight, vibrating with anger. She planted her fists on her hips and stared Spenser down. Everyone shifted in their seats uncomfortably.

"I just saw Brock at the house," she started, her voice as tight as the set of her body. "I thought you arrested him, Sheriff. What is he doing out?"

"Okay, first of all, you don't just barge into my office," Spenser growled as she got to her feet. "And frankly, I don't care what your last name is, I will not tolerate you storming into my office like you own the place."

"Oh, but I can. My last name guarantees that I can own this place if I want. Need I remind you, Sheriff, that your position is elected?" she sneered.

"I'm well aware of that fact, Aspen," Spenser said. "But guess what? I don't care. Nobody is going to tell me how to run my department. And nobody is going to disrespect me or the officers who work under me. We work for the people of this town. Not for any one family, no matter how rich or well-connected. If you want to talk to me, you call. You don't just barge in here. Am I clear?"

Aspen glared hard at her and looked like she was going to threaten and try to throw her weight around further but eventually backed off under Spenser's withering gaze. She patted her black hair and quickly composed herself.

"I apologize, Sheriff," Aspen said. "It was just a little upsetting to see Brock back at home after I assumed he had been arrested."

"Officially, we brought him in for questioning," Spenser said. "We couldn't hold him, though, because we have nothing to charge him with. We cannot prove he did anything to your mother. Unfortunately, gut feelings or hunches do not equal proof."

"But he lied about where he was—about having an affair," she said.

"He did lie initially. But then he told us to further conceal his affair, he hid out at his cabin," Spenser told her.

"Cabin?"

Spenser nodded. "Brock has a family cabin he apparently never disclosed to your mother. He says he goes there to get away sometimes. And he said he was there for the three days he was supposed to be in California."

"And you believe him?"

"The evidence we found at the cabin corroborates it," Spenser said gently. "He hid out there because he believed your mother was at the house and if he came home early, she would know he was cheating on her. I've even had my team out there searching the woods for the last couple of days, Aspen. We didn't find anything. And certainly, nothing implicating Brock in your mother's disappearance."

Aspen took a moment, seeming to process what Spenser had just told her. "But he had to have done something to her," she said softly as if the words she was speaking didn't quite compute for her.

"We're still running down leads and looking into a few things. We're not giving up on this, Aspen," Spenser said. "We will not stop looking until we know what happened to your mother. I promise you that."

"It's him. It has to be him," she said.

"And if it is, we will find out and arrest him," Spenser said. "But for now, go home. Be with your sister. She needs you. And I swear that I will call you the moment we know anything."

Aspen nodded absently, a numb look on her face. But she turned and walked out of the conference room without another word, leaving Spenser and everybody else to watch her go.

"That girl is more invested in Brock Ferry being guilty than even Amanda is," Jacob said.

"Yeah, but you can't help but understand it. She needs somebody to blame," Ryker said.

Through the window in the conference room wall, Spenser watched Aspen walk through the front doors and into the afternoon beyond, once again wondering why the girl was so strident in her belief that her stepfather was responsible for whatever happened to her mother.

CHAPTER TWENTY-SIX

"Sorry to call you so early," Young said. "But I figured you'd want to be here."

"You figured right," Spenser said.

They stood on a narrow dirt road that bisected fenced-in fields of the Beal Dairy Farm. Cows wandered the fields, some grazing, some looking at them. The sun had barely crested the horizon to the east, its golden rays chasing away the dark purple and blue hues of the night. A soft breeze rustled the tall grass in the field beside them, carrying the rancid and unmistakable odor of death. Thick, scattered clouds overhead were painted in vivid shades of red and orange as dawn began to assert itself, signaling

THE LIES IN THE FALLS

the start of a new day. And with the new day, the answers they had been seeking were hopefully coming along with it.

Young leaned against the hood of the Bronco and gestured over to an older man standing with Deputy Summers. He held a leash, the Golden Retriever on the other end of it sitting patiently beside him. The man was visibly shaken, and Summers appeared to be trying to comfort him. A pair of cruisers were parked on the dirt road ahead of the Bronco, their blue and white emergency lights flashing. The boxy white cargo van that belonged to Noah Arbery parked near the cruisers told her they were indeed dealing with a dead body.

"What do we know so far?" Spenser asked.

"This property belongs to Larry Beal," Young said. "He called in a dead body in his well early this morning. Summers was on duty when the call came in. She drove out here to check it out and sure enough, she found a body in the well. That's all I know at this point."

Spenser felt like a bowling ball had landed in the pit of her stomach. It was news she'd been expecting. But even expecting it didn't keep it from feeling like a hammer blow to the midsection. She took a minute to collect herself and swallowed hard.

"Do we know who it is yet?" Spenser asked.

"I mean, I think we can probably hazard a guess," Young said. "But until Arbery gets the body out of the well, we can't say for certain. Not officially anyway."

"Right," Spenser muttered. "Okay, well, let's go talk to Beal and see if we can start piecing this all together."

Spenser and Young walked over to Summers and Beal. The younger deputy gave Spenser a nod then walked over to where Arbery and his team were working to get the body out of the well. Beal was a tall, rail-thin man in his early sixties with ebony skin and a full head of silver hair. His hands shook and he had a haunted look in his eyes that told Spenser he was not familiar or comfortable with seeing dead bodies.

"Mr. Beal," Spenser said. "Good morning."

"Not sure if I'd call it good," he grumbled, his voice deep and resonant.

"Of course," Spenser said then smiled down at the dog who looked up at her and wagged its tail. "And who is this?"

"This here's Winston," he said.

Spenser crouched down and scratched Winston behind his ears. He wiggled and panted, his tongue lolling out the side of his mouth, enjoying the affection as much as Annabelle did. Winston licked her face, making Spenser laugh.

"He likes you," Beal said.

"I like him," Spenser replied. "I'm a big fan of dogs."

She stood up again and as she glanced over at Arbery and his team, the smile on her face faded as the gravity of the situation sunk in all over again.

"Is this all your land, Mr. Beal?" Spenser asked.

He nodded. "Been in my family since before I was born. We ain't a big operation but we've managed to do our thing for decades now."

"Can you walk me through what happened this morning? How is it you came to discover—what you discovered?" Spenser asked.

"I'm an early riser—always wake up before the sun to walk Winston here then turn the cows out to let them do their thing," he told her. "Anyway, we were walking down this road here on account of I saw a car that shouldn't have been here last night—"

"You saw a car out here?" Spenser interrupted. "Around what time was that?"

"It was a little after one, I suppose," he said. "I have trouble sleepin' through the night anymore. My bladder has me up a few times a night and all."

"Can you describe the car?" Young asked.

He shook his head. "Unfortunately, I can't. Didn't have my glasses on and I can't see much without them. I just saw the taillights."

"This is private land, isn't it?" Young asked.

"Yes ma'am. But every now and then, people get turned around out here. If they don't cause me no trouble, I see no reason to cause them trouble," he said. "Honestly, I didn't think nothin' of it. They eventually moved on and I went back to bed."

THE LIES IN THE FALLS

The breeze carried the scent of decomposing flesh combined with the pungent stench of cow manure so thick, Spenser had to cover her nose. Beal chuckled.

"City girl, huh?" he asked.

"Afraid so," she replied with a wry grin then took a beat to compose herself. "So, what led you down here this morning?"

"Well, like I was sayin', I took Winston out on his mornin' walk. We came down here on account of I wanted to check the fences to make sure whoever was out here last night didn't cut 'em or nothin'. Kids do that sometimes... some of these environmental groups don't think cows should be fenced in or used for milkin' or some such nonsense," he said scornfully. "Anyways, when we got down here, Winston started actin' all squirrely. We went through the gate and into the field and he made a beeline for the well. I saw right away the lid had been pried off and when I got closer, I smelled it. You don't mistake that smell for nothin' else."

"No, you don't," Spenser agreed.

"Anyways, I wasn't sure what had gotten down in there, so I pushed the lid off the well and shined my flashlight down there. That's when I saw her," he said. "After I caught my breath, I called your department straight away and... well... here we are."

"Here we are," Spenser repeated with a grimace. "So, there's nothing you can tell us about the car that was out here last night, Mr. Beal? Didn't recognize it or..."

He shook his head. "I wish I could tell you more, Sheriff. Believe me. I'd love to be able to help catch whoever did this terrible business here."

Spenser looked over to see that Arbery and his people were pulling the body out of the well. They laid it gently down on a tarp they'd laid out on the ground beside it. She turned back to Beal.

"Okay, Mr. Beal, we appreciate all your help," Spenser said. "We're going to do our thing here, so feel free to head back up to your house. We'll call you if we've got follow-up questions."

He nodded and looked eager to be away from the scene. He tipped his hat to her and quickly turned away, ushering Winston along with him as they scurried back up the road toward the large house that sat at the end of it. With Beal on his way, Spenser turned and led Young over to the old brick and wood well that sat crumbling and decaying near the fence at the edge of his property—a relic of a bygone era.

"Jesus," Spenser muttered.

On the ground at their feet, the remains of a woman were stretched out on the blue plastic tarp Arbery had spread out. Her eyes bulged in their sockets, her body gray, waxy, and bloated, and her skin was beginning to slough off. Despite the decomposition that was ravaging her body it was clear to see the signs of violence that had claimed her life. She had a ragged wound cut so deep into her neck it nearly reached her spine.

"Damn, she was almost beheaded," Young said.

Spenser said nothing but continued to study the corpse at her feet. In addition to the wound in her neck, smaller puncture wounds dotted her body. Spenser lost count after thirty. She'd have to rely on Doctor Swift to give her the accurate and final count. Her gaze drifted back up to the woman's wide, bulging eyes. Her mouth hung open, her face forever frozen in a rictus of the fear and agony that had gripped her in the final moments of her life.

Spenser raised her gaze to Young. "This is Wendy Gilchrist, I assume?"

She nodded. "It is."

They stared at the woman's corpse in silence for a few moments, each of them lost in their own thoughts. Spenser would need Doc Swift to confirm it, but given the condition of her body, she was relatively certain that Wendy had been dead the entire time they'd been looking for her. Dead even before whoever was dressed like her had boarded that train to Connecticut. Wendy Gilchrist had been murdered and under their noses the whole time. And whoever had done it went to great lengths to throw them off the scent.

"This took a lot of anger," Spenser mused, her tone tinged with sadness. "This took a lot of anger and a lot of hate."

"She may have ruffled some feathers in her time, but I honestly can't think of anybody who hated Wendy enough to do… this," Young said. "Who could have done this?"

"That's what we're going to find out," Spenser replied.

CHAPTER TWENTY-SEVEN

"**A**RE YOU OKAY?"

Spenser looked up from her plate and nodded. Ryker was looking back at her with an expression of gentle concern on his face. She offered him a wan smile.

"Yeah, I'm fine," she said.

"You don't look fine."

She shrugged. "I'm fine. I mean, it's not like I knew her."

"That doesn't mean somebody's death doesn't impact you," he said. "It's never easy to see the things you see, Spense. Go easy on yourself."

"I guess I'm just disappointed," she replied. "I mean, I knew the likelihood of finding her alive was slim. But I guess deep down, I was hoping for a different outcome. I guess I was hoping she really was off somewhere getting her head on straight."

She cast a glance around their table, making sure nobody was listening in. To that point, they had kept a lid on the discovery of Wendy Gilchrist's body. Spenser didn't want word leaking until they'd processed the body and had collected any forensic evidence that remained on it. She wasn't optimistic about there being much left since the water in the well would have likely washed away much of anything that might have been there.

"Have you notified the daughters yet?" Ryker asked.

She shook her head. "I wanted to be done processing all the forensics before we let them know," she said softly. "I want to be able to turn the body over to them for burial as quickly as possible. As corny as it sounds, I want them to be able to start healing."

"That doesn't sound corny. It sounds like somebody with a caring heart."

Spenser pushed the food around her plate, her appetite mostly non-existent. After finishing his errands and tending to his store, Ryker had shown up at the office late in the afternoon and asked her to dinner. Wanting to get away from the madness for a while, Spenser had quickly agreed and accompanied him to one of the better seafood restaurants in town. Once they'd gotten there and had ordered their food, though, Spenser found that she wasn't all that hungry. But knowing she'd need the fuel the food would give her for what was to come yet—and to keep from being rude and wasteful—she'd forced herself to eat most of what was on her plate.

She set down her fork and picked up her wine glass, taking a sip as she sat back in her chair. She'd tried to keep the mood light and the focus of the evening away from work, but the details of the case wouldn't let up. The image of Wendy Gilchrist's gray, bloated face and that ragged, deep neck wound wouldn't stop scrolling through her mind. It wasn't the grisliest crime scene she'd ever seen—not by a long shot. But something about Wendy's death was sticking with her in ways others in her career hadn't. Why that was, Spenser had no clue.

"What's bothering you about the case?" Ryker asked.

"What makes you think something's bothering me?"

He gave Spenser a wry grin. "Because I know you, Spenser Song. I can see it on your face."

She laughed softly. "I'm not sure I'm comfortable with anybody knowing me that well."

"Well, you're going to have to get used to it, I'm afraid," he said.

"It's something that Larry Beal, the dairy farmer, told us—"

Spenser took another sip of wine, giving herself a moment to organize her thoughts. She replayed the conversation with Beal in her mind again. It was a conversation she'd thought about so much since that morning, she knew it verbatim and always got hung up on the same thing. She took another drink then set her glass down.

"Beal said that he woke up around one that morning and saw a car stopped on the road out by the well where we found Wendy," Spenser said. "I don't know for sure, but it got me wondering if the killer dumped the body in the well that night."

"It might have just been somebody that got turned around out there," Ryker offered.

"Yeah. That's what Mr. Beal thought as well. And maybe that's right," she replied. "But my gut is telling me the two are connected."

Ryker sipped his wine and looked at her thoughtfully. "Okay, walk me through this. What makes you think they're connected?"

Spenser gnawed on her bottom lip for a moment then sat forward. "It seems obvious that Wendy was killed somewhere else. I don't think she was attacked at the well. So, if she was killed somewhere else, the killer would have needed to dispose of her body," she said. "Sticking her in an unused well at the edge of a field would be a good place to do it."

"But why now?"

"Maybe the killer had to wait to dispose of her for some reason. Maybe he couldn't risk moving her until now," Spenser said. "It just strikes me as a strange coincidence for Mr. Beal to see a car stopped right out by his well mere hours before he found her."

Ryker paused and seemed to be considering her words. Spenser had nothing to back that thought up yet. She had no hard evidence.

"Given the decomp of the body, wherever she was being kept is likely going to have some evidence of that," Spenser said. "There's likely going to be fluid from the body seeping and skin from the slough."

Ryker grimaced then chuckled to himself. "You make the most stimulating dinner conversation, my friend."

Spenser returned a smile. "Sorry. I've been focused on this all night instead of just enjoying the break and time with you."

"No, it's all right. I'm just teasing you," he replied. "I can see how much this is bothering you. You need to figure this out. I'm glad you trust me enough to talk it out with me."

"Aside from Amanda, you might be the only person I can talk this out with," she told him. "You always have a great perspective and insights. You help me see things in ways I often don't."

"You don't give yourself enough credit. You're brilliant in your own right, Spenser."

"That's sweet of you to say. But one thing I've learned is that I don't have all the answers and I always need fresh perspectives."

"And that's one reason I say you're brilliant."

She smiled at him and they enjoyed the companionable silence that spun out between them for a few moments.

"Okay, so what's your next move?" he asked.

"I'm waiting for Arbery to give me his findings. Once we have that, we will hopefully have some idea who our killer might be," Spenser said. "Either way, I'm going to have to go out to inform Aspen and Dallas. I've already got a warrant in the works to search the Gilchrist house. If there are traces of blood or decomp, we're going to find them."

"And if there's nothing there? Or if Arbery doesn't find anything useful?"

"Then we're totally screwed. We'll be back at square one and no closer to finding out who killed her," Spenser said.

"You are going to figure this out," Ryker said. "I've seen you do a lot more with a lot less."

"I appreciate your confidence in me. I just don't know about this one."

"Have faith in yourself. You're too stubborn to fail."

"I wish I had a fraction of the confidence you have in me," she said, then paused. Ryker reached across the table and gave her hand a gentle squeeze. The sincere compassion and care she saw in his eyes made her heart swell to the point she thought it might burst and she found herself reflecting on their journey together to that point.

"You know, you didn't like me very much when we first met," Spenser said.

"But I like you now. And that's what matters," he replied with a grin.

"And I like you, too. A lot," she said then quickly clamped her jaw shut, shocked she'd heard those words come out of her mouth.

Ryker squeezed her hand again and smiled softly. Spenser felt her heart fluttering in her breast as a shaky smile crossed her lips.

"Let's get out of here. And let's put thoughts of the case out of your head for a while," he said. "Maybe unplugging from it for a while will help you see more clearly in the morning."

"That sounds like a wonderful idea to me," she said with a warm smile and her heart thundering in her chest. "And you might just be right about that."

CHAPTER TWENTY-EIGHT

"Looks like somebody had a nice evening," Young said.

"What are you talking about?"

"I'm talking about that sparkle in your eye and that glow in your cheeks," she replied.

Spenser laughed. "Oh my God, shut up. That's not even true."

"It's very true," she said. "You also don't seem able to make eye contact with me, which, oh by the way, is another dead giveaway."

Spenser's face was hot, and she struggled to keep the stupid schoolgirl smile off her lips. She focused on the road and tried to ignore the woman in the passenger seat grinning at her like a fool. Spenser refrained from saying anything because Young was clever enough to twist whatever came out of her mouth into some suggestive double entendre.

"So, I take it you and Ryker had a nice dinner last night?" Young asked.

"We did," Spenser replied cautiously.

"And how was... dessert?"

"Don't make me fire you," Spenser said as her cheeks burned like they were on fire. "It wasn't like that. There was no walk of shame involved."

"No? Are you sure about that?"

"I'm very sure about that. After dinner, we went back to his place, had a few glasses of wine, and talked," she said. "Then I went home. Alone."

Young sighed dramatically as she rolled her eyes and threw her hands in the air. "What am I going to do with you? It's all right there for the taking, woman!"

"You sound exactly like Marley right now."

"We only want the best for you," Young said.

"Which I appreciate. But we're taking things very slowly. That's by design. Neither of us wants to jump into something we're not ready for. We're enjoying spending time together and getting to know each other."

"You realize at the rate you two are going, you're both going to be too old to enjoy spending naked time together—not without breaking a hip or something."

Spenser laughed and shook her head. "We're going to be just fine. I promise you. But sex isn't high on our list of priorities right now. We want to be smart about things."

Young blew out another breath and laughed. "All right. That's fair. I'll stop hassling you about it for now. On the other hand, I make no promises about tomorrow."

"I appreciate your consideration—as well as your concern for my love life."

"I take my duties as your undersheriff seriously."

"I wasn't aware monitoring my love life was one of your duties."

"You should probably read the job description more thoroughly then."

Spenser laughed as she pulled into the lot behind Doctor Swift's clinic and parked. Almost immediately, her good humor vanished, and the smile fell from her lips. She glanced at Young who seemed to be having the same reaction. Her expression was as grim as the one on her own face felt. They climbed out of the Bronco and headed across the lot to the back door of the clinic.

Doctor Swift was already waiting for them when they stepped through the doors. His face was pensive, his body stiff. Rather than his normal prissy, impatient, and disdainful look, Swift's expression was even darker and grimmer than the one on Young's face. It wasn't difficult for Spenser to see he was taking the case personally. That it was hitting him hard. She didn't need to ask if he was friends with Wendy. She could see it all over his face.

"Good morning, Sheriff Song," he said, then nodded a greeting to Young. "Undersheriff."

"How are you holding up, Doctor Swift?" Spenser asked.

He shook his head. "This is a terrible business we're in."

"I can't disagree with you."

"I've known Wendy for close to forty years," he said, his voice thick with emotion. "She could be a hard woman, but she was kind at heart. She didn't deserve to die like this."

"No. No, she didn't," Spenser replied softly. "Nobody does."

"Indeed," he said, then took a beat to gather himself. "Please. Come into the autopsy suite. Mr. Arbery is already here."

Without waiting for a reply, he turned and walked through the door and into the autopsy suite. Spenser led Young into the room. Mostly stainless steel and white tile, the room was cold and sterile, a room that was lifeless. Spenser had never felt comfortable in morgues. The air never seemed to move and even when you spoke in a normal tone of voice, it sounded like a whisper. It was as if the dead housed within the bank of refrigerated drawers on the far side of the room were somehow stealing both the oxygen and sound around them.

On the steel table in the center of the room, Wendy Gilchrist's body lay beneath a sheet. Swift had stitched the gaping wound in Wendy's neck, leaving a raised, puffy scar that looked a lot like something off Frankenstein's monster. The puckered skin from the sutures Swift had stitched in after performing the autopsy poked out from beneath the covering. Her skin was still gray and waxy, her body still bloated, and her eyes were wide open, fixed on a point far beyond this world. Doctor Swift had managed to close her mouth which helped erase the look of terror that had been etched into her features when they'd pulled her out of the well.

"Sheriff," Arbery solemnly greeted her. "Undersheriff."

"Good morning, Doctor Arbery."

Her forensic examiner stood on the other side of the table and was joined by Swift. The two men looked down at Wendy, matching frowns on their faces, as a heaviness settled down over the room so thick, it was almost suffocating.

"I know this is difficult, but it's imperative we put aside our feelings and keep our professional focus," Spenser said. "I didn't know Wendy, but I get the idea she would have demanded no less. And she deserves that. All victims do. Now, let's get our heads on straight and figure out who did this."

"Agreed," Swift said with a firm nod.

"Okay, good. What do we know, gentlemen?" Spenser asked.

"I can say with relative certainty that the neck wound was the fatal blow," Swift reported soberly. "It was a complete severing of the carotid artery—the killer almost beheaded her…"

His voice, still thick with emotion, trailed off and he took a moment to gather himself. A moment Spenser was more than happy to give him. It was the first time Spenser had seen Swift display any emotion other than annoyance, and she found the experience somewhat disconcerting. It humanized him in a way she didn't think possible. Swift cleared his throat and ran a hand over his face before raising his gaze again.

"Excuse me," Swift said. "As I was saying, exsanguination would have occurred within minutes. The rest of the stab wounds—forty-seven in all—appeared to have been post-mortem. Or at least, very close to the time of death."

"The neck was cut from behind, going right to left, which would seem to indicate the killer is left-handed," Arbery said. "I also do not believe she was in that well for very long. In fact, based on my examination, I'd say she was dropped in just before her body was discovered."

That jibed with Spenser's thinking about Beal seeing the killer depositing Wendy's body into his well a few hours before he'd found her. It still left a host of questions unanswered, the most prominent of them being the question Ryker had posed over dinner: Why now? Why did the killer sit on Wendy's body for all those days before running the risk of moving her? Why not leave her where she was?

As Spenser listened to Swift and Arbery alternating telling her what they'd found, she considered the questions running around in her head. And all roads kept coming back to Brock Ferry. As she pondered the question of why risk moving Wendy now, she thought perhaps he felt the walls starting to close in on him. He wasn't a stupid man and had to know they would search the house at some point. Perhaps he was trying to act preemptively by getting rid of the body in a place he believed she wouldn't likely be found.

As those thoughts fired through her mind, Spenser tried to pump the brakes. She feared she was putting the blinders on—the same blinders she'd admonished Aspen and Dallas for wearing. In any investigation, Spenser always strove to keep an open mind. To never focus in on any one person until the evidence was incontrovertible. And that wasn't the case at the moment. Still, she kept thinking back to everything Brock had said and done from the start, and in her mind, it was making him look guiltier than sin.

"We did not find any skin beneath the fingernails. Which unfortunately means we're not going to have blood DNA to compare with any potential suspects," Swift said.

"That makes sense if she had her throat cut from behind," Spenser said. "There wouldn't have been much of a struggle."

"Right," he said sadly. "Likely not."

"We did, however, find several hairs caught in her clothing," Arbery said. "Unfortunately, there were no follicles attached to the strands, so again, no DNA."

Not having any DNA to compare was a major blow. DNA was the gold standard and the sort of incontrovertible evidence that locked down most any case. Not having it was a blow, but it wasn't fatal. There were still other ways they could connect a suspect to a murder.

"What color is the hair you found, Dr. Arbery?" Spenser asked.

"Blonde," he replied. "I know you're thinking they may be a match to Wendy's husband, and they very well may be, but they could have been on her body through a simple transference. They live in the same house, so it's very likely she picked them up through normal, everyday activity."

"It's possible," Spenser agreed. "But is it possible she picked them up in a struggle? Could she have pulled them out herself?"

"It's possible, of course," Arbery said. "But if that were to be the case, I would have expected to find follicles attached to the strands."

"But it is possible to tear out strands of hair and not get the follicles along with it, right?"

"Certainly. It's possible."

"Good. That's all I need then," Spenser said. "Drs. Arbery and Swift, please go over the body and all her clothing again. See if you can find anything else we can use. Anything at all."

Swift nodded. "We will."

"What's next on your to-do list, Sheriff?" Young asked.

"We're going to scoop up Brock again and throw him in the box. If we don't have DNA, we're going to need a confession," Spenser said. "So, we're going to go lean on Brock as hard as we can to see if we can't get him to crack."

"Good. Finally," Young replied. "I've been looking forward to this for a while now."

"Good. Then let's do it."

CHAPTER TWENTY-NINE

THE HOUSE AROUND THEM WAS IN CHAOS. EVERY DEPUTY on duty was in the Gilchrist home. Spenser had ordered them to search every nook, every cranny, and every space in between looking for anything that could conceivably be considered evidence. Arbery and his team were doing the same. Rather than searching for evidence, though, Spenser had tasked them with searching for evidence of a crime scene. She needed to find some proof that Wendy had been killed in that house.

As they were executing their search warrant, Spenser had called Aspen, who was up at school, and asked her to bring Dallas to the house. It was time she delivered the bad news and told them where they were with the investigation. Standing there, looking them in the eye, Spenser felt her mouth grow dry and her stomach churn. Delivering a death notice was never easy. But something about delivering it to two girls who were so young, knowing they were now alone in the world, made this one even more difficult.

"Girls," Spenser said. "Thank you for coming out and meeting with me. And I'm sorry for the chaos here at the house."

"Of course," Aspen said. "I trust you have some news."

"It's not going to be good news. Not if she's meeting us in person," Dallas added.

Spenser stood on one side of the island in the kitchen while Aspen and Dallas stood on the other. Their faces were pale, eyes wide, and wore matching expressions of trepidation. After Spenser and her men had taken hold of Brock, cuffed him, and threw him into the back of their cruiser. She had Young escort the man as he yelled, screamed, and protested his innocence down to the station and threw him into an interrogation room. She'd told Young to babysit him. To let him cool his heels in the box until she was ready to talk to him.

"I'm afraid it's not good news," she said softly. "We've found your mother."

The girls exchanged a look, a myriad of emotions crossing their faces in the blink of an eye. Aspen's eyes shimmered and welled with tears. Dallas lowered her gaze and stared at the countertop, her face tight, dark, and unreadable. Unlike her older sister, Dallas didn't wear her heart on her sleeve and was better able to conceal her emotions.

"She's dead, isn't she?" Aspen asked.

"I'm so very sorry, but I'm afraid so," Spenser said gently.

Aspen grabbed her sister's hand, and they stood in silence with their heads down. Spenser gave the girls a moment to process it. After a couple of minutes, Aspen, still clutching her sister's hand, raised her gaze. Her cheeks were wet with tears as they streamed down her face. Dallas' expression was blank.

"I assume since I don't see Brock here that you've finally arrested him?" Dallas finally said.

"Based on new evidence, we are detaining him again for questioning," Spenser said. "But I need to caution you that we don't have a proverbial smoking gun. It is still possible that we are going to have to release him. It's also still very possible he didn't kill your mother."

They both shook their heads in unison. "He did it, Sheriff," Aspen said. "I know it with every fiber of my being. He was cheating on her and he knew if she found out, he was going to get nothing, so he killed her. I know that as sure as I know my name."

"And believe me, if the evidence bears that out, he will be prosecuted to the fullest extent of the law. I'll give you my word."

"What new evidence?" Dallas asked.

"I'm afraid I can't discuss the particulars of an ongoing investigation," Spenser told her.

"Sheriff, please. We need to know," Dallas replied with the first hint of emotion in her voice that Spenser had heard.

Spenser sighed and looked off for a moment, trying to put some order to her thoughts. She couldn't compromise the integrity of the investigation by giving them all the details, but she could see how desperate they were for some bit of information and felt the cold stab of guilt. She gave it a little more thought then nodded to herself. There was a way she could split the difference.

"I can't give you specifics," Spenser said. "But let me just say we've developed some forensic evidence as well as proof of a potential financial motive that has led us to reconsider Brock. What we've found is what led us to bring him in for further questioning."

The girls shared another look, some bit of silent communication passing between them. Their expressions were unreadable to Spenser, but she had no doubt being as close as they were, the girls had their own language. She didn't doubt they knew what the other was thinking without having to use words. After a moment, they both turned back to Spenser.

"A financial motive?" Aspen asked.

"Yes. I'm afraid I can't tell you more than that right now, but we believe this financial angle we've uncovered is a solid motive—especially if your mother had tumbled onto it," Spenser said. "Again, though, I need to caution you to manage your expectations. It's still possible these leads we're following end up not panning out. May not be what it looks to be at first blush. So, I don't want to give you false hope, girls. It's the last thing I want to do. I just want you both to keep an even keel as we go through our investigation."

"We understand," Aspen said.

"Yeah. I guess so," Dallas muttered.

"But you sound fairly confident that you've got Brock in a corner," Aspen added. "Or am I reading you wrong?"

The girls were desperately grasping for some thread of hope to hold onto—hope that their mother's killer would be brought to justice. That the person who took Wendy away from them would not get away with it. It was something Spenser could not only understand but something she could relate to. She was still seeking justice for the murder of her husband. She knew what it felt like to be fed false hope and be made to believe things that just weren't true.

When you were grieving, there was nothing worse. And she'd vowed she would never do that to another person. She'd vowed that she would always be as honest and straightforward as she could be with them and help them manage their expectations.

"Let me just say, that at the moment, it doesn't look good for him," Spenser replied. "But investigations are never a straight line, girls. There are always unexpected twists and turns along the way and just because something might not look good for Brock right now, it doesn't mean he did it. It only means we've got cause to look at him. But things change. They always change during an investigation. Do you understand what I'm saying?"

The girls nodded and looked to be struggling to keep themselves from being discouraged. One of Arbery's assistants— Vanessa Ortiz—stepped into the kitchen and shifted on her feet uncomfortably as she waited for Spenser's attention.

Spenser turned. "Yes?"

"I'm sorry to interrupt, Sheriff. Noah's in the basement and sent me up here to get you," she said. "He said he has something you need to see."

Spenser gave her a nod. "Tell him I'll be right down."

"Of course."

She turned and headed back to the basement as Spenser turned back to the Gilchrist girls. They looked back at her with inscrutable expressions on their faces. Spenser saw the grief in their eyes. She saw the pain of their loss reflected in their faces. But there was something else flickering behind that pain. They were both so guarded with their emotions, though, so tightly controlled, Spenser couldn't identify it.

Neither girl seemed comfortable expressing her emotions so Spenser thought it might be a shame. She thought it was perhaps fear and uncertainty about their future now that their mother was gone, and they were looking to her for answers. It was a thought that made Spenser as uncomfortable as showing their emotions made them.

"I should get downstairs, but if either of you need anything, if you need to talk or whatever—I'm just a phone call away," Spenser said. "I mean it. Any time, day or night, I will always pick up for you."

"Thank you, Sheriff," Aspen said softly.

"And believe me, it might not feel like it right now, but you will get through this. Both of you," she said. "You're both incredibly strong young women on your own, but lean on each other. Help one another get through this."

Dallas looked away, hiding her face from Spenser. Aspen still clutched her sister's hand and gave Spenser a nod and a weak smile.

"Thank you, Sheriff. We appreciate everything you've done—everything you are doing," Aspen said. "And please… just keep us in the loop?"

"You have my word."

Spenser gave them an encouraging smile then turned and walked down the hallway, finding the door to the basement, and took the flight of stairs. The concrete room was large and unfurnished, but it was clean and neatly organized. Racks of shelves lined three of the four walls with neatly labeled boxes lined up on every shelf.

Arbery had marked off a six-by-six section of the basement floor off to the right with cones and tape while he and his team were clustered by the washer and dryer against the wall across from the staircase. He looked up when Spenser reached the basement floor.

"Sheriff, you need to see this," he said.

Spenser walked over and he handed her a plastic evidence bag with a gray t-shirt inside. According to the tag, the shirt was XXL. It was a man's shirt. The plastic crackled as Spenser held it up and turned it over, looking at it closely. She noticed right away there were dark stains the color of rust on the gray fabric and knew instantly what it was. Blood. Her heart thundering against her breast and her stomach churning, Spenser raised her gaze to Arbery.

"Where did you find this?" she asked.

"Vanessa found it behind the washer. It looks like it had fallen back there. But that's not all. Come over here," he said.

Arbery walked her over to a mop bucket and pointed out the dark brown smears on the handle of the mop that stuck out of it. The inside of the bucket was dry, but Spenser saw the rust-colored ring. It was as if it had been filled with bloody water that had since been dumped out but whoever did it hadn't bothered to wipe the bucket out. Even more than that, there was a pair of rags at the bottom of the bucket that had been soaked with blood at one point, turning the formerly white fabric the same rust color as the stains on the t-shirt.

Arbery pointed to the area he'd taped off and Spenser immediately noticed an area of dark, discolored concrete on the ground within the square he'd laid out.

"On the ground over there, we found more dried blood and evidence of bodily decomposition. I expect we'll find the DNA matches that of Wendy Gilchrist," Arbery told her. "We have also found evidence of blood on the ground and the walls. Somebody went to a lot of effort to clean it up, but they weren't thorough enough and left plenty behind for us to find."

"So, this is our crime scene," Spenser said.

"It would seem so," he replied.

"Okay, so, Wendy is killed down here in the basement and her body is left here on the ground until it was safe to move," Spenser mused to herself.

"I can't say that for certain, but I can tell you it seems very definitive that she was murdered here on the basement floor," Arbery cut into her thoughts.

It seemed to line up with the theory she'd been working with. Brock killed Wendy and left her down here, moldering. But why? Because the girls had come home from school unexpectedly? She remembered that he'd said that. Leaving her down there in the basement might have been risky, but then Spenser recalled the girls said they stayed in one of the guest houses on the property when they came home. They couldn't stand being in the house while Brock was here.

But he hadn't been in the house. Had he? He was hiding out at his cabin to keep his infidelity from being discovered and they had receipts to prove he'd been there during the time Wendy was killed. Unless... unless he'd come home early and she had discovered his infidelity. Maybe then he'd gotten into it with Wendy, killed her, then used those receipts to establish his alibi up at the cabin, and only moved her body when he realized Spenser and her team were starting to close in on him.

Some things were lining up, but other things weren't. Not quite. There were holes in her theory. Things that she still needed to work through to make it all make sense. But given the evidence available to her at that moment, the reasonable conclusion was that Brock Ferry had murdered Wendy Gilchrist. He'd killed his wife. He'd lied to her about his whereabouts. He'd lied to her about his having an affair. Was it so far outside the realm of possibility to think that he'd lied to her about murdering his wife?

Absolutely not. It was not only possible, it was likely. And if there was one thing Spenser hated more than anything, it was being lied to.

"Good work, Doctor Arbery," Spenser said. "Please keep at it. Find everything you can that we can use to nail this man's coffin shut once and for all."

"I will. Of course," he replied. "What are you going to do?"

"I'm going to squeeze him as hard as I can," she said, her voice low and tight. "I'm going to squeeze him until I make him squeal and he confesses everything."

CHAPTER THIRTY

"WHAT IN THE HELL AM I DOING HERE AGAIN?" Brock all but shouted at her.

Young was already inside leaning against the wall with her arms folded over her chest when Spenser walked into the interrogation room. She slammed the door behind her, making Brock jump in his seat as fear flashed across his face. He quickly composed himself and pointedly yanked on the chain that locked him to the table making it rattle and clink.

"Can you please remove these cuffs, Sheriff?" he asked.

Spenser took her seat at the table and silently glared at him. His face darkened with anger, he rattled his chains harder, his expression more pointed.

"Sheriff?" he growled. "My cuffs? Unlock them."

"Shut up," Young growled right back.

Still not speaking, Spenser reached into her bag and pulled out the plastic evidence bag with the t-shirt inside that Arbery had given her at the scene. It landed with a thump when she tossed it onto the table in front of him then leaned back and stared at him. She watched him closely, scrutinizing every movement and gesture, watching his eyes and expressions as he took in the evidence bag sitting in front of him. He finally looked up at her, his expression wary.

"What is this?" he asked.

"It's a Seattle Seahawks t-shirt. Double XL… a man's size," she said. "We're testing the hair and DNA from the shirt, but we both know it's going to come back as yours."

"Yeah, so? It's my T-shirt. That's not a secret," he replied. "But I haven't worn it in weeks and have no idea what the stains all over it are."

"Those stains are blood, Mr. Ferry. Blood we're almost certain will come back as belonging to Wendy Gilchrist."

He stared at the shirt for another moment then shook his head as if he wasn't comprehending what she was saying. Spenser let him sit in silence. Let him work it out for himself. It took him a minute but when he did, his mouth fell open and he looked up at her with wide eyes and a dumbfounded expression on his face.

"No. Uh uh," he said. "You are not going to pin this on me."

"We have Wendy's blood on your clothing. We have her blood and bodily fluids on the floor of your basement. We have—"

"I was at my cabin. You verified that!"

"Your alibi could have easily been manufactured," Spenser said.

"We did the math, Brock," Young said. "You could have easily murdered Wendy then driven back to your cabin with more than enough time to buy that fast food to establish your alibi."

He shook his head. "That's crap. That's absolute crap. I did not kill her!"

"So, you keep saying," Spenser replied. "Everything we're finding keeps pointing to something different, though. Everything we're finding points to you, Mr. Ferry."

"This is not happening. This. Is. Not. Happening," he said, mostly to himself.

"I'm afraid it is happening," Spenser replied. "And believe me when I tell you that this is as real as it gets."

"I'm telling you, I didn't do this."

Spenser pulled a file folder Jacob had prepared for her out of her bag and tossed it onto the evidence bag. With his limited range of motion, Brock flipped it open and looked at the pages inside with an expression of confusion and bewilderment on his face.

"He's a good actor, isn't he?" Young asked.

"Oscar-worthy."

"What in the hell are you guys talking about? What is all this?" he asked.

"Let's talk about you skimming off the company till, Mr. Ferry," Spenser said.

He stared at them with something akin to astonishment on his face. But then he shook his head as his expression deepened, the shock fading and the anger taking over. Brock finally managed to settle himself down and stared at them, schooling his face to be as blank as he could possibly make it.

"What in the hell are you people talking about?" he demanded.

"Look at all the documents there. It's all right there," Spenser said.

He glared at them scornfully and pushed the file away, clearly uninterested in the contents. Spenser had to admit, if only to herself, that if he was putting on an act, he was doing a pretty good job of it. It was almost convincing. But she'd bought his act before and wasn't about to give him the benefit of the doubt again. Like the old saying went, fool me once, shame on you, fool me twice, shame on me and all that.

Young pushed away from the wall and perched on the corner of the table. She leaned forward and stared him in the eye. He flinched then leaned back in his chair as if trying to put as much physical distance between them as he could. Cuffed to the bolt in the table as he was, though, Brock wasn't able to create very much.

"The Cliff Notes version is that you set up an offshore account and have been skimming money from the company's accounts and setting yourself up with a tidy little nest egg," Young said.

"You're insane. You're both absolutely insane," he said. "I didn't do any of that. This is absolute garbage."

"Mr. Ferry, we've found an offshore account with your name attached to it," Spenser said. "We've also found corresponding deposits from accounts linked to Emerald Timber."

He shook his head and uttered a laugh that was completely devoid of humor. "This is insane. Is there anything else you want to try to pin on me? The Kennedy assassination maybe? Or maybe you want to blame me for global warming? Selling nuclear secrets to the Chinese?"

"If we uncover evidence of those things, we'll charge you with them," Spenser said. "Right now, all we have on you is evidence of murder and embezzlement."

"This is ridiculous," he said. "I'm obviously being set up. Somebody is trying to frame me here, Sheriff. Surely you see that."

"That's original," Young said.

"It's also true," he snapped.

"Okay, let's pretend for a second that's true," Young replied. "Who's trying to frame you? And why would anybody go to the trouble?"

He fell silent as he sat back and seemed to be racking his brain. Clearly, he thought there was a list of potential suspects. Brock took a minute then looked up.

"My best guess is that Aspen and Dallas are behind this," he said. "They've hated me from the minute I started dating their mother. They'll do anything to get me out of the way."

"So, what you're telling me is they're so upset that you're dating their mother, that to get you out of their lives, they… killed their mother?" Young asked. "Are you actually listening to yourself?"

He glowered at her, his face darkening. "Fine. What about Anderson Collins? Maybe he found out about me and Elayna and this is his way of getting me out of the picture and exacting a little revenge?"

"That would only have legs if Mr. Collins had access to the Emerald Timber banking information and accounts. Which he doesn't," Young said.

"How do you know? He's a money guy. Maybe—"

"Okay, look. Enough of this. I'm going to lay this out for you in very plain, unvarnished terms," Spenser said. "So, I need you to pay attention. Are you listening?"

Brock stared at her with a clenched jaw and rage burning in his eyes. But he was silent and he was listening. That was a good start. Spenser knew the evidence they had was good. Solid. But it was also circumstantial. They couldn't put Brock in the house the night Wendy was murdered. Not definitively. And to that point, there was still no murder weapon. While the DA might be able to wrangle a conviction out of the evidence they'd gathered, a decent defense lawyer might be able to cast enough doubt on the case to win an acquittal. It was fifty-fifty. And Spenser wasn't willing to hand her case over to the DA with what amounted to a crapshoot. What Spenser desperately needed was a confession.

"Good," Spenser said. "Now, we have Wendy's blood on your clothing. We have blood in your basement. We have evidence of her decomposing body in your basement. We also have her blood on rags and in your mop bucket. Somebody cleaned up the basement but didn't do a thorough job. Add all that to the bank account in your name and embezzled funds and what does that add up to, Mr. Ferry?"

"It adds up to a frame job. That's what it adds up to," he grumbled.

"No, that adds up to murder one and life in prison without parole," Young said.

"With the evidence we have, you are going to prison for a very long time," Spenser said. "But if you walk us through what happened and tell us what led up to you killing your wife, I will personally talk to the DA and let him know that you've been forthcoming and cooperative. I can try to talk him into a reasonable plea deal—"

"I'm not going to do anything like that because that never happened," he said, his voice rising. "I will not confess to something I didn't do."

"Mr. Ferry, all the evidence we've gathered says otherwise," Spenser said.

"Then your evidence is wrong. Or you're reading it wrong," he snapped. "Or maybe you're just so invested in hanging me that you're not looking for the real killer."

"The real killer. Really?" Young asked. "You're going to go with the OJ defense?"

"Okay, I'm done with this. This is your last chance to cooperate with us," Spenser said. "Walk us through the night of the murder and I'll do what I can to help you with the DA."

"I'm done talking to you," he said. "I want my lawyer."

"That's probably a good idea," Spenser said as she got to her feet. "And for your sake, I hope you have a good one. You're going to need all the help you can get."

Spenser led Young out of the interrogation room feeling disappointed and frustrated. They'd needed a confession to put the final nail into Brock's coffin and were walking out with nothing. She hadn't wanted to turn the case over to the DA without something incontrovertible. But it looked like she had no other choice. Brock wasn't talking, so a roll of the dice it was going to be.

CHAPTER THIRTY-ONE

IT TOOK A COUPLE OF DAYS TO GET HIM FULLY BOOKED AND processed, but Spenser was finally set to be free of the millstone that was Brock Ferry. Word about Wendy's murder had finally broken and it had sent shockwaves through town. It seemed to be the fifty-plus demographic who were most affected by Wendy's death—the folks who'd grown up with her or knew her when she was a kid. Wendy's murder had cast a definite pall over Sweetwater Falls.

Spenser walked into the holding cells and stood at the bars looking in at Brock Ferry. He was still stretched out on his bunk, an arm flung over his eyes, pretending to be asleep. Rather than the leading man and model he looked like when she'd first met him, a couple of days in her holding cells had left Brock looking a little rough around the edges. He was accustomed to living a pampered life of privilege. Prison was not going to agree with him.

"I know you're awake," Spenser said. "Come on, get up. On your feet."

"What now?" he muttered. "Going to draw and quarter me in the town square?"

"Pretty sure they outlawed that a long time ago," Spenser replied.

"I'm sure that must pain you."

"Not really," Spenser said. "I can think of far more creative ways to execute somebody if that's what I really wanted."

"Like framing them for murder?"

"Are we still banging that drum?"

He finally sat up on his bunk and looked at her. A thick layer of stubble covered his chin and cheeks, his eyes were bloodshot, and he looked like he'd aged ten years in the couple of days he'd been a guest in her facility. Yeah, prison was definitely not going to agree with him.

"I'm going to bang that drum from now until the day I die because it's true. I did not do this, Sheriff," he snarled. "I'm an innocent man and somebody is setting me up."

"Okay, well, that's between you, your lawyer, and the King County DA now," Spenser said.

"Are you really going to let this happen?" he asked. "Are you really going to let this miscarriage of justice happen?"

"I'm not letting anything happen. My part in this play is over," she said. "What happens next is up to the DA now. If you're innocent, I expect that would come out at trial. You'll have your day in court, a chance to plead your innocence, and present your theory that you've been framed."

"Please. Like the accused murderer of the late, great Wendy Gilchrist is going to be able to get a fair trial in this state," he sneered.

"You know, you're starting to sound like a broken record here. Everybody but you is to blame for this. You're the victim of some vast conspiracy," Spenser said.

"Because that is the truth, Sheriff."

"And like I said, you'll have your day in court to present all that," she said. "My job is to collect evidence and turn it all over to the DA who decides how best to proceed. That's my part. Now, let's go. On your feet. I need to get you prepped for the marshals who are taking you up to a facility in Seattle."

He got to his feet grudgingly, his face a mask of anger blended with resignation. Brock sighed and ran a hand through his hair.

"This is wrong. This is just wrong," he said.

"Turn around and approach the bars then place your hands through this slot and cross one wrist over the other," Spenser ordered.

He complied and when he had his hands through the slot, Spenser put a pair of handcuffs on him then ordered him to step forward and he shuffled a couple of steps away from the bars. Spenser opened the cell then stepped in and took hold of him, one hand on the small chain between the cuffs and the other on his shoulder.

"Come on, your ride is waiting," she said.

"This is a travesty," he said. "You're letting this travesty happen, Sheriff. I want you to know that you are letting an innocent man be sent to prison… probably for the rest of his life."

"The offer I made before stands," she said. "Talk me through what happened the night you killed Wendy and I'll put in a word with the DA. He might be able to offer you a deal that includes the possibility of parole at some point. You might not die in that concrete box."

"Like I said before, I'm not going to confess to something I didn't do."

"Okay. Let's go then."

Spenser walked Brock out of the holding cells and through the bullpen. The deputies who happened to be in the office all stopped what they were doing and turned to watch him go. The hostility in the air was thick. Even Alice, normally fairly mild-mannered, glared daggers at the man. Spenser walked him over to the two large men in US Marshal windbreakers.

"He's all yours, gentlemen," she said.

Like a magician, the man on her right deftly unlocked the handcuffs and put a pair of his own on, then handed Spenser's pair back to her with a grin.

"I see you've done that a time or two before," she said.

"A time or two," he replied.

"Thank you, Sheriff," said the other.

As they walked Brock out of the station, Spenser noticed that Mayor Dent was standing just inside the doors watching the procession. Although she looked satisfied, Spenser couldn't help but see the tinge of sadness in her eyes. When the doors closed and Brock was gone from their sight, Dent turned to Spenser and gave her a small smile as she walked over to her.

"Can we talk in your office?" Dent asked.

"Of course."

Spenser led the mayor through the bullpen and into her office, softly closing the door behind them. Dent dropped into one of the chairs in front of her desk as Spenser walked around and took her seat on the other side.

"I thought I'd feel some sort of elation watching him being taken away for trial," Dent said. "Instead, I still feel… a little empty."

"I think that's natural. Especially given that this is just the first step," Spenser replied. "Like you noted, there's still a trial to come."

"And how are you feeling about that? Did we get the right guy?"

Spenser let out a big sigh. "I mean, all the evidence we collected points to him. I'm not going to lie to you, Maggie. There are weaknesses in the case—"

"What kind of weaknesses?" Dent cut her off.

"Like we can't put Brock in the house with Wendy the night of the murder. There are receipts in Brock's cabin that put him there the day Wendy went missing—the day we believe she was murdered," Spenser answered. "It's still very feasible he made sure to have receipts in his cabin to establish his alibi, then came back to town and murdered Wendy, then slipped back out and hid out at his cabin for a few days. And we still have no murder weapon. But you can bet Brock's attorney is going to make hay with that—

THE LIES IN THE FALLS

and I can't honestly say it's not enough to cause a little reasonable doubt."

Dent pursed her lips and seemed to think about it for a moment. "What else do you have in the way of evidence, Sheriff?"

"We've got his t-shirt with Wendy's blood all over it. We have the mop bucket, rags, and the decomp tissue on the basement floor. We also have Brock's hair on Wendy's body," she replied. "But again, any defense attorney worth their salt can cast those things in a very different light. We don't have a direct link putting Brock in the house the night she was killed. The entire case is circumstantial, I'm afraid."

"I'm no lawyer, but that all sounds pretty solid to me."

"It might be enough. It should be enough," Spenser replied. "But you know the games lawyers play. Plus, you can never predict what a jury is going to do."

"Do you think we have the right man, Spenser?"

She pursed her lips and thought for a moment before answering. "I think the evidence says we have the right man."

"You're equivocating. We promised each other we'd only ever be blunt and truthful," Dent said. "So, let me ask you again. Do you think we have the right man?"

"All right, if you want my honest answer, I'm going to say… I don't know. But my gut isn't evidence and all the physical evidence we have says he is," she replied. "But my personal feeling, which is utterly irrelevant, is that I don't know."

"What's your hesitation?"

Spenser shook her head. "I don't know that, either. All I know is that there is something in the back of my mind that's giving me pause. There's just something in the back of my mind that's bothering me. It feels like I've got a splinter just under the skin and I can't get it out. It's just sitting there nagging at me. But I can't put my finger on what it is."

"That's ominous," Dent said.

"It also might be nothing. There are just a few loose threads I haven't been able to tie up to my own satisfaction. That doesn't mean they're relevant or important," Spenser told her. "It also doesn't mean we don't have the right guy. Like I said, everything is pointing to him. But you know how I am with loose threads."

She laughed softly. "I do. And I've told you before that not everything gets wrapped up perfectly and with a neat bow on top. Real life is often messy and has loose threads flapping in the breeze every which way."

"That is true," Spenser said. "And this may be one of those times."

"Well, in that case..."

Dent reached down into her bag and brought out a very pricey bottle of scotch. She set it down on Spenser's desk then pulled a pair of plastic tumblers out of her bag and set those next to it. Dent opened the bottle and poured them both a couple of fingers worth of the amber liquid and slid one of the glasses over to Spenser. She picked up the glass and waved it under her nose, inhaling the aroma with a groan of pleasure. Dent picked up her glass and raised it to Spenser.

"Congratulations on closing the case, Spenser," she said. "Thank you for handling this so quickly and so efficiently and bringing Wendy's killer to justice. It doesn't bring her back, but we can all rest a little easier knowing the piece of garbage who took her from us will rot in a concrete box for the rest of his miserable days."

"I can drink to that."

Spenser leaned forward and they tapped glasses. She settled back in her chair and took a short sip of the scotch, relishing the burn as it slid down her throat. It hit her belly and Spenser felt her insides explode with warmth.

"My God that's good," Spenser said.

"Right? This was one of my dad's favorites."

"He had excellent taste in liquor."

"That he did."

They sipped in silence for a few moments, basking in the warmth the scotch had ignited in them as well as the sense of camaraderie and companionship between them. Dent sat back and sighed as she stared into the amber liquid in her glass.

"God, I miss her," Dent said.

"It sounds trite, but she's always going to be with you," Spenser said.

"Yeah, you're right. It does sound trite."

They shared a laugh together, but Spenser knew Dent believed what she'd said. The mayor nodded and took another sip.

"I feel bad for those girls. They've got nobody in the world now," Spenser said.

"I hope one day they realize what they lost and come to appreciate their mother for who she was and all she did for them," Dent remarked.

"I thought they were close?"

"It depended on the day. You know how unreasonable teenagers can be. What kid gets along with their folks twenty-four-seven? And believe me, those girls can be a handful. They're spoiled and what we call high maintenance. Wendy always wanted them to have the best of everything," Dent said with a chuckle. "There were a lot of fights and a lot of resentment when they were growing up. But once they went off to college, that all started to change, and they did grow a lot closer. Still, there were days when it was touch and go. But I know this is going to hit them hard at some point. I just hope there's somebody in their lives who can help keep them from going off the rails when it does."

"Maybe you should be that person, Maggie. You and Wendy were close. I have no doubt she'd be glad to see you help guide the girls," Spenser said.

She stared into the bottom of her glass as if the answers could be found there. "Yeah, maybe. I just don't know if I'd be able to get through to them. But maybe."

"Don't sell yourself short. You're great with people," Spenser said.

"You're buttering me up. You must be getting ready to ask me to champion something on your behalf with the City Council," Dent said with a laugh.

"Not just yet. But I'll let you know when I have something I need you to crusade for on my behalf," Spenser replied.

"Thank you, Spenser," Dent said, holding her gaze. "I know you have doubts, but this will bring a lot of us some semblance of peace. So, thank you."

"Of course," she replied. "But I was just doing my job."

She'd done her job, but that little voice in the back of her head kept whispering incessantly, telling her that job wasn't yet done.

CHAPTER THIRTY-TWO

"**Y**OU DON'T LOOK LIKE A WOMAN WHO JUST SOLVED one of the biggest cases this town has ever seen," Ryker noted.

"No?" Spenser asked. "And what does that woman look like?"

"A little happier," he replied. "I don't see that smug little smile of satisfaction you usually have when you get a win."

Spenser laughed. "I do not get a smug smile."

"Oh, you absolutely do," he said. "We can ask Amanda if you need confirmation."

"Yeah, that'd be a reliable and unbiased answer."

"Are you suggesting your protégé would be so unscrupulous as to lie?"

Spenser grinned. "Nothing of the sort. She will, however, agree with you just to poke at me."

"Yeah, I can't really argue with that."

They walked along, enjoying the companionable silence between them. The night was cool and growing colder. Thick clouds blanketed the sky overhead and a slight breeze made Spenser pull her coat around her a little tighter.

"You do seem pretty tense," Ryker said, his tone serious. "Tenser than I would have expected given that you closed a high-profile, high-stress case."

"Your powers of observation are truly scary sometimes, Ryker Makawi," Spenser said. "A normal person might be disturbed by them."

"Well, I suppose it's a good thing you're not a normal person then, isn't it?"

Spenser laughed softly and elbowed him in the ribs as they walked along admiring the holiday décor in the main town square. It had been a couple of days since she'd sent Brock Ferry to Seattle and things seemed to be getting back to normal. Or some reasonable facsimile of it. The light poles had all been wrapped in red and white foil, looking like giant candy canes, all the storefronts had been painted with Christmas flair, and an enormous tree was being set up and decorated in preparation for the lighting ceremony.

Spenser greeted the people on the street they passed. The square was crowded but subdued. People spoke in quiet tones, and the energy as well as the joy Spenser had seen from the people during the Founder's Day carnival had all but evaporated. The pall brought on by Wendy Gilchrist's death seemed to be lingering.

"So? What is it that's bothering you about the case?" Ryker pressed.

"Why don't we talk about something else?" Spenser said. "We always talk about work, and we should be focusing on other things. Like us, for instance."

He laughed softly. "Because you are a woman who is consumed by her work. You are the job and will never allow yourself to relax and focus on other things—like us—until your mind and heart are settled," he said. "And right now, I can see that you are far from settled. There is something gnawing at you about it. So? What is it?"

"Honestly? I don't know. There's just something that keeps nagging at me. I've been trying to figure it out but it's like I'm grasping at smoke," she replied.

"Do you think you have the wrong man and Brock Ferry didn't actually kill her?"

She shook her head, a frown touching her lips. "I just don't know. The evidence all lines up—the bloody shirt, the offshore bank account, the traces of Wendy's body in the basement—all of this evidence points to him."

"But?"

"But… I don't know," she said. "I'm probably just overthinking this. Like Maggie said the other day, not every case is going to be wrapped up and topped with a perfect little bow. This is probably one of those cases."

"You? Overthink something? Perish the thought."

She laughed and elbowed him again as they continued to walk. Spenser tried to shut her mind off and just let herself enjoy the evening. Enjoy her time with Ryker. He was a good man, and it made her feel terrible that she was sometimes so consumed by work that it cut into their time together. She believed him when he said he didn't mind sharing her with the job, but it bothered her. She knew herself well enough to know she probably wouldn't have been so gracious if she had to share him with his job.

Spenser wished she could learn to shut off her mind. Learn to maintain a healthier work-life balance and focus on enjoying moments like these. She knew how fleeting they could be. Knew that moments of joy and bliss like she was feeling could be taken away from her in the blink of an eye and that she should give herself over to them. She should allow herself to revel in them. Soak them all up and hold onto them tightly because moments like those—moments of pure joy and love—were rare and unfortunately, not permanent.

But like he said, if she could shut that part of herself off, she wouldn't be her.

"Let's try to talk about something else," Spenser said with a soft smile. "I'll try to stop thinking about work."

"Good luck with that," he replied with a laugh.

Spenser giggled. "I said I'd try. I never said I'd be successful at it."

"Fair enough," he replied, still smiling as he gestured to the mammoth tree in the town square. "Have you finished your speech?"

"Not even close. I have no desire to do that," Spenser replied. "I don't understand why the mayor or a member of the City Council doesn't light the stupid thing. That seems to be the more appropriate choice."

"It's tradition. Back when the town was founded, the first sheriff—Fred Teller, I believe his name was—was a tremendously respected figure. People in Sweetwater Falls looked to him for safety, guidance—he was more powerful than any political figure," Ryker explained. "So, when this whole tree lighting ceremony business started, Fred Teller was the natural choice to light it. He provided the people with hope and inspiration. And it's a tradition that's endured."

"I suck at speeches."

"I honestly can't think of anybody better to give this town hope and inspiration again. And I think given all that's happened this year, they need it," he said. "Besides, in case you haven't noticed, I think you've helped restore the respect and reputation the sheriffs of old around here used to have, so it seems fitting you do the lighting."

"I don't know about that."

"I do. And so does everybody else, Spenser," Ryker replied seriously. "I hear people talk. And I hear a lot of them talking about their respect for you. You're winning them over."

She smiled as she slipped her arm through his and leaned her head on his shoulder as they walked down the midway between the rows of booths set up by independent vendors. Some she'd seen during the Founder's Day carnival and others were just getting started. Strings of lights hung from poles overhead and Christmas music reverberated through the air all around them. Spenser couldn't deny that it felt good to know she was winning over the people of town. It felt good to hear the people respected her.

But Spenser was realistic enough to know that respect didn't always translate to votes. She knew people with money and influence had the power to sway an election. She'd seen horribly unqualified and cruel people elected to office on a wave of support whipped up by money, ignorance, cynicism, and even hate. Maybe that was a jaded way to see things. Maybe that made her a cynic at heart. But it seemed to be the way of the world. The people of Sweetwater Falls might respect her today, but that could change overnight depending on who decided to run against her and how much money they had and how much influence they wielded.

"Don't overthink your speech," Ryker said. "Just speak from the heart and be yourself. It's what the people around here love about you. You're genuine and you've got a good heart. They see that. They respond to that."

She turned to him and took his big hands into hers. Gazing up into his warm, dark gaze sent a shudder through her heart and brought a smile to her lips.

"I'm sorry I'm so consumed by work," she said.

"Don't be. It's one of the things I respect and admire most about you," he said. "You don't take shortcuts and work a case until it's done. Not everybody does that. Your predecessor certainly didn't. I—and everybody in town—respect your willingness to sacrifice your own peace of mind to make this town safe. To make it more just."

Sliding her hand around the back of his neck, Spenser stood on her tiptoes and pulled Ryker down to her. Her body exploded with warmth and the crackle of electricity as their lips touched. She gave herself over to the sensations rocketing through her body. Spenser was trying to live in that moment. To savor it. To commit it to memory. It was a lesson Trevor had tried to teach her in what felt like another lifetime, but it hadn't taken. That was something she was trying hard to correct now that she felt like she was being given another chance.

It was interrupted, though, when she felt a presence to their right. She slowly and reluctantly pulled away from Ryker and turned to find a tall, thin young man standing there with an embarrassed look on his face. Equal height to her, he was trim with sharp, angular features, narrow shoulders, and a prominent Adam's Apple. He had a pale complexion, a somewhat shy demeanor, and seemed a little socially awkward. Spenser had never met him before but the midnight black hair, thick and shaggy, and eyes so blue they were almost silver told her exactly who he was.

"Brendan Gilchrist," Spenser said.

"Forgive me for intruding on your time like this," he replied, his voice soft as a feather. "I was told that you're Sheriff Song?"

"I am," she said.

"H—how did you know who I am?"

"Your eyes and your hair," she told him. "You look exactly like your sisters."

"Oh. Yeah. I guess we do… look alike, that is."

He shuffled his feet and slipped his hands into the pockets of his jeans. He wore a long-sleeved black t-shirt but no coat and black and white Converse hi-tops.

"What can I do for you, Brendan?" Spenser asked.

He ran a hand through his thick, dark locks. "I, uh… I wanted to say thank you for catching the man who killed my mother," he said quietly. "She and I didn't see eye-to-eye on a lot of things, but she was still my mother."

"Of course," Spenser replied. "And I'm so sorry for your loss. It's never easy to lose somebody we care about."

"No, it's not. I just wish… I wish we'd been able to patch things up before…"

His voice trailed off and he looked away, his face clouding over with emotion. He sniffed loudly and his body shook as he struggled to fight back his tears. Spenser didn't need to be a psychic or a psychologist to see Brendan was struggling with the weight of the guilt he carried over not having mended fences with his mother and knowing that now, he'd never get the chance.

Brendan drew in a long, shaky breath and let it out, taking a couple of moments to gather himself. Spenser glanced at Ryker, silently apologizing for the interruption in their evening. He squeezed her hand, his lips curling upward slightly, as he signaled his understanding. She couldn't believe he was so patient with her. She was grateful for his understanding, but the patience and grace he gave her was uncommon.

Finally in control of himself, Brendan gave her a shaky smile. "Anyway, I just wanted to thank you for bringing my mom's killer to justice. I appreciate how hard you worked to do it."

"Of course, Brendan," Spenser replied. "I know it won't fill the hole in your hearts, but I hope it brings some peace to you and your sisters."

"I hope so, too," he said.

"What will you do now?" Spenser asked. "I mean, who is going to take over the company?"

"Oh, nobody... at least, nobody named Gilchrist," Brendan said. "None of us want to run it, so we're going to sell the company."

"You're selling the company?"

He nodded. "Yeah. I mean, it's no secret I never wanted to take over. I have my own thing going and have bigger plans," he told her. "Aspen and Dallas have no interest in it, either. Never have. Apparently, there's already a buyer lined up and we're going to be signing the papers after the funeral. I'll be able to use my share of it to fund my start-up."

Spenser was taken aback. That was the last thing she'd been expecting to hear, and it left her feeling flatfooted for a moment.

"That seems quick," was all Spenser could think to say.

"My understanding is that this has been in the works for a while now. I was surprised that my mom would sell the company, but I guess it makes sense given that none of us wanted to run it. So, maybe she figured it would be better to cash out and enjoy the rest of her life," he said. "Honestly, from my perspective, the sooner we finalize the deal and divide the proceeds, the better," he said. "I just want to say goodbye to my mom and get back to my life."

"What are the girls planning on doing?" Spenser asked.

He shrugged. "No idea. Knowing them, probably partying. Trying to establish themselves as social media influencers—as if that's a viable career path," he said with barely disguised contempt. "But they seem to think they're going to build an empire that way, so more power to them, I guess."

Spenser frowned and let her mind spin with this new information and thought she felt some of the loose threads that had been bothering her so much starting to pull together and be woven into a larger tapestry. The full picture was still out of focus and opaque, but she thought she was glimpsing the broad shape of it.

"Anyway," Brendan said. "I just wanted to say thank you, Sheriff. I appreciate everything you did for our family."

"Of course. It was nice meeting you, Brendan," she replied. "And good luck to you."

He gave her a tight smile and a nod then turned and walked away. Spenser gnawed on her bottom lip as she watched him go.

"You've got that look on your face again," he said.

"What look?"

"That look of a woman on a mission."

"I suppose I am," she said. "If you don't mind sharing me with the job for a little while, I need to get back to the office. There's something I need to look at."

"Lead the way."

CHAPTER THIRTY-THREE

Spenser sat in the conference room on one side of the table and Ryker sat across from her, watching as she pawed through all the reports and paperwork generated as they'd worked the case. Two large banker's boxes sat in between her and Ryker, lids off, contents strewn across the top of the table. She picked up the evidence bag with Brock's bloody shirt in it, looked at it again, then tossed it aside. There was nothing new to be gleaned from it.

"Might I ask what put this bee in your bonnet?" Ryker asked.

"What Brendan told us put this bee in my bonnet."

"Which part?"

"About the girls brokering the sale of the company."

"What about it?"

"It's all happening a little quickly, don't you think?"

Ryker shrugged. "It makes sense. If none of the Gilchrist children have any interest in running the lumber empire, why not move quickly to cut ties with it?"

"Yeah, on some level it makes sense," Spenser said. "And this may ultimately be nothing more than a fruitless fishing expedition. But I appreciate you indulging me."

"Of course," he said. "If this will help you find that closure to the case you've been lacking then by all means, throw out a line and keep fishing."

The door to the conference room opened and Jacob bustled in with his laptop in hand. He dropped into his chair at the table and booted up his computer.

"Sorry to call you in tonight," she said.

"It's fine. I'm happy to help," he replied. "But I thought we closed the Gilchrist case?"

"We did. But there are a few questions that have been lingering that I want answers to," she said. "It very well may be academic and pointless, but I just need to satisfy my curiosity."

"Okay, well, I looked into the sale of Emerald Timber like you asked, and from the company filings I've dug up, it looks like it's legit. It appears to be on the up and up," Jacob said.

"And who's the buyer?"

"Evergreen Lumber and Milling," he replied. "Eric Bass is the CEO and has signed all the paperwork authorizing the pending sale. But here's the thing, all the preliminary paperwork on record was filled out more than eight months ago. Nothing is finalized yet, but the exploratory paperwork and original offers were made back then."

Spenser frowned. "Is it possible Wendy was actually trying to sell the company?"

"I honestly doubt it," Ryker said. "The company is her family's legacy."

Jacob gave her a sly smile. "So, I did a little more digging and was looking through Bass' correspondence from around that time—"

"Do we want to know how he got into the private correspondence of the CEO of a major company?" Ryker asked.

"We've learned there are some questions we don't want or need answers to," Spenser replied with a soft laugh.

"All you need to know is that I am good at what I do. Very good," Jacob said.

"So good the FBI would probably take an interest," Ryker noted.

"Maybe. But we'll never know because they'll never catch me. That's how good I am," Jacob said with a leering smirk. "Anyway, according to Bass' correspondence from around that time period, Wendy Gilchrist emailed him directly and started the process of selling the company. She also insisted on strict secrecy and that he wasn't to mention it to anybody or the deal would be off."

"Huh," Ryker said. "I wouldn't have guessed that."

"I wouldn't have, either," Jacob said. "So I looked again and on closer inspection, I noticed there was a slight deviation in Wendy Gilchrist's company email address and the email address used to contact Bass to get the ball rolling on the sale."

"Meaning, somebody was posing as Wendy to initiate the terms of the sale," Spenser said.

"Which also explains why they insisted on absolute secrecy. They couldn't afford to have Wendy get wind of what was going on," Ryker said.

"That stands to reason," Spenser said. "Just out of curiosity, what was the negotiated price for Emerald Timber?"

"Three hundred and fifty million," he answered. "Given what Emerald Timber pulls in a year, it would be a bargain. It seemed like Bass knew the person posing as Wendy was motivated to sell and took advantage of that."

"Or perhaps the person posing as Wendy just wasn't experienced or a very strong negotiator. They held the cards and could have squeezed him for more," Ryker said.

Spenser nodded. "Probably both," she said. "Now, we just need to figure out who was posing as Wendy Gilchrist. Jacob, have you been able to glean anything from those email communications?"

THE LIES IN THE FALLS

He shook his head. "Unfortunately, no. All I can tell you is the IP address tracks back to Emerald Timber. Whoever sent the emails was at the company's location."

"Which tracks back to Brock," Ryker said.

"Yeah. Maybe," Spenser said.

"I think it makes sense," Jacob offered. "Brock negotiates a secret sale of the company then, when he has all those ducks in a row, he kills Wendy."

"Except for the fact that he didn't stand to inherit the company or any proceeds from a sale," Spenser said. "The prenup was clear on that. So, how would he have hoped to see any of that three hundred and fifty million?"

"He must have had an accomplice," Ryker said.

"Or, he might have been able to challenge the prenup in court," Jacob added. "He could have filed a suit—"

"There's no way he would have won," Ryker said.

"Unless his goal wasn't to win, but to be such a nuisance, the Gilchrist kids pay him off just to make him go away," Spenser mused. "It's a risky gambit because he might have ended up with nothing. But I kind of think the girls hate him so much, they might have paid him just to get them out of their lives once and for all."

"But that leaves the problem of the sale of the company," Ryker said. "If Wendy didn't actually negotiate the sale—"

"But as far as the kids know, she did," Spenser said. "The girls aren't very engaged with the family business and if they're presented with papers saying their mother set the sale in motion, I don't see Aspen or Dallas questioning it. Given what Brendan told us, I tend to think they'd sign the papers just to be done with it and start their social media empire or whatever it was they're talking about doing."

"And dangling three hundred and fifty million in front of a couple of kids who want nothing to do with the company anyway might be a good way to make them not look too hard at the provenance of the sale paperwork," Jacob added.

Ryker nodded. "Yeah. That's probably likely."

Spenser looked at everything on the table and let the information Jacob was passing on sink in. It was all interesting. Anecdotal, but interesting. From where she was standing, it helped cement the idea that Brock Ferry murdered his wife. He set things in motion that might net him a slice of the pie by selling the company out from under the kids. Despite all she'd learned, Brock Ferry remained their prime suspect.

And yet, something still lingered in the back of Spenser's mind that continued to bother her. Some nagging voice that kept whispering in her ear, kept telling her to look deeper. Telling her the picture wasn't yet complete and there was something she still wasn't seeing. Telling her the loose ends that had been plaguing her remained and were still preventing her from seeing the full and complete picture.

"You still don't look convinced," Ryker said.

"I'm not one hundred percent sold on all this yet," she replied.

"What's still stuck in your craw, Sheriff?" Jacob asked.

Spenser pursed her lips and looked again at the evidence and reports spread out on the table in front of her, trying to make sense of it all. Trying to will herself to see the complete picture. But it remained tantalizingly just out of reach. It was like looking at a stereograph and not being able to see the image hidden within it. The frustration within her was almost boiling over.

"You know, one of the things I keep circling back to is the most obvious and unanswered question," Spenser started.

"What's that?" Ryker asked.

"The woman on the train station platform. We still haven't figured out who that woman was," she said with a frown. "We know it wasn't Elayna Collins. But who was she?"

"Is it possible she's somebody Brock paid to get on that train?" Ryker asked.

"What, you mean like an actor?" Jacob asked.

Ryker nodded. "Yeah. Somebody he paid to help sell that illusion."

"I mean, I guess it's possible," Spenser replied, her tone thick with skepticism. "Something about that doesn't feel right, though."

"So, this mystery woman is Brock's accomplice," Ryker said. "Is it possible he had another girl on the side? Somebody who might have helped him?"

"I haven't found a trace of anything," Jacob said.

"Yeah, but to be fair, you didn't know about Elayna Collins at first, either," Ryker said.

"That's fair," Jacob said.

"Everything's changed," Spenser said.

"How so?" Ryker asked.

"Now that we have this information about the sale of the company, here's the problem I'm having with all this," Spenser started. "If Brock was moving behind the scenes to sell the company, intending to murder Wendy the whole time, why go through the trouble of creating the illusion of his wife getting on the train in the first place?"

Ryker and Jacob both fell silent as they pondered her question. They sat back in their chairs and seemed to be trying to come up with an answer—and judging by the looks on their faces, neither one was coming up with anything.

"Jacob, can you call up the image of the woman on the train platform?" Spenser asked.

"Coming right up."

The screen on the wall lit up and came to life as Jacob's fingers flew over the keys. Spenser got to her feet then walked over and stood closer to the screen as the image she'd asked for came up. Spenser stared closely at the grainy, black and white photo, scrutinizing every pixel of it. She once again got the sensation of staring at a stereograph and knew she was looking at it too hard. She took a step back and closed her eyes then drew in a deep breath and held it for a ten count before slowly exhaling, letting her thoughts settle.

When she was ready, Spenser opened her eyes and looked at the still image from the security feed again, trying to see the picture within the larger design. She took in the figure of the woman. Stared at the large, floppy hat and the oversized sunglasses. Spenser focused on the shape of the woman's nose. Her chin. Her fingers. She tried to see them all individually but also put them all together to take them in as a whole.

And still, she saw nothing.

Beating back the waves of frustration that washed over her, Spenser kept her calm and continued to slowly and methodically search the image of the woman on the train platform. She hoped to find something within the image that would lead her to the answers she sought. Something that would clear the opacity in her mind and reveal the larger picture she was so desperately searching for.

And then she saw it.

Spenser's eyes widened and her mouth fell open into a perfect "O" as a powerful wave of adrenaline surged through her veins. Spenser's mouth grew dry, and her heart started to thunder in her chest. She looked again, just to be sure she was seeing what she thought she was seeing. And when the image didn't change, when Spenser realized the opacity had been cleared away and she was seeing what she'd been searching for the entire time, she felt a charge like electricity coursing through her veins. She turned to Ryker and Jacob, her body trembling with excitement.

"I know who the woman on the platform is," she said. "And we have some work to do."

CHAPTER THIRTY-FOUR

"Thank you all for coming in today," Spenser said.

She looked around the table in the conference room. Young and Jacob were seated on one side while Aspen, Dallas, and Brendan Gilchrist all sat on the other. Dallas wore her usual dour and disinterested expression, Aspen looked curious but pensive, and Brendan sat slumped back in his chair simply looking sad and like he wanted to be anywhere else in the world. Though he sat just a couple of feet apart from his sisters, he couldn't have been further away. The wall of ice between the siblings was palpable.

"What are we doing here, Sheriff?" Aspen asked. "I don't mean to be rude, but we're in the middle of planning our mother's funeral."

"Of course. And I appreciate you taking the time out to come down," Spenser said. "There have just been a few developments in your mother's case, and I promised to keep you in the loop."

"Developments?" Aspen asked. "Did that piece of garbage finally confess?"

"Not exactly," Spenser replied.

"Then what new developments are there?" Aspen pressed.

"Before I get to that, there are a few things I wanted to get a little clarification from you on," Spenser said as she got to her feet.

A look passed between Aspen and Dallas while Brendan sat forward, an expression of curiosity crossing his face.

"The first thing I wanted to ask about was the sale of your family's company," Spenser said. "Did your mother talk to you about her plans to sell?"

Aspen nodded. "She did. I think about what, eight or nine months ago now, Dally?"

Dallas nodded but remained silent while Brendan shook his head. "No," he said. "She didn't mention it to me."

"Because you weren't part of the company, Brendan," Aspen said, her voice acidic. "You had your chance but walked away from it. So, why would Mom talk about it with you?"

He shrugged. "Relax. I was just answering the question."

"Don't talk to me like that," she snapped.

The saying there was no love lost between them would have been a vast understatement and it left Spenser wondering where the source of that divide stemmed from. Had Wendy pitted her children against each other the way her brother Baker said their father had? Was there just a natural rivalry between them that had morphed into outright hate and hostility? Was there some other external—or internal—factor that had driven a wedge between the siblings?

"Did your mother ever tell you why she wanted to sell?" Spenser asked. "The company has been in your family for generations. It's your legacy."

"It's not my legacy," Dallas said sharply.

Aspen put a hand over her sister's hand and gave it a squeeze, shooting her a quick look as she did. Once Dallas had lowered her gaze again, Aspen turned back to Spenser.

"What she means is that our mother knew none of us—not even him," she said dismissively gesturing to her brother, "we all have our own things going on and we weren't interested in taking over the company's operations. Our mother wanted us to be able to do what we wanted in life rather than be saddled with that responsibility. She wanted us to have the choice she never had."

"She never said any of that to me," Brendan remarked.

"And why would she?" Aspen spat bitterly. "Again, you left. You made your choice and weren't privy to the conversations we had with Mom. She wanted for Dallas and me to live our best lives and do what made us happy."

"That doesn't sound like the Wendy Gilchrist I remember," Brendan muttered.

"Yeah, well, she changed," Dallas retorted as she glared at her brother. "Not that you would know since you were never around."

Brendan rolled his eyes and sat back in his chair but fell silent.

"Sheriff, I need to ask you again… what is this all about?" Aspen asked.

"We'll get there. Please, just indulge me," Spenser replied. "I just want to dot my I's and cross my T's. We don't want your mother's killer walking away, right?"

Aspen's shoulders slumped but she nodded. "Right. Of course not."

"Good. Thank you," Spenser said. "So, were you and Dallas involved with the negotiations of the company's sale?"

Aspen shook her head. "No. That was, as they say, above our pay grade. Our mother was handling all the details."

"That's interesting because over the past few days, we've been going through all of your mother's correspondence and paperwork and there is nothing suggesting she was in the midst of negotiating a sale of the company," Spenser said. "We did, however, find a shadow email account that was being used to correspond with Eric Bass, the CEO at Evergreen Lumber, facilitating a secret back channel negotiation. The email address being used to correspond with Mr. Bass was similar to your mother's company email address."

A moment of silence, thick and heavy, hung over the conference room. Aspen and Dallas cut a quick glance at one another, a silent bit of communication passing between them. Brendan sat forward again, his curiosity piqued. Aspen cleared her throat and turned to Spenser.

"Perhaps our mother didn't want the details of the sale leaking and conducted the negotiations in secret," she said. "She always played her cards very close to the vest."

"We considered that. But there was absolutely nothing in any of her papers—not even the papers in the safe in her office—that indicated a sale as imminent," Spenser said. "A sale as large as your family's company is a complex thing that requires public filings, contracts—it's complicated. But we spoke with the legal department at Emerald Timber, and they had no knowledge of a pending sale, either. There is absolutely nothing indicating the sale was coming."

"Well, maybe she was working it out with her personal lawyer," Aspen offered. "With as secret as this sale seemed like it was, it would make sense that she didn't go through the company's legal department."

Spenser got to her feet and folded her arms over her chest as she started to pace behind Young and Jacob on her side of the table, her lips pursed, a thoughtful look on her face.

"No, see, we talked to her personal attorney—what was his name?"

"Freeman," Young said. "Brady Freeman."

"Right. Brady Freeman," Spenser said. "We spoke with him, and he didn't seem to know anything about a sale, either. Your mother hadn't said a word to him on the down-low or otherwise."

Dallas sighed and rolled her eyes dramatically. "Is everybody in this room really this dumb?"

"Apparently so," Spenser said. "Why don't you enlighten us, Dallas?"

"Emails coming from within the company using a company email address made to look like our mother's?" Dallas spat. "It's obvious that Brock was trying to do something shady."

"We had that thought as well," Spenser said. "But I'll tell you what, let's come back to that."

"Are we going to be here much longer?" Dallas complained.

"Jesus, Dally, relax," Brendan snapped. "It's like you don't want them to find out who murdered our mother or something. I don't care if we're here all night—"

"Nobody asked you, Brendan," she growled. "You're not even around. It's not like your opinion on any of this matters anyway."

"She was my mother, too," he spat back.

"Both of you, shut up," Aspen said forcefully then looked at Spenser. "I'm sorry for them, Sheriff. But how much longer is this going to take?"

"Not much longer. I promise," Spenser said. "Girls, can you tell me what your relationship with your mother was like?"

"It was fine," Aspen said. "We were close. We got along well—"

Brendan snorted, cutting her off. "Yeah. Right."

Aspen rounded on him. "Shut up, Brendan."

"Sheriff, they were always at each other's throats," he said. "My sisters were always teaming up on our mother and they fought like cats and dogs."

"That's not true. That's not true at all," Aspen countered. "Besides, it's not like you were here. How would you even know?"

Brendan rolled his eyes and looked away. Aspen glared at him, her cheeks flushed, and her face etched with anger. Dallas was slumped back in her chair, staring off into nothing, the look of irritation Spenser had come to think of as her normal expression on her face.

"Girls, can you tell me where you were on the day your mom went missing?" Spenser asked.

"We were up at school," Aspen answered. "It wasn't until we came home and realized she was missing that we called you, Sheriff. You remember that."

"I do remember when you called," Spenser said. "But how could you have been up at school when your cell phone records put you here in town?"

The two girls looked at each other, communicating silently. Brendan seemed to finally realize where Spenser's questioning was going and he sat up, suddenly looking intrigued—and appalled. Aspen turned back to Spenser and shook her head.

"That's not possible, Sheriff. As I told you, we were up on campus," Aspen said. "And frankly, I don't appreciate what you seem to be suggesting. We're grieving."

"Well, I'm sorry about that," Spenser said. "Just bear with me here."

Spenser nodded to Jacob, and he tapped a few keys on his laptop. The screen on the wall lit up and he brought up a screen that showed the pings from both girls' cell phones. Spenser walked over to the screen and pointed to the two sets of dots that were overlaid on the map.

"Aspen, those blue dots represent your phone. And Dallas, the red dots are yours," Spenser said. "As you can see, both sets of dots are in Sweetwater Falls the day your mother went missing. Not in Seattle."

The girls were both silent for a long moment. They exchanged a look but neither girl seemed to know what to say. Spenser could see the tension building within the girls. Dallas sniffed loudly and adopted a sour, dismissive expression.

"It's obviously some sort of technical glitch," she said. "We weren't here. We were on campus the day our mother went missing."

"Okay, let's move on to something else then," Spenser said. "We looked into that offshore account that was attached to Brock where the embezzled funds were being stashed."

"I spoke with the manager of that offshore bank. After we sent him a copy of the warrant we obtained for the account, we had quite a lengthy conversation," Young said. "It turns out the account wasn't set up by Brock. The man I spoke with distinctly remembers a woman setting up the account with him."

Aspen bristled. "Well, say what you want, that phone conversation doesn't prove what you seem to be implying."

"No, I'm aware of that," Spenser said. "But the audio recording of the call between the bank manager and this mystery woman should go a long way toward helping us figure out who actually set up that account since it doesn't seem that it was Brock."

THE LIES IN THE FALLS

Aspen's face darkened and her lips curled back in a sneer. She looked like a woman who realized the house of cards she'd built was starting to crumble all around her. She got to her feet and grabbed hold of her sister's hand.

"We're done here," she growled. "We don't have to sit here and listen to this."

"Okay, but before you go, I just want to show you one more thing," Spenser said.

The girls got up and grabbed their bags, slinging them haughtily over their shoulders. Spenser nodded to Jacob and with the tap of a few keys, the image from the train station platform came up. Still standing beside the monitor, she pointed to the bag the woman in the still image had over her shoulder.

"Do you recognize that bag?" Spenser asked. "Dallas? Does that bag look familiar to you?"

Her eyes narrowed and she looked like she was about to be sick. Spenser walked over to her and plucked the bag off her shoulder then set it down on the table. She pointedly looked at the bag in the still image then at the bag on the table in front of her. Spenser tapped Dallas' bag.

"You know, if I didn't know better, I'd say this bag is the same bag on the shoulder of the woman in that still image," Spenser said.

Dallas groaned and suddenly looked shaky. She swayed on her feet, her legs trembling and looking like they might give out beneath her. Aspen grabbed her sister's hand and squeezed it tight. She looked at Spenser with an expression bordering on rage.

"Brock Ferry murdered our mother. We didn't do anything, Sheriff," she said with a sneer in her voice. "You can't prove anything."

"That's for the DA to decide," Spenser said. "And the DA already thinks we've proven enough to release Brock from custody."

"You what?"

"Did I stutter?"

Aspen looked at her sister, her jaw clenching and unclenching and her hands balled into fists at her sides. She took a couple of beats then turned back to Spenser.

"I think we're done talking to you, Sheriff," Aspen said. "If there's anything else you want to talk to us about, you'll need to go through our attorney."

"Aspen, that is probably the smartest thing you've said today."

They turned to leave but the door to the conference room opened and a pair of Spenser's deputies stepped in, blocking their way. Spenser nodded to Young who jumped out of her seat with barely controlled enthusiasm.

"Aspen and Dallas Gilchrist," Young said. "It gives me great pleasure to say, you are both under arrest for the murder of Wendy Gilchrist."

CHAPTER THIRTY-FIVE

"I can't believe it," Dent said. "I simply cannot believe it."

"I'm really sorry, Maggie," Spenser said.

They sat alone in a room together backstage the night of the tree-lighting ceremony. The sound of a local band playing Christmas tunes on stage echoed back to them, the light and festive atmosphere clashing with the somber mood that hung heavy over them. Dent hung her head, an expression of absolute misery on her face. Knowing it was going to be another devastating blow to her, Spenser hated delivering the news. It had to feel like Dent had not only lost her best friend but a pair of girls she'd thought of as her nieces in one fell swoop.

"Why?" Dent asked. "Why did they do it?"

Spenser shook her head. "On the advice of their very high-priced criminal defense attorney, the girls aren't speaking. I have a sinking feeling we may never know. Not for sure."

"If you had to hazard a guess?"

"If I had to hazard a guess, I'd say that Wendy wasn't thrilled with the girls wanting to build their brand on social media and not be involved with the day-to-day operations of the company. I think, perhaps, Wendy was squeezing them to abandon their plans and take over Emerald Timber once she stepped down. Maybe she even threatened to cut them out altogether if they didn't do as she wanted. So, maybe feeling like they had no other options, they murdered their mother and set their stepfather up to take the fall. In the meantime, they brokered the secret sale of the company intending to cash out and wash their hands of the business altogether," Spenser said. "Again, that's purely conjecture. I have absolutely nothing to back any of that up. It's just a theory I developed when I was putting it all together."

Dent was silent and seemed to be thinking about what she'd just said. Eventually, she sat back in her chair and nodded.

"That's plausible. It sounds as reasonable as anything I can think of," Dent said. "I know Wendy was very forceful and she very much wanted the girls to follow in her footsteps. Continuing her family's legacy was incredibly important to her. But why go through the whole charade of making it look like Wendy had gotten on a train and disappeared?"

"Honestly, I don't know. I guess that after they murdered Wendy, Dallas panicked and freelanced that bit. There really was no reason for it," Spenser offered with a shrug. "Except for that obvious slip-up, the girls set everything up pretty well. Between the offshore account, the bloody clothes in the basement, and everything else, they'd built a pretty solid case against Brock. If not for Dallas going to the train station, we might never have looked in their direction."

"Devious. Absolutely devious," Dent said. "I never dreamed those girls could be that… evil. I mean, I knew they were a handful, but I would have never guessed they were capable of doing something like that. Never in a million years."

"I don't know that they're necessarily evil. But they are young and full of themselves. And worst of all, they're incredibly selfish and want to do what they want," Spenser said.

"What they did is evil," Dent replied.

"We're all capable of doing terrible things, Maggie. Good people sometimes do terrible things. Don't beat yourself up for wanting to see the best in them. Honestly, I did the same exact thing. So, give yourself a little grace," Spenser said. "Honestly, I can't believe I missed it at first. It was right there the whole time, but I let myself get so invested in the girls and how they must have been feeling after losing their mother that I blinded myself to what was sitting right in front of me. If I'd picked up on that bag earlier on, we could have closed it a lot sooner than we did."

"You should take your own advice and not beat yourself up about it," Dent said. "The important thing is that you figured it out and the right people are behind bars."

"Yeah, she's not good about taking her own advice, which is usually pretty good."

They both looked up as Ryker slipped into the room. He nodded to Dent in greeting then offered Spenser a warm smile.

"Am I interrupting?" he asked.

"Of course not. Pull up a chair," Dent replied. "We're just having our own little pity party back here. You're more than welcome to join."

"If it helps, I don't come empty-handed," he said.

Ryker walked into the room with a carry-tray bearing three red cups with green sleeves around them. He handed one to Dent and one to Spenser then pulled a chair over and sat down with his hands wrapped around his own cup.

"Hot chocolate—Kelli's special brew," he said with a mischievous grin.

Spenser raised the cup to her nose and inhaled deeply, a smile stretching across her face. "Special brew, huh? Smells like hot chocolate with peppermint Schnapps to me."

"I will neither confirm nor deny," he said.

"This is amazing and exactly what I needed right now," Dent said after taking a sip.

A young woman poked her head into the room and smiled. "Mayor Dent, Sheriff Song? You're on in five minutes."

"Thank you, Ashlynn," Dent said.

Spenser turned to the mayor. "I think we should start a new tradition and have the mayor deliver the holiday address."

"Nice try," Dent replied. "But the people out there hear from me enough. They want to hear from you. And I'm not brave enough to try and switch up tradition on them. I'm half-afraid they'll show up at my house with their torches and pitchforks."

"I can confirm the people love their traditions here and are resistant to change," Ryker said.

"Very resistant," Dent agreed.

"Wonderful," Spenser groaned.

They sipped their cocoa in silence for a few moments, each of them seemingly lost in their own thoughts. Dent wrapped her hands around her cup and raised her gaze to Spenser.

"I think one of the things I'm having the hardest time accepting is that what the girls did seems so extreme. I mean, why murder their mother?" she asked.

"Money, I'd wager," Spenser said. "If Wendy was threatening to cut them off if they didn't fall into line... Well, the threat of losing out on that kind of money can be enough motivation to do all kinds of extreme things."

"The promise of a quick three-hundred-and-fifty-million-dollar payday is also a great motivator to do something that extreme and wicked," Ryker added.

"But Wendy didn't even cut Brendan out. Not entirely," Dent said.

"I don't think the girls wanted to risk the possibility Wendy might do something extreme if they didn't do as she asked, so they acted first... before she could make any changes," Spenser said.

Dent shook her head. "I'll never truly understand this."

"You'll go crazy if you try," Spenser said. "As you've told me so many times before, sometimes you'll never get all the answers you want. Life isn't always neat and tidy and not every problem has a solution that comes neatly wrapped with a nice little bow on top."

A wry smile tugged at the corner of her mouth. "I hate it when you throw my own words back in my face."

"Sometimes, you're wise and your words make sense," Spenser said with a grin.

"I assume Brendan is in line to inherit everything now," Ryker said. "Any idea what he's planning on doing? Is he going to go through with the sale?"

Spenser shook her head. "No idea yet. He's talking about keeping the company but bringing somebody in to run it for him."

"Brendan is a smart kid," Dent said. "I'm sure he'll make the right decision."

"Mayor Dent? Sheriff Song? It's time," Ashlynn said.

"Last chance, Maggie," Spenser said.

"I'll pass."

"You suck."

They got to their feet and Ryker grabbed hold of Spenser's hand as they walked out of the room and out onto the stage beside the giant tree. It looked like the whole town had turned out. And despite the bombshells that had rocked Sweetwater Falls to its very core, the mood among the crowd seemed upbeat and light. Far more so than Spenser had assumed it would be.

The band—Charlie and the Silver Notes—was a staple in town. Known for their lively music, they played a lot of local events and were always a crowd favorite. The five older men, all of them with shoulder-length silver hair, matching beards, and paunches around their middles, were decked out in hideously ugly Christmas sweaters and Santa hats. They smiled as Spenser and Dent stepped out of the back and onto the stage.

"Ladies and gentlemen, let's give it up for Mayor Maggie Dent and our kick-butt, hard-working, take-no-prisoners sheriff, Spenser Song…"

Applause and cheering erupted from the crowd. Dent cheered along with them and pushed Spenser forward. Ashlynn came over as Spenser stepped to the microphone and presented her with the comically oversized red button that when pushed, would light the tree. Her stomach churning and her heart fluttering, Spenser looked out over the crowd, trying to take heart in seeing the smiles among the people. She cleared her throat and the cheering started to taper off. As Spenser gathered her thoughts—silently cursing herself for not preparing any remarks—she noticed the soft, white flakes falling from the sky.

The year's first snow.

It was beautiful, peaceful, and just as it always had back in New York, filled her with a sense of optimism and unbridled joy. She cast a look back at Ryker who nodded and gave her an encouraging smile, his eyes filled with nothing but warmth for her. Spenser smiled back as her heart swelled inside of her.

Spenser turned back to the microphone. "Well, first of all, thank you all for coming out tonight and Merry Christmas..."

AUTHOR'S NOTE

Thank you for joining Spenser Song on another exciting adventure in Sweetwater Falls! As we wrap up this journey, I can't help but feel your curiosity about what's next for Spenser, so allow me to give you a sneak peek.

In the upcoming chapter, Spenser finds herself entangled in the impending trial of her former FBI partner, bringing the pursuit of justice for the darkest chapters of her life tantalizingly close. However, peace shatters when a routine day at her office transforms into a high-stakes shooting investigation. Engaging with the victim's shaken wife, Spenser senses an ominous undercurrent of terror. Despite the seemingly ordinary couple and tranquil neighborhood, Spenser's instincts lead her to uncover hidden secrets behind the burglary. As she delves into the couple's history, unexpected twists unravel, exposing a concealed side to the seemingly pleasant pair. The suspect pool expands, encompassing both inmates and neighbors, while the investigation takes unexpected and bizarre turns. In the Falls, sweetness often masks the most bitter realities.

Your feedback is invaluable to me, and let me just say that I am all ears. I want to know what delighted you and where I can improve so that I can continue to craft the best reading experience for you. As an independent writer, I rely on your support to keep writing and delivering pulse-pounding and entertaining reading experiences like this one. Please consider leaving a review to let me know your thoughts on this book. I'm looking forward to you reuniting with Spenser and Ryker in the enchanting world of Sweetwater Falls in the next addition!

If you're yearning for another riveting mystery, consider joining FBI agent Blake Wilder in *'The Inmate's Secret,'* set to release in a month. In this tale, Blake is basking in the holiday spirit when an unexpected phone call from an old high school friend leads her to a challenging murder case. Reluctantly, she visits her friend in prison, only to be begged to investigate his case and prove his innocence. He's serving a life sentence for a crime he swears he didn't commit. While glossing over his case, she uncovers potential discrepancies in the original investigation and realizes her friend has been keeping secrets from her. And as Blake dives deeper into the case, she finds a trail of illicit affairs, abuse, incompetence, and a shocking twist that no one saw coming.

Thank you again for your continued support. It is because of YOU that I have the motivation to keep going and keep delivering the stories you love. By the way, if you find any typos or want to reach out to me, feel free to email me at egray@ellegraybooks.com

Yours truly,
Elle Gray

CONNECT WITH ELLE GRAY

Loved the book? Don't miss out on future reads! Join my newsletter and receive updates on my latest releases, insider content, and exclusive promos. Plus, as a thank you for joining, you'll get a FREE copy of my book Deadly Pursuit!

Deadly Pursuit follows the story of Paxton Arrington, a police officer in Seattle who uncovers corruption within his own precinct. With his career and reputation on the line, he enlists the help of his FBI friend Blake Wilder to bring down the corrupt Strike Team. But the stakes are high, and Paxton must decide whether he's willing to risk everything to do the right thing.

Claiming your freebie is easy! Visit
https://dl.bookfunnel.com/513mluk159
and sign up with your email!

Want more ways to stay connected? Follow me on Facebook and Instagram or sign up for text notifications by texting "blake" to 844-552-1368. Thanks for your support and happy reading!

ALSO BY
ELLE GRAY

Blake Wilder FBI Mystery Thrillers

Book One - The 7 She Saw
Book Two - A Perfect Wife
Book Three - Her Perfect Crime
Book Four - The Chosen Girls
Book Five - The Secret She Kept
Book Six - The Lost Girls
Book Seven - The Lost Sister
Book Eight - The Missing Woman
Book Nine - Night at the Asylum
Book Ten - A Time to Die
Book Eleven - The House on the Hill
Book Twelve - The Missing Girls
Book Thirteen - No More Lies
Book Fourteen - The Unlucky Girl
Book Fifteen - The Heist
Book Sixteen - The Hit List
Book Seventeen - The Missing Daughter
Book Eighteen - The Silent Threat
Book Nineteen - A Code to Kill
Book Twenty - Watching Her

A Pax Arrington Mystery
Free Prequel - Deadly Pursuit
Book One - I See You
Book Two - Her Last Call
Book Three - Woman In The Water
Book Four - A Wife's Secret

Storyville FBI Mystery Thrillers
Book One - The Chosen Girl
Book Two - The Murder in the Mist
Book Three - Whispers of the Dead
Book Four - Secrets of the Unseen

A Sweetwater Falls Mystery
Book One - New Girl in the Falls
Book Two - Missing in the Falls
Book Three - The Girls in the Falls
Book Four - Memories of the Falls
Book Five - Shadows of the Falls
Book Six - The Lies in the Falls

ALSO BY
ELLE GRAY | K.S. GRAY

Olivia Knight FBI Mystery Thrillers

Book One - New Girl in Town
Book Two - The Murders on Beacon Hill
Book Three - The Woman Behind the Door
Book Four - Love, Lies, and Suicide
Book Five - Murder on the Astoria
Book Six - The Locked Box
Book Seven - The Good Daughter
Book Eight - The Perfect Getaway
Book Nine - Behind Closed Doors
Book Ten - Fatal Games
Book Eleven - Into the Night

ALSO BY
ELLE GRAY | JAMES HOLT

The Florida Girl FBI Mystery Thrillers
Book One - The Florida Girl
Book Two - Resort to Kill
Book Three - The Runaway
Book Four - The Ransom

Made in United States
Troutdale, OR
03/25/2025